240

IT DIDN'T TAKE ME LONG TO PUT TOGETHER A MENTAL LIST OF MOTIVES AND CANDIDATES

There was good old hatred. Talk about a plausible motive! When it came to pure loathing, nobody could generate it like Niki.

There was Galena. "I shall be here long after Niki and his friends have departed," she had said. And how about Tricia? Didn't she have good reason to hate the man who disgraced her in public? And Jonquil, her big moment ruined? And Jonquil's mother, for the same reason? And who knew how many others there were? The way Niki operated, he'd probably made enemies with half the people he met—stagehands, the people who worked in the canteen—the list could be endless. The problem was, nobody but me was interested in exploring it.

D1010265

Also by Carole Berry

THE LETTER OF THE LAW
THE YEAR OF THE MONKEY

GOOD NIGHT, SWEET PRINCE

Carole Berry

A DELL BOOK

GOOD NIGHT, SWEET PRINCE

Prologue

At the altar, the bearded patriarch of the Russian Orthodox Church in New York swung the big brass censer, sending curls of incense wafting over the open coffin. He uttered words that possibly a dozen people in the packed cathedral understood.

Surging crowds had pushed me to a center pew where, like the other mourners, I stood holding a lighted candle. I would have preferred a spot at the back of the church. To be honest, I would have preferred skipping Nikolai Koslov's funeral altogether. I admired him as a dancer, but I had known Niki all too well to like him.

Up in the front row were the luminaries. There was the mayor, flanked on one side by Michael Devereux, artistic director of Gotham Ballet, and on the other by the U.S. ambassador to the Soviet Union. Behind them stood rows of celebrities—ballet greats, stage personalities, familiar faces from television.

Around and behind me, filling the cathedral, were the real mourners, the ballet fans who had worshiped Niki. Here were the damp handkerchiefs and eyes glistening with tears. None of these people had ever met the Reigning Prince of

Ballet. Believe me, if they had they might have thought twice about dragging themselves out in the rain to go to his funeral.

The most stolid attendees, by far, were the men lining the walls at the back of the church. They didn't pretend to mourn. Not a hankie in sight. They watched—watched us and watched each other. The KGB—their awful suits gave them away—watched the FBI. The FBI, or CIA or whatever they were, watched the KGB. When my cab pulled up outside, both factions had representatives wandering through the rain, mumbling into walkie-talkies and writing down license plate numbers.

As far as our government was concerned, the murderer was behind bars. The Soviets, of course, continued to tell the world what they thought of Niki's terrible death. For days, newspaper headlines had screamed quotes about Western decadence in general and drugs in particular.

Speaking of the papers—and how could I speak of Niki without speaking of the papers?—the cathedral's massive double doors were jammed with reporters and photographers waiting for celebrities to file past, hoping for one more pungent quote, or maybe a photo of a famous face disfigured by grief.

What a sideshow! But why should I have expected anything else? From the moment Nikolai Koslov hit Manhattan, it was Standing Room Only everywhere he appeared. His final appearance was no exception.

1

Like most New Yorkers, my first look at Nikolai Koslov came by way of a picture on the front page of the *Times*. The photographer had caught him suspended mid-leap, legs straight and at an angle to his body, toes pointed. His torso was bent at the waist and his arms swept up in a semicircle. And that face, all cheekbone and flashing eyes, surrounded by a halo of hair. How could this be a mere mortal, this man who seemed to soar with eagles? Under Nikolai Koslov's photo the caption read, BOLSHOI STAR IN TRIUMPHANT UNITED STATES DEBUT AT METROPOLITAN OPERA HOUSE. STORY ON P. 42.

Jostling my fellow commuters, I flipped to the entertainment section. What a rave! The critic had gone crazy with superlatives. The Bolshoi dancers gave new meaning to the word *magnificent* and new life to the New York ballet scene. The ballerinas were sublime, beauty incarnate, and Nikolai, "The Reigning Prince of Ballet," was movement personified and glorified.

The article transported me, not that it takes all that much. I imagined myself onstage, on my toes. Nikolai's hands encircled my waist. His powerful arms began their lift. The audience was breathless. I was rising off the stage, light and graceful as a butterfly, when the motorman's voice shattered my daydream.

"Columbus Circle station. Change for the B, the D, the number one train on the upper level."

The A train screeched to a stop. Nothing like a ride on the subway to bring your head down from the clouds.

Tucking the paper into my tote, I followed the crowd out of the cavernous Columbus Circle station into the blazing July morning. Eight forty-five and already the thermometer on the Gulf & Western Building read eighty-six degrees.

As I turned up Broadway toward Lincoln Center, both my hairdo and my spirits wilted. I was on my way to what I was sure would be my less-than-triumphant debut with the Gotham Ballet Company, as temporary data-input clerk in their fund-raising office, a debut that had no relationship, or resemblance, to Nikolai Koslov's.

Temping had been the last thing on my mind when I began my latest job hunt. Just back from a long vacation in Europe, I had armed myself with suit, briefcase, and fabricated resume and set out to take corporate New York by storm. The problem was, I'd grown used to spending my days in jeans and sweaters and letting my hair do more or less what it wanted. Corporate New York didn't look so good when I compared it to windy afternoons on a twenty-one-foot sailboat and nights in Copenhagen's jazz clubs.

Still, I almost took the job at the Midtown accounting firm. The man in personnel let the M word pass his lips. Specifically, the MT words: *management trainee*. I couldn't do it, though. The sea of gray faces rushing through the halls, the crush of gray suits buffeting me on the elevator, the gray flannel wallpaper all depressed me. I had walked out of the accounting firm thinking that almost anything would be better. I was wrong.

The moment I laid eyes on Tricia Van Rensselaer, the ballet company's fund-raising director, I thought of the Designer Daywear department at Bloomingdale's. Whenever I've wandered through the Adolfos and Chanels on my way to the markdown section at the back of the store, I've seen Tricia-like women. They are, until gravity finally wrests control, ageless. They are thin, with regular features, whether by birth or scalpel. They dress quietly and expensively and wear their hair in gleaming pageboys. Tricia's shiny brown hair looked as if it wouldn't ruffle in a hurricane.

In general, dressing for success eludes me. That morning I hadn't tried. I wasn't looking for success at Gotham Ballet. I was looking for an easy, hang-out kind of temp job. Tricia greeted the elevator that whisked me to the subbasement of the theater with an impatient expression that grew stonier as she took in my sandals, stockingless legs, and cotton skirt.

"Miss Van Rensselaer? I'm from Pro-Team Temporary Secretaries. My name is Bonnie. . . ."

"Yes, yes. I know." There is nothing lower than an office temp, her look said.

My last permanent job had ended six months earlier. My employer's chief executive officer had been murdered, an incident that planted the kiss of death on my budding career in tax shelters. A trip to Europe with a boyfriend and a series of temp jobs had occupied me since. It was a situation that couldn't go on forever. The boyfriend appeared to be a thing of the past, and my bank account wasn't far behind him.

Actually, I like temping. Temps aren't held to the same standards that plague other employees. If a regular employee shows up looking as if she's spent the night on a park bench, she's had it. A temp can go around looking as if she *lives* in the park and her employers will shrug and roll their eyes and say, "What can you expect? She's a temp."

That morning, I didn't even get my last name out before Tricia Van Rensselaer was leading the way down a long, dingy corridor, high heels beating into the vinyl flooring like a pile driver. Tricia from behind was as intimidating as Tricia from the front. This was a woman whose shoulders would never slump, whose navy linen dress wouldn't dare wrinkle.

"You can call me Tricia," she said over her shoulder as she whisked through the maze of corridors. "I certainly hope you know what you're doing with that computer. My so-called assistant seems to have lost our entire list of patrons."

I trotted behind her through a door into a terrible mess of an office. It was so cluttered it was hard to imagine anyone working in it, but the two desks and chairs meant that it was intended for two people. It was intended for me. On the desk closest to the door sat the offending computer. A woman stared at the monitor, looking baffled.

"Our temp is here, Abigail. Maybe she can figure out what you've done."

Without a word the woman pushed her chair back from the desk. I took her place in front of the computer with no idea of what to do.

"If you could tell me the problem . . ."

Tricia glared at her assistant. "The problem is that yesterday afternoon we had input our patrons' names up to the D's, and this morning we have a blank. Look at this!" She whacked the monitor with five buffed fingernails. "Nothing! Nada!"

Abigail sighed. She was about my age, but that's where I hope the resemblance ended. Though the potential for good looks was there—regular features, fine skin, and a decent enough figure—Abigail seemed faded. Her gray-flecked brown hair was badly cut and lifeless, her shoulders sagging, her expression tired. As for her outfit, I'm sorry to admit that she and I shared the same rung on the career dressing ladder. At a suburban garden club meeting her madras wrap skirt, sleeveless polo shirt, and espadrilles might have been at home. In a Manhattan office—well, I don't know if you can buy madras wrap skirts in Manhattan.

"I can't imagine what went wrong. There was nothing

there when I turned the machine on. I couldn't even find . . ."

The woman spoke with a Southern accent, genteel and slow. Much too slow for her boss. Tricia put her hands on her hips. "I'm sure you couldn't!" When she turned back to me, her toes were already tapping. I was expected to do something, and fast.

For a second or two I fiddled around with the offending machine. The computer looked brand-new. It was humming away, but the monitor remained black as night. It didn't take a genius to figure out what was going on. Bending under the desk, I located the tangle of cords. Sure enough, one plug dangled loose on the floor. I held it up.

"Anybody have a screwdriver?" A few seconds later, with the help of a nail file, I had put Gotham Ballet's fund-raising office back in business.

I didn't expect to have bouquets of roses thrown at me for connecting a terminal, but when I crawled up off the floor I did expect a thank-you. Just goes to show that I didn't know my new boss well. Tricia, I would later discover, took things such as laugh and frown lines as seriously as she took her job. Her lips stretched about an eighth of a millimeter, which for her was tantamount to a handstand.

"One of the cleaning women must have knocked the plug out," she said. "Now, Abigail, you can explain to Bonnie how I like things done. I'll be at Citicorp, then Exxon. If that nickel-squeezing rodent is looking for me, I can't be reached. See you tomorrow."

To me she said: "Try to get through that list today, would you? I'm getting tired of all these delays. Our autumn season will be here before we know it."

Tricia barked a few more orders at Abigail and left, heels clacking.

Abigail pressed her wrist to her forehead, a dramatic gesture for someone who looked as if she didn't have an ounce of drama in her. "Hardly nine o'clock," she said, "and already I'm getting a sick headache."

"Who's the rodent?" I asked.

"Elliott Pierce, our administrative coordinator. He and Tricia can't stand each other. She's convinced he got the job because he's Michael Devereux's nephew."

"It probably didn't hurt. Have you worked here long?"

"About a year. I'm Abigail Jeffreys. I'm glad you're going to help out," she added wearily. "I can barely cope."

On cue, a stack of envelopes tumbled over the edge of her desk. As Abigail slowly bent to retrieve them, I looked around at the glamorous world of ballet my temp agency had promised. The desk fought for space with an odd assortment of file cabinets, a jumble of boxes, and several thigh-high stacks of phone books. The furniture could have come from a junk store and the walls hadn't seen a paintbrush in years. Above us, exposed fluorescent tubes filled the room with an eerie blue-gray light. One of them buzzed and sputtered on and off. The one amenity we did have was a veritable blizzard of air-conditioning, blasting through a dust-coated vent in the concrete block wall.

I sat back behind the monitor. "I suppose we could survive a direct nuclear hit on New York City."

"It's actually all right when Tricia's not around. And that's most of the time. I hope you stay a while. The computer absolutely throws me." Abigail went into a quick explanation of how the fund-raising office worked and what I would be doing. The latter took only a minute. Let's face it: data entry isn't brain surgery.

I was right about the computer being new. Until a few weeks earlier the office had done everything on typewriters, keeping information about donors in file cabinets. The plan now was that once the donors' names and addresses were in the computer, additional notes about them—their businesses, their other artistic and charitable interests—would gradually be added.

"Do *you* ever visit potential donors?" I asked.

The question seemed reasonable enough to me. Not to my officemate.

"Me?" She was clearly surprised by the idea. "Even if I wanted to, Tricia wouldn't hear of it. She's very possessive about her position. Thinks it's a birthright. She's old New York society. Her family goes back to Peter Stuyvesant. Oh . . ." Hesitating, Abigail glanced down at her watch. "I'll bet if I hurry . . ."

How did I know Abigail was going to ask a favor? I can't say for sure, but I felt it coming. Maybe it was the way her head tilted when she looked up, or maybe her sweet smile.

"You'll cover the office if I run upstairs for a few minutes, won't you?" she asked. "There's someone I'd like to talk to."

"Sure." I nodded at the phone on her desk. "What should I say to callers?"

"Tell them someone will get back to them," she answered. With that, she disappeared for a good hour.

I spent the morning typing names and addresses and taking phone messages. Talk about low stress! I could have done something else at the same time—learned Spanish by tape or listened to recordings of the great books.

By lunchtime the dingy subbasement was getting to me. Craving sunlight, I stepped out of the theater's employee entrance into a blinding white-hot day. After buying a hot dog from one of the vendors on Broadway, I settled myself on the rim of the Lincoln Center fountain. It was a good spot for eating and people-watching.

Groups of teenagers, their distinctive toes-out walk identifying them as ballet students, strolled around the plaza. Musicians on their way to a dress rehearsal, curiously formal in their white shirts and black jackets, carried instrument cases through the doors into Avery Fisher Hall. Above me, huge red banners announcing the Bolshoi's visit flapped almost soundlessly in the hot summer gusts.

The banners left no doubt about the big draw. At the

center of each, Nikolai Koslov was silhouetted in his signature leap. Posters on the kiosk in front of the Met announced in big red letters, THE REIGNING PRINCE OF BALLET.

If I glanced over my shoulder, I could see the growing lunchtime line at the Met's box office. Over the past dozen years ballet has experienced a tremendous rise in popularity in the United States. These days, more people attend ballet performances on a yearly basis than either football or baseball games.

Unfortunately, my temporary employer, the Gotham Ballet, though once one of the finest ballet companies in the world, had not received the full benefit of this wave of support. In his youth and well into his thirties, Michael Devereux had been a wonderful dancer with a few tolerable choreographed works and no management experience to his credit. Devereux had taken over artistic direction of Gotham Ballet eight years earlier, adding the saying "The World's Most Exciting Dance Experience" to its advertising. Since then the company had danced its way into mediocrity, exciting fewer critics and fans every year. As artistic director, Devereux was widely considered out of his depth. To someone who didn't follow the ballet world closely, the man's most exciting feat was probably his marriage to the company's fiery prima ballerina, Galena Semenova. It had been brief and volatile.

After lunch, I passed the Gotham Ballet box office on my way back inside. On Monday nights there's no performance, but even so it was a shame there wasn't a soul waiting to buy tickets for later in the week.

"Slow day," I said to the man behind the ticket window.

He looked across the plaza at the crowd by the Met. "Not next door. Every time a bunch of Russians comes to town our loyal fans defect."

"You have Russian dancers."

He waved his hand in a dismissive gesture. "Our Russians are old, tired Russians."

When I got back to my desk Abigail wasn't around so I

went straight into my list. I was up to the H's—Harper, Harris, Harrison. The afternoon threatened to be endless. Their names were running together until I could hardly keep them straight.

"Ahem!"

I looked up, startled. What kind of person actually says "ahem"? A man of about thirty was standing in the office door, arms crossed over his narrow chest. He had a bleached-out look about him—pale skin, pale eyes, a mop of pale hair falling over his forehead—and no reason whatever to look cocky. He did, though, as if the sight of me at my PC was just about the silliest thing imaginable.

"And just who might you be?" he asked.

I'm afraid his attitude didn't bring out my best. "Well, I might be an office temp, but on the other hand, I just might be the boss."

He sniffed. "Cute. I wasn't aware we could afford temps. Once again, Tricia has bypassed me. Where *is* the wicked witch of the west corridor, anyway? She's not in her office."

What a silly man! This had to be the infamous Elliott Pierce.

"Tricia's calling on sponsors," I said.

He rolled his eyes. "Some of us work, and some of us 'call on sponsors.' Tell her to see Elliott as soon as she gets back. As always, her expenses are out of line. The woman is addicted to taxicabs. Why can't she take the subway? I take the subway. Millions of people just like me take the subway."

It occurred to me that if Tricia was as choosy about her traveling companions as she was about her appearance, he had just answered his own question. This notion made me smile, something Elliott may not have been accustomed to. I don't suppose many people smiled in his presence. His lips worked, but there was no more sarcasm.

"Please tell her," he finally said.

Ten minutes later Abigail fluttered into the office, eyes

aglow and cheeks flushed red. Something had certainly perked her up during her extended lunch hour.

"Elliott was here," I said. "He wants to see Tricia."

She slammed the office door and propped herself on the edge of her desk. "I couldn't care less," she said breathlessly. "You're not going to believe what's happened!"

"What?" By then I could have used some excitement. The World's Most Exciting Dance Experience hadn't delivered.

"Niki is going to observe the advanced girls class this afternoon at four. My daughter is going to sneak me in the back door to watch. This could be the chance we've been waiting for."

"Slow down," I said. "I don't know what you're talking about. Who is Niki?"

"Who is Niki?" Abigail drew back and eyed me as though she was dealing with an idiot. "Haven't you seen the posters? The Reigning Prince of Ballet, that's who! Nikolai Koslov."

"You know him well enough to call him Niki? I'm impressed."

She shook her head. "Of course not, but everybody in the dance world calls him Niki. My daughter, Jonquil, is a student at the ballet school. We expect Michael Devereux to invite her to join the company."

"She must be very good."

"She's wonderful! Michael told me he thinks she'll go far. It's awfully competitive, though. You wouldn't believe the things those girls will do to get ahead." Abigail paused. Her forehead wrinkled. "I got Jonquil new tights just the other day. I hope she wears them instead of her usual rags. Do you realize what it would mean if Niki singled her out in class?"

For the next two hours, Abigail couldn't stop talking about the wondrous, beautiful, and precocious Jonquil. The spirit that put color in my co-worker's cheeks was her daughter's dance career. The work suffered, both Abigail's and mine. She was far too distracted to get anything done, and I had to contend not only with my mountain of potential donors but with the phone, which rang incessantly as she paced the office.

At a few minutes before four, as I typed my way resolutely into the K's—Kahn, Kaiser—Abigail asked suddenly:

"Would you like to come with me, Bonnie?"

I glanced up from the monitor. The idea was appealing. "I better not," I finally decided. "Tricia wants this list by tomorrow. And what about the phone?"

"I'll stay late to input the rest of the names. We'll let the phones ring. If it's important they'll call back. Please. If Niki notices my child I'm going to need someone to hold me up. I'm already a wreck." To illustrate, she placed her hand on my arm. Her fingers were ice-cold.

"Please," she said again.

One flight up from the subbasement is the basement, where the prop rooms, some dressing rooms, and several rehearsal studios are located.

I followed Abigail to the back door of one of those studios. Nikolai's impending appearance was no secret. The crowd was two-deep, mostly with young men.

"The advanced boys. They don't have class right now," Abigail explained, straining to see past them.

"Hi, Mrs. Jeffreys."

The speaker, a good-looking young man with a mop of blond curls, received a thin smile and an unenthusiastic "Hello, Chris" from Abigail. He received a bit more from Abigail's daughter. The wispy girl in pink tights and a leotard who pushed through the crowd and took Abigail's arm gave him a bold wink.

"Hurry up, Mom," the girl said. "There's a place by the wall where you can stand."

Abigail and I followed her daughter into a big oblong room. The walls were lined with mirrors. Two wood barres ran along the walls, one about three feet above the floor, the other about six inches higher. Young women in leotards and leg warmers were sprawled all over the floor. Some were chatting excitedly, some knitting, some reading.

While Abigail introduced me to her daughter she straightened the little topknot of hair atop Jonquil's head. What a cute girl! Her light red hair didn't take well to a bun, tumbling over her forehead and ears. A band of freckles crossed her pug nose. Other than that she looked every inch a ballerina. She stood about an inch more than my five feet four inches, and was several pounds less than my weight. There seemed to be nothing more than the thinnest layer of muscle between her skin and bones.

Two sharp claps and a command—"Girls!"—brought the girls to the barre. In a far corner of the room a pianist began playing a tinny piano. Jonquil quickly joined the other girls at the side of the room, left hand on the barre, heel-to-heel and toes out in first position.

Madame was a tiny ball of fire in black tights. Her face belonged on a sixty-year-old, but from the neck down she could have been one of her students. They called her simply "Madame." She called the students—even the older ones— "girls." That is common practice in the ballet world—female dancers are girls, males boys.

Once Jonquil joined the other ballerinas I could hardly tell one from the next but for differences in height. All wore their hair in tiny knots atop their heads. All had thin arms and backs, and powerful legs. All wore pastel tights and leotards and white toe shoes. Breasts and hips were not terribly in evidence.

Only one stood out—a brown-haired girl with skin several shades darker than the others. She was at the far end of the barre and was the shortest girl by a couple of inches. The heaviest, too. To call her voluptuous would be lunacy, but compared to her classmates she was almost curvy.

"Who is that girl at the end?"

Abigail glanced at the young woman. "She's new. Carmen Garcia. I haven't met her, but Jonquil likes her." Abigail tilted her head and stared hard at the girl. "I can tell you one thing right now: she'll never make it with the layer of fat she's carrying around. Michael prefers thin ballerinas. She better get rid of that name, too, if she wants to get anywhere. Carmen is all right, but Garcia is not a name for a ballerina!"

"Is Jonquil a stage name?"

Abigail gave me a cool smile. "Hardly! I chose her name carefully when she was born. Jonquil Jeffreys has a nice sound for a performer. Not *too* stagy, you know."

Abigail had very definite ideas about what made a ballerina. As the class proceeded, with Madame calling out exercises more and more rapidly—"Tendu front. One two one two"—in heavily accented English, she kept up a whispered commentary. This one was too slow, that one had no extension, another wasn't musical enough.

To me, they all looked terrific. I used to dance. Not ballet. I was a tap dancer and did chorus line work when I could get it. I don't often succumb to the "if only's" where my dance career is concerned, but I felt a pang of something— envy or regret—as I watched these young women. If only I'd tried harder. If only I'd given it another year or two. If only . . .

The double doors at the opposite end of the rehearsal room opened with a bang. The pianist paused. Jonquil and the other ballerinas were suddenly as awkward as any other teenagers. The boys standing near me stopped whispering, and Madame, who had been paying some particular attention to Jonquil, stood even straighter.

Through the door filed the stars. First came the great Galena Semenova. She was casually dressed in white slacks and a yellow shirt, with big dark glasses covering much of her face and her dark hair hidden by a scarf, but she was regal—in her height, more than five feet seven inches, in the way she held herself, even in the upward tilt of her chin. Flamboyant and wildly emotional, Galena was a rare creature in the ballet world. The nature of the profession calls for strict discipline:

Galena Semenova had thumbed her nose at discipline, at least in one area, and she'd made it big.

Her marriage to Michael Devereux when he was a principal dancer with the company had been viewed by the dance press and public as something ordained by the heavens. A recent defector from the Soviet Union, she had called Michael her White Knight. Their blissful union of beauty and talent had dissolved within months. "The marriage threatened our working relationship," was Galena's explanation to the press. After nursing her post-Devereux blues with the usual Argentinean polo players and French skiers, Galena found "true love at last" with a leading tenor from the Met. A year or two later, true love struck again. Right now Galena was single. It was a state that probably would not continue long. I admired her tremendously.

Michael Devereux entered the room behind her. What a handsome man! He had to be in his late forties, but with his dark eyes, full lips, and thick black hair falling over his forehead, he looked as good as he had twenty years earlier. A small scar slanting over one cheekbone gave his sensual appeal a devilish cast. Just looking at him made me weak in the knees.

A big, bulky man followed Devereux into the room. He was wearing a terrible plaid sport jacket, a wide brown tie, baggy pants, and heavy, rubber-soled shoes. This was no dancer. His long, careful look around the room came to rest at the back entrance, where I was standing. Turning my head slightly, I saw that another stranger had joined our little crowd—another big, clunky man.

The young dancer, Chris, was behind me. "KGB," he whispered. An old joke popped into my head. Question: What's the Moscow String Quartet? Answer: The Moscow Symphony Orchestra after its U.S. tour.

This second man's glance took us in, one by one. Then he looked across the room and nodded.

The first bulky man stepped to the edge of the door. And then He walked into the room. The Prince! Nikolai Koslov.

Looking back, I realize that it was nothing more than Nikolai's reputation that caused my breath to catch in my throat. To be blunt, the Reigning Prince of Ballet was a bit on the short side, with knobby knees and a backside so developed by all that leaping and lifting that, seen from the rear, he resembled one of those horses that pull beer wagons. His hair, which shone like a halo in photos, was in reality a dull light brown.

Unlike Devereux and Galena Semenova, Nikolai was in practice clothes. I watched Devereux introduce Nikolai to Madame. A quick conversation between the three, and it was decided that Nikolai would partner a ballerina in a pas de deux from *Giselle*. Jonquil, standing behind Madame, was an obvious choice.

As the pianist began to play I glanced at Abigail. Her lower lip was gripped between her teeth. When Nikolai took Jonquil's hand, Abigail grabbed my wrist with ice-cold fingers. The girl rose on pointe, as cool as if she danced with Nikolai every day.

The scene in the center of the room could have been part of a dream. In motion, the coltish, adolescent Jonquil was beautiful. And Nikolai—even now I can't think about that first time I saw him dance without getting shivers. The pianist blazed on, no longer tinny but symphonic. When Nikolai placed his hands at Jonquil's waist to begin a turn, Abigail's fingers threatened to cut off the circulation in my hand.

And then, in one awful instant, the magic ended. Jonquil's ankle buckled. Her pointe shoe slipped across the wooden floor. An instant later her leg shot from under her. She went down hard on her knee and then her hip. The music stopped dead and the room fell quiet. Abigail's nails dug into my flesh. "Get up," she whispered. "You can do it!"

Rubbing her knee, Jonquil pushed herself up. At her side, Madame talked softly. Jonquil nodded, but when she got to her toes her leg trembled.

Nikolai was already looking beyond her to the other ballerinas. He said something in Russian to Madame.

"Carmen!" the teacher called. The girl at the end of the barre wasn't as cool as Jonquil. From across the floor I could see her catch her breath, see tension grip her. She walked to the center of the floor as Jonquil limped off. The pianist started again. Nikolai took Carmen's hand and they began the pas de deux.

Releasing her grip on my wrist, Abigail fled into the hall. I wanted to stay and watch but I followed, rubbing the four clearly etched nail marks in my flesh.

"It's just one fall," I said to my weeping officemate as I handed her another paper towel from the rack on the ladies' room wall.

She splashed more water on her face and rubbed the towel roughly over her skin.

"Just one fall, but why did it have to happen at the most important moment of her life?"

"It happens," I said. "She's only seventeen. She'll have other important moments."

Abigail shook her head. "If you had any idea of the sacrifices I've made to get that child the best schooling. I have a husband, you know, and a beautiful home in Atlanta. I don't have to work for that bitch Tricia. . . ."

I didn't believe that dance careers were that fragile, to be made or broken so easily. "It's not that big a deal, Abigail. I used to be a dancer. Dancers fall all the time, especially in class. I've seen dancers fall onstage during performances. Even the stars fall. I'll bet Nikolai falls!"

"You were a dancer?" She gazed at me with teary eyes.

"Yes. Not ballet, but I've been in a few shows."

Her tears stopped. For a moment I thought I'd comforted her.

"I was a dancer too," she said softly. "I studied for years. And look at us now. I'm sharing two dumpy rooms in a fifth-floor walkup with a kid who doesn't appreciate anything I do for her, and you . . . you're an office temp!"

That did it! Enough coddling. "I've got work to do," I said. "Are you coming?"

She took a couple of steps toward the door, then leaned back against a sink and touched wrist to forehead. "My sick headache is coming back. Would you mind terribly if I went home?"

"It's not up to me, Abigail, but you can't expect a temp to run that office. And I thought you were going to work on the list tonight."

She shuddered. "I can't go back. I just can't. Not with my head pounding. The office doesn't take much running, Bonnie. You wouldn't be able to stay tonight, would you? Work on the list?"

"Okay, but I'm on overtime after five."

"That's no problem. Give me your time card and I'll forge Tricia's initials on it."

P-y-r-y-t, I typed into the computer. What on earth kind of a name was that? Rubbing my eyes, I looked at my stack of three-by-five cards with cautious optimism. The M's had been hellish. The S's loomed ahead, God-awful as crossing the Sahara on foot. But the stack was shrinking.

It was after nine. Down the hall the cleaning staff called to each other over the roar of a vacuum-cleaner. The office was even gloomier than it had been during the day, but without Abigail and the phones interrupting I was getting a lot done. P-y-z-z-e-l, I typed. First name Maynard, no less. The poor soul. Some parents are vicious.

"'Scuse me, miss." An old black man pulled a big green barrel into the office and started dumping our trash cans into it. "You seen that mouse anywhere 'round here?"

"Mouse?" I lifted my feet a few inches off the floor. "Do we have mice?"

The old man laughed. "We've got everything. Mice,

roaches, water bugs big around as your fist. Last week one of those little dancers found a rat in the dressing room. Had fangs like a doberman. Foam coming out of its mouth. Must of had rabies. Bet they heard her screaming all the way up in Harlem."

The skin on my back prickled. "If I see a rat in this room, they'll hear me in the Bronx."

The old man brandished his broom threateningly. "You just call me, miss. I'll take care of it for you."

A few minutes later he and the other janitors disappeared and an eerie silence fell over the subbasement.

I was well into the R's when something rustled outside the office. Walking to the door, I peered down the hall. The maintenance people had left the trash barrel and some cartons against the wall. There it was again—a scraping noise. Goose bumps broke out all over my body. A mouse. Maybe a rat. A rabid rat! It was going to come out of those cartons in a second and come straight at me in a crazed rush, and there was nobody to hear me scream. Then I heard a noise from the other direction, behind me. It sounded like a leather-shod foot sliding over the floor. I held my breath and listened. There was a different noise now, the squeak of a door hinge. Or a rat!

Calm down, I told myself. You're giving yourself the willies over nothing. "Anybody there?" I called, my voice shaking. Silence. I looked back into the office. The computer hummed away, the fluorescent bulb buzzed and flickered. And there sat my cards, the ominous S's waiting.

"The hell with this," I said out loud. "I'm getting out of here."

I closed down the computer quickly, grabbed my purse, and left, pulling the office door closed behind me but not locking it. Maybe I'd get in early and attack those S's.

At the end of the first hall I had to pass the rustling cartons. I approached cautiously, ready to run if anything moved. Sure enough, one of the cartons shifted. I scooted past, hugging the opposite wall.

I was near the main corridor when I heard the clank of the elevator arriving. If I hurried I could catch it before the door closed. I turned the corner fast, but then something stopped me cold. Two men had gotten off the elevator—the two big men who had accompanied Niki in the practice room. Their backs were to me. One of them nudged the other and gestured with his arm. I could hardly believe my eyes. In his hand was the biggest gun I've ever seen outside of a Dirty Harry movie. Heart pounding, I stepped back around the corner.

I slipped off my shoes, picked them up, and tiptoed quickly back down my hall, past the cartons and barrels and into my office. Thank God I'd left the door unlocked. I stepped into the dark room, turned the lock behind me, and let out a huge sigh of relief. I would call the security office upstairs, tell them that the basement was crawling with gun-toting Russians, and not come out until I heard a nice unaccented American voice on the other side of my door.

I had taken only a few steps toward the center of the dark office when a noise came from somewhere near Abigail's desk. A big noise. My heart jumped. I was trapped between a doberman-toothed, foam-spitting rat and the Russians. Without thinking I reached back to the wall and switched on the lights.

The fluorescent bulbs came on, sputtered, and then the bad one blew with such a huge pop that I caught my breath. That was sure to send the rat into a frenzy. I put my shoes back on in case it went for my feet, then stretched toward Abigail's desk for the phone. Before I had it in my hand, there was a voice outside my door. The knob turned. The lock held.

"Who is in there?" The voice came from a man with a thick Russian accent.

I held my breath. The rat was silent.

He tried the knob again. "Who turns on the light?"

"It's just me," I called.

"Who are you?"

"Bonnie Jean Indermill," I snapped, giving him the dubious force of my full name. "Pro-Team Temporary Secretaries."

That stopped them. A smattering of whispered Russian conversation followed. The KGB probably doesn't use temps. "You are alone?" the man finally asked.

"Of course I'm alone. And if you don't go away I'm going to call Security."

A second later the voices retreated up the hall. Forgetting all about the rat, I raced to Abigail's desk and grabbed the phone. I had my finger on the button when something rubbed against my calf. My heart flip-flopped and I was on top of my desk in an instant.

I waited, stapler in hand, for the rat to make his move. I didn't plan to staple him. I planned to throw the thing at him. The Scotch tape dispenser would follow, then the pencil cup. A hailstorm of office supplies would pound that rat to smithereens. Seconds passed, then minutes. Except for the buzzing of the lights the room was quiet. Maybe the rat had gone away. Maybe my little commotion had frightened him.

Okay, Bonnie. You can't spend the night like this. Lowering myself onto my stomach, I lay across my blotter and hung my head over the desk's edge until I could see through the jumble of chairs to the shadowy space under Abigail's desk.

Feet! A pair of feet, in socks and shoes, attached to ankles! For a second I grew light-headed and almost toppled face first off that desk. The feet were moving. Legs stretched out from the dark hiding place. A torso emerged. Shoulders, finally a head, with sloping cheekbones and straight brown hair.

"I am Nikolai Koslov. I wish to defect."

2

When I looked back on it several days later, I had to wonder at the speed and ease with which Nikolai Koslov gained U.S. asylum. The tremulous search for a sponsor, the nerve-racking wait for a green card common to many immigrants play no part in the life of a superstar.

On that first night, when Niki crawled out from under the desk and announced his intention, my whispered call to the security office quickly brought a brigade of police officers and immigration officials to Nikolai's rescue. We weren't out of the building before our bulging ranks were joined by a mob of reporters and photographers. How they'd gotten word of Nikolai's defection I don't know, but they turned out in force, microphones and cameras ready. Seconds later Michael Devereux and Galena Semenova pushed through the crowd. By the time we reached the cars waiting at the curb we must have numbered two dozen.

Behind us trailed the Soviet Union's gloomy gang—the two KGB men, whose gun had miraculously disappeared—and several other people claiming to be members of the diplomatic corps.

It was a circus! Everyone talking at once, microphones shoved in our faces, flashes popping in our eyes, engines racing, ready. Nikolai had taken a hard grip on my hand. I wasn't sure what was in store for me when I climbed into the car after him, but I can't claim I didn't go eagerly. It was enormously flattering to be Nikolai Koslov's life raft in these unfamiliar waters.

We were taken to a government office in a building on the east side of town. There Nikolai met with some U.S. officials, then spent half an hour by himself contemplating his decision. Now, knowing so much more about Nikolai, I suspect he spent those thirty minutes mapping out the next move in his career. But who knows? When he walked out of that quiet room and announced, in broken English, that his decision to seek asylum in the United States stood, his little speech brought a lump to my throat. As he spoke about leaving his beloved country because he needed to grow as an artist, his own eyes grew damp. Only later would I discover that acting is part of a Russian dancer's education.

The press ate it up. A reporter shoved me aside to get to Niki. A photographer blocked my view of the great man. Nikolai began moving toward the door, taking his entourage with him. Minus one. Me! I tried pushing my way back into the crowd. My effort got me a crushed foot. Seconds later, without so much as a parting glance my way, the Prince of Ballet left surrounded by his court.

For a moment I was sort of hurt. There I was, Nikolai's savior, owner of the hand he'd desperately clutched less than an hour before, standing alone in a corner of this dreary office building.

I followed a couple of stragglers from the Soviet contingent out the door. The night air was clammy and uncommonly still. A streak of lightning cracked the sky. A crash of thunder followed, and then the heavens opened wide.

The downpour went through my thin summer blouse in seconds. Up the block the yellow light of an empty taxi appeared. Waving frantically, I ran through the rain. The Soviets got there first. As the cab they had stolen from me sped away, its tires splattered my skirt with mud from the gutter. An omen of what was to come.

New York was a natural stage for Niki. Both were teeming with talent, ambition, and ego.

He embraced the city with a passion. It returned his affection. Onto his well-developed form flowed the admiration of the common man. During his first week in the Free World, the entourage of photographers that followed Niki everywhere caught him eating a hot dog at a Yankees' game, gazing fondly at the Statue of Liberty from the deck of the Staten Island ferry, kissing a Chinese baby on Canal Street, and hugging an Italian grandmother on Mulberry Street. The man was born for the camera.

By his second week in New York, it became clear that Niki was also born for the good life. Photographers caught him beaming and accepting a pair of handmade cowboy boots and an invitation to "come on down for a real barbecue" from the governor of Texas, dining with the mayor, and attending a charity ball with the queen of New York society on his arm. Street vendors gave way to four-star restaurants. Niki had arrived.

Interestingly, he had arrived without his wife of five years. That was the one blotch the papers turned up to tarnish the godlike reputation following Niki around. In Niki's rush for freedom, Irena Koslova, research scientist at a supersecret nuclear facility near Kiev, had been forgotten. His wife actually had distant relatives living in Brooklyn, but when reporters asked Niki if he planned to visit them, he answered with a shrug. When reporters mentioned his wife, which of course they did, he managed to get teary-eyed. "I shall miss her terribly, but because of her work, she is not permitted to leave Soviet Union. Someday . . ." At that point his shaky command of English invariably went to pieces.

More than a week passed before I saw Niki again. During that time, my stock around the Gotham Ballet Company rose about a thousand percent. I'm embarrassed to say that I did nothing to discourage the prestige that attached itself to me.

My underserved role as resident expert on the life and loves of Nikolai Koslov turned my shabby half office into a popular visiting place for clutches of young ballerinas, made all but inarticulate by their admiration for me and love for Niki. They had the idea that Abigail was my supervisor, so they kept out of the way until she left the office. Lucky for them, that happened frequently. As soon as she was gone, the dancers appeared. The first would grab Abigail's chair, the next her desk top. Others propped themselves on cartons of mailing labels and stacks of phone books.

"But what's he really like? You know, *really*."

My reluctance to share the "down and dirty" on Niki whetted their starving appetites and later they'd be back: "What if his wife can never leave Russia? Will he get a divorce?"

Needless to say, Abigail doted on me, never failing to bring me a cup of coffee when she returned from her wanderings. And with each cup came the tilt of her head, the smile, and a little hint that I might return the favor by reintroducing her daughter to Niki's attention.

The reason I kept up my pretense had little to do with a desire to share Niki's limelight. The fact is, my new celebrity-by-association had given my job hunt a healthy boost. Tricia was being unbelievably nice, talking about my innate talent for fund-raising, about how with her backing I might go places in the field. Hard to believe that she, an expert in swaying the public, could actually fall for a lot of press hype, but fall Tricia did, and since she couldn't get next to Niki she figured I was the next best thing.

Not long after Niki's defection she waved a bribe in my face. We were stuffing envelopes together. The office had suddenly become a democracy. Tricia, with several hundred dollars' worth of black linen on her, stuffed right alongside her lowly office temp.

"I understand the company is adding to its administrative budget," she said. "There's going to be enough money for a new person. That's something you might want to think about. Starts in the neighborhood of eighteen thousand."

"That's not a very good neighborhood, Tricia."

"They might go as high as twenty. Are you interested?"

In New York City, twenty thousand dollars doesn't get you much of a neighborhood either. On the other hand, I was enjoying the work. I shrugged. "Possibly."

She nodded. "I'll tell Michael. Oh, Bonnie, if I may change the subject for a second. When you see Niki, could you sound him out about joining Gotham Ballet? He keeps putting Michael off about his decision."

I had no more chance of swaying Niki's career decisions than I had of making waves at the next summit conference, but Tricia didn't have to know that.

"But Tricia," I explained patiently, "he's been in the country less than two weeks. After all . . ."

"They might be able to go as high as twenty-two thousand on that job. Michael has always been willing to listen to me, and if I were to explain how good you are at this work . . ."

Twenty-two thousand dollars. On that, I might be able to squeak by. "I'll speak to Niki about Gotham Ballet the next time I see him."

Fat chance of that, since it looked as if Niki had already forgotten I existed, but if my little pretense got me started in my fund-raising career, why not?

As things turned out, my relationship with Niki was far from over.

Two unattached women, high and dry on a hot Saturday night. My friend Amanda Paradise wasn't optimistic about our situation but she hadn't stopped trying. She tilted her head to the side so that her long dark hair fell over one eye like a 1940s glamour queen. She swept it back with a dramatic swing of her head, then glanced around the sidewalk café through half-open eyes. That move having gathered no attention, she thumped her elbows back on the table.

We were at Dos Sombreros, one of the trendiest of the many trendy restaurants on Manhattan's West Side. Though the service was almost nonexistent and the noise level excruciating, the quasi-Mexican food was pretty good and the prices not too bad for the Lincoln Center area. Both the big indoor dining room and the outdoor café where Amanda and I had eaten were packed. Less than a block from Lincoln Center, Dos Sombreros attracted show-biz types in droves—dancers, singers—as well as people who wanted to be seen and people willing to pay to see them.

"It's not as if we're ugly or anything, Bonnie," Amanda said. "I'll bet most of the men in here are gay. That's the problem. Oh," she groaned. "Things couldn't be worse."

"Sure they could." I sank my spoon into my custard dessert and took a taste.

"How? We don't have boyfriends, we don't have jobs. I'm . . ." She leaned toward me so she could lower her voice. "I'm going to turn thirty-two this year and I've never even been married. At least you've been married!"

"It wasn't all that great. Want a taste?" I asked, extending a spoonful of custard her way. "It will make you feel better."

"Pass the lips, look out hips!" she singsonged, pulling away. "You know, Bonnie, you shouldn't have broken up with Derek. He's probably the last available man in Manhattan."

"I doubt that," I said with more conviction than I felt.

"I'd gotten so used to you as a couple," she mused.

So had I, but there's that other M word. The big M word. I'd said it to Derek. On that awful night I'd said it quite a few times.

I can't remember how it started, but I recall myself edging up on the forbidden territory, dropping a word or two about commitment. He'd been puzzled. Commitment? What did I want from the relationship? Wasn't what we had enough? Good times, good sex, good this, good that.

Not good enough! That's when I said the dirty M word, the one that goes hand in hand with the H word: *husband*. I'd said it so loud that his entire apartment building knew what I wanted from the relationship. Marriage!

The word had come up from nowhere. Until it blasted from my lips like a flame from a stoked furnace, I hadn't known it was in me. I mean, I'm not nuts—I'd known it was in there somewhere, but I'd thought it was secure, concealed where it would never give me away. When it burst out it shocked me almost as much as it shocked Derek. But there was no taking it back.

"Why do you want that so much?" he had asked. A perfectly sensible question considering I'd been there before and hadn't wanted it then. I'd been married before I was twenty, and the only thing good about the experience had been its short duration: eight months, from march down the aisle to divorce court.

I couldn't explain why I wanted it, but I wanted it, and after six months of never breathing the word, I wanted it immediately. Derek didn't want it. Then or ever, it seemed. The next week he had left on a sailing trip. Since then—a period of several weeks—I'd had two postcards.

Amanda found the entire business mind-boggling, and never missed a chance to talk about it. I should call him, she said. Write him. Camp out on his doorstep. Anything to win back the last available man in Manhattan.

It was only by chance that I was spared a lecture that evening. I spotted Jonquil, Carmen, and Chris dodging traffic on their way across Broadway. The three looked as if they had been performing. Their hair was damp and their faces scrubbed and rosy.

Amanda's glance followed mine. "He's cute, Bonnie, but he's with two girls."

When the trio reached the restaurant door, Chris disappeared inside, leaving the girls on the street. Catching their eyes, I waved.

"You know them?" Amanda asked.

"They're dancers. The redhead is Abigail's daughter, Jonquil."

Amanda peered into the restaurant. "Where did the guy go, anyway? I didn't recognize him. Is he a principal?"

She was referring to the hierarchy of dancers. At the bottom of the ladder were members of the corps, and at the top the principals, those whose names commanded attention. In between those two groups were the soloists—up-and-coming dancers who had been promoted from the corps and now aspired to principal status.

"His name's Chris Lansing. He's a soloist. Apparently he's going to be promoted to principal this year. He's already gotten his own dressing room. I think he's twenty-three," I added pointedly.

"Oh." She half stood in her chair to look into the restaurant. "He's kind of young, I guess. Probably gay, anyway."

"I don't think so. I think he and Jonquil are dating."

By then Jonquil and Carmen had made their way through the squeeze of diners. They slipped into the empty chairs at our table.

"Hi, Bonnie!"

I introduced the two girls to Amanda. They were both impressed by her, I could tell. Amanda is a beauty. She works at it. Almost the first words out of Carmen's mouth were, "I love your hair. Where do you get it cut?"

For the next few minutes everything was hairdressers, which led naturally to makeup and clothes. I have a limited appetite for that sort of thing.

"Where did Chris go?" I finally asked.

"To see the Old Man," Carmen said with a giggle.

Jonquil gave her friend one of those "shut up" looks. "Carmen's kidding," she said as she glanced into the restaurant. "That's what she calls the men's room. The Old Man."

"Yeah," Carmen said brightly. "Just like ladies your age call the girls' room 'the little girls.'"

"Carmen," I said, "I've never called a rest room 'the little girls.'"

Amanda started to say something when a commotion on the sidewalk interrupted her and, for that matter, everyone else around.

The curbside door of a huge white limousine had just been opened by a uniformed chauffeur. The high-heeled sandals and long bare legs of a well-known starlet emerged. She wiggled out of the seat onto the sidewalk, tossing her short blond curls and tugging her flared white minidress just far enough over her thighs to keep her out of jail. She alone would have caused enough of a stir, but when she turned toward the car's dark interior and put out her hand, guess who joined her on the sidewalk.

"Would you look at that," I said.

"Wow! What a hunk!" That, of course, was Amanda.

"I don't think he's so attractive," I said.

Carmen squinted at the limo. "Who? Who is it? I took my contacts out. I'm blind without them."

"Don't you have glasses?" I asked.

"Glasses? You've got to be kidding. I wouldn't be caught dead—" She stopped abruptly. My almost new, rose-tinted glasses were sitting on my nose. "I mean," she stammered, "on some people, like you, they look great. But on me . . ."

I took off my glasses and handed them across the table. "Be my guest."

"It's Niki!" Thrusting my glasses at me, Carmen began frantically straightening her hair.

"Oh no," Jonquil groaned. "What if he remembers that I'm the one who fell? I hope he doesn't see us."

"Why, that's Nikolai Koslov with . . ." a woman at the table next to ours gasped.

The hounds caught the scent, not that either of their prey

was elusive. As the celebrity couple made their way toward the restaurant's entrance, culture vultures and autograph hounds mobbed them. To the delight of the crowd, the starlet did a Marilyn Monroe over a breezy subway grate. A photographer emerged out of thin air. And then there was another. Both cameras aimed at the starlet.

Niki watched his date cavort for a second, but then his attention wandered. As he glanced around, his look was impatient, bored. And then—

"Bonnie-e-e!" His arms stretched wide.

All eyes were back on Nikolai. The crowds parted as he made his way to my table.

"The woman who saves me," he said loud enough to be heard by everyone around. Bending down, he planted a big kiss right on my lips. Flashes exploded. Before I could say a thing, he had taken a chair from the next table and pulled it between the two ballerinas.

"My charming partners from the ballet school."

"Niki! We've got a reservation!" The starlet, standing by the door, had shouted over traffic. Niki rolled his eyes and leaned into the center of the table. "Manager's idea I be seen with actress. Not my type," he added.

How special we felt, being part of Niki's crowd. Carmen was speechless and Jonquil was positively scarlet. "I don't usually fall," she said. "My mother almost killed me."

Niki smiled. "Bah! Is nothing. I fall, everybody fall." As he said this his glance traveled to the fourth member of our party. "And Bonnie, what is other friend's name?"

"This is Amanda . . ." I began. A microphone was suddenly there. A young woman at the end of it yelled a question across the table.

"Do you think you'll be joining Gotham Ballet?"

Niki reached across the table and grasped my shoulder. "With such a friend as Bonnie there, perhaps." Another burst of flashes followed.

"Niki!" the starlet called again, her voice ragged.

He shrugged and pushed back his chair. "Must go. Until later," he added, his eyes looking into Amanda's.

"Until later?" I asked her as Niki and his entourage made their noisy way through the tables and into the restaurant. "What did you do? Grab him under the table?"

"Of course not! Do you think he liked me? I can't believe how sexy he is. I'd do it with him in a minute."

"I'm in love," Carmen sighed.

Jonquil squealed with laughter. "He's not that cute!"

I had to laugh, too. I'd seen examples of who Amanda would do it with. Her recommendation counted for nothing. Amanda and I had met on my last permanent job. She'd been having an affair with one of the executives, a man so froglike in every respect that no amount of kissing could have made a prince of him.

"He kissed you right on the mouth," Amanda said. "Did it feel fantastic?"

"Unbelievable. He must do barre exercises on his lips."

To tell you the truth, I was sure Niki's kiss was his way of saying to the crowd watching his starlet date, "Pay attention to me!" Still, I can't complain that I got nothing out of that public smack on the mouth. I got a permanent job.

Niki and the starlet made the Saturday afternoon paper. BALLET GREAT CONSIDERING GOTHAM BALLET. I was nowhere mentioned but it didn't matter. Jonquil and Carmen told half the company about the kiss, Tricia got the story through the company's well-nourished grapevine, and so it goes. Nikolai Koslov and I officially joined the Gotham Ballet on the same hot summer day.

As you might imagine, his arrival was greeted with a lot more fanfare than mine. By Monday at noon, Niki had made it official, signing a one-year contract with Michael Devereux in front of the usual reporters and photographers. And Monday at four, Tricia called me into her office.

She was wearing another crisp linen number. This one

was rose with an ivory lace collar. I would have done almost anything for a job where I wore dresses like that.

"If you still want it, the position is yours. Twenty-two thousand dollars." The expression that accompanied these words was not a study in enthusiasm. I suspect a rough translation of it was, "You delivered; now I'm paying off."

Who cared? Not me! Though I lacked even the most rudimentary qualifications for the position of fund-raising assistant, and though the whopping $22,000 a year was nothing to write home about, I wanted that job.

"Thank you. I'd like that very much."

She extended her hand. I grasped it. We had a deal.

I went straight to Bloomingdale's.

3

"Nice outfit, Bonnie," Tricia said the following morning. It *was* nice—a pale green linen sheath and bolero jacket. In that outfit I could solicit funds from any corporate president in the world. The green sheath and the other new outfits in my closet were the result of a three-hour delirium at Bloomingdale's Career Dressing Summer Savings Spectacular. My charge card had taken the brunt of it. A fund-raiser can't go around looking like some aging flower child, can she?

Tricia wasn't sufficiently in awe of my new wardrobe or of my friendship with Niki to do anything crazy like give me a decent place to work.

"I know you and Abigail don't mind sharing," she said.

No, Abigail didn't mind. Abigail's attitude about the workplace gave new meaning to the word *relaxed*. Tricia could have put a gorilla at my desk. As long as it didn't threaten her daughter's future, Abigail wouldn't have minded. She might even have asked it to cover the phones during her frequent absences from the office.

I, on the other hand, minded. Clutter confuses me, and when things are already confused it makes me crazy. Looking around that horrible little office and realizing that it was my new home for eight hours a day almost gave me a panic attack. I beat down a wave of claustrophobia and put an expression on my face as bland as Tricia's and as accepting as Abigail's.

"It's fine."

"Good. I'll leave you to settle in. Stop by at four and we'll go to Michael's party." She raised her head a millimeter and gave me a look through half-closed lids, so that her stare came down the bridge of her aristocratic nose. "I'm amazed Niki didn't mention it to you."

I smiled. "He has so much on his mind."

"I suppose so."

The party was an informal office affair being held in one of the rehearsal rooms to welcome Niki and other new members of the company. My great friend Niki hadn't invited me and my status with Tricia had dropped a couple of notches. Now I had to find a way to buddy up to him, at least while Tricia was watching.

I turned to my work. No sooner was my nameplate glued to the door than my phone was ringing. I was responsible for following up on our begging letters—keeping computer records on who might be written off, who might be squeezed a little harder. With Niki joining the company, donations were expected to quadruple and I was going to be real busy. On my last job I'd been paid handsomely for doing nothing, which was fine until management decided to cut the extraneous staff. After that, I'd expected a pink slip in every envelope that crossed my desk.

That wouldn't be a problem on this job. From what I'd seen, my only problem—if I ignored the fact that my salary barely covered life's necessities—was going to be Abigail. I can deal with having too much to do, at least for a while, but I have trouble going at a lunatic pace while the person sitting next to me spends her days languishing like a hothouse orchid thrown into a weed patch. And when Abigail wasn't languishing, she was too taken up with her daughter's career to bother with the office. Why Tricia tolerated her mystified me. In the patience department, I looked like Gandhi next to my boss.

That morning Abigail's wheedling started as soon as Tricia left.

"Tricia told me you'd be in charge of these," she said, handing me a stack of responses to our begging letter. "I'll be sure to give them to you. If you write out your answers, I'll type them. I'm not very fast, but . . ."

"Thanks, Abigail," I said, "but I'm a good typist. I'll do them myself."

"You're sure now?" She ran her fingers nervously through her hair. A few strands of gray caught my eye. "Tricia didn't give you much space to work in, did she?"

"It will be okay," I said. "I've got everything I need here."

"Oh, I didn't mean you wouldn't be able to get your work done. You're so smart and likable, you'll do well no matter where they put you."

Though several of my ex-employers might have argued that point, I thanked Abigail. "I better get moving on these letters." I started thumbing through the stack.

"I was wondering . . ."

I kept my eyes down. "Yes?"

"Did you get a chance to talk to Niki? About Jonquil, you know. I thought you might just mention . . ."

Finally I glanced up. Abigail's shoulders were hunched and her hands were folded over each other. Lying to her made me feel like a creep, but I wasn't about to jeopardize my job by admitting that the only time I saw Niki was when he needed to use me for one thing or another.

"Jonquil's surely soloist material," she continued. "And she's not too tall. She might make a perfect partner for Niki, don't you think? That time she fell was nothing. It's not like she falls all the time. Or like no one else ever falls. Any dancer with enthusiasm is bound—"

The idea of sharing an office with Abigail had made me irritable. I interrupted.

"What about your own life, Abigail?"

She stopped short, confused. "My life?"

"Yes. Maybe you should start thinking about yourself. You've got that nice home and your husband. Jonquil's going to be eighteen in a couple of months. She might want to take an apartment with some other girls . . ."

She was shaking her head. "No, no. Jonquil's career is the most important thing in my life. I've put everything I have into it."

"But at this point isn't everything up to her, and luck?"

"Not if I can help it." Compressing her lips stubbornly, Abigail turned to her desk.

Tricia at work. What a line she had!

"One of my mother's best friends married a Boylston. The Westchester Boylstons, of course. What a coincidence. I've known Harry and Joan for years. They're like my own family. And you say your wife is related . . ."

This who's who was being directed into a telephone. The phone on Tricia's desk. Her expression had nothing to do with her words. Her voice was all excitement, her face complete boredom. I'd caught her in the midst of her solicitation calls, sinking her teeth into some sucker.

While she babbled I looked around her office. In the battle for square feet Tricia hadn't done badly. It wasn't baronial, but it wasn't a corner of a corner either. In the battle for furniture she'd done about as well as the rest of us, which wasn't well at all. But she'd added little touches to improve the situation: a lithograph of Balinese dancers, a couple of framed posters. On the wall behind her desk she'd hung a framed coat of arms. Swords crossed over some hodgepodge. I couldn't make out the words over the swords.

"Lunch?" Tricia was saying. "I'd adore it. I feel as if I already know you. No, no. Anywhere you suggest would be marvelous. I'm looking forward to it." She hung up and jotted something on her calendar.

"A nouveau riche philistine! Doesn't know the first thing about ballet. What do you suppose he does for a living?"

From Tricia's tone I expected to hear that the guy ran a bordello or something. "I can't imagine," I said.

"Owns a car dealership! What we have to go through to get funds to support this company. You'll find yourself sitting across the table from people who are one generation from a trailer park."

At that moment Tricia was doing just that—sitting across from someone who was one generation from a trailer park. I resented her remark terribly but kept my mouth shut.

"I don't suppose you have any corporate contacts, do you?" she asked.

She expected a swift no. I surprised her.

"As a matter of fact, my favorite uncle is a vice president at ——" I named a Fortune 500 company.

This uncle, though no part of my life, is not a figment of my imagination. My mother assures me he is alive and well in New Jersey. The last time we met was at my high school graduation, when he shook my hand and gave me a savings bond.

Tricia's eyebrows rose at the mention of his firm. "Very nice. That's one you can cultivate."

"I intend to." My eyes wandered up to the coat of arms.

"We should prefer death to disgrace." Tricia snapped these words at me with such force that for a crazy second I thought she was threatening me.

"Pardon me?"

"The Van Rensselaer family motto. From Cicero."

I nodded. "Oh." I suppose death is better than some things, but disgrace? It's always seemed to me that the best way to handle disgrace is to brazen it out.

Tricia picked up her phone again. "I have one more call to make before we go upstairs. Just be a second."

A minute later she was going on to some other refugee from the working class about all their schools, relatives, and friends in common. To listen to Tricia, you'd have thought she went to school with half the people in New York and was related to the other half.

I wasn't naive enough to think that she wanted my company at the party because she liked me. What she wanted was a personal introduction to my great pal Niki. I figured I'd play it by ear. If the mood of the party was loose enough, maybe I could work up the nerve to fling my arms around him and give him a big smack on the lips like he'd given me in the café. That would settle Tricia's hash!

Her telephone fawning threatened to go on forever. Finally I stood and gestured. I'd be back in a minute.

The air-conditioning vent in the ladies' room ceiling was sending a blast of noisy, icy air over my head and down my back. I pulled my feet up under me in the narrow stall and breathed as quietly as I could. There are few things more embarrassing than being caught eavesdropping on personal conversations. Especially nasty personal conversations.

I hadn't intended to listen so long. It's just that before I could come bursting noisily out of the cubicle, Abigail and Jonquil's argument grew so hot and heavy that I wouldn't have shown my face for the world.

"What if I don't want to flirt with him?" Jonquil had been saying when they walked into the rest room. "What if I think he's yucky?"

"Niki is not 'yucky,'" her mother said. "And I wasn't suggesting you flirt with him. I said 'Be friendly.' Let the man know you're alive."

"Friendly? Sure. You'd like it if I told him I'd sleep with him, wouldn't you?"

Water started running into one of the sinks. Then there was a scraping noise. This was turning into a shoving match.

"Ouch!" Jonquil cried. "What's the matter with you?"

"What's the matter with me? You can ask that after everything I've given up for you? What kind of a daughter are you? One of these days, Niki is going to be running this company . . ."

"I didn't ask you to give up anything. I wish you'd go back to Atlanta. You just wait. As soon as I get my Granny Foote's money, I'm finding my own apartment—"

Abigail interrupted. "Ten thousand dollars doesn't go as far as you think, young lady. Now, I'm going up to the party. When you get there, I don't want to see you off in a corner giggling with that bum Chris. Circulate!"

The ladies' room door swung closed behind Abigail. Now if Jonquil would go I could get out of the cubicle. My calves were killing me.

She was in no hurry. She went into a stall a couple down from my hiding place. I was as quiet as a mouse and I suppose the air conditioner camouflaged my breathing. I heard the rustling of plastic and a scraping noise, followed by a long, loud sniff. The poor kid, crying. A little more scraping, and another long, loud sniff. The plastic rustled again. Maybe she wasn't crying at all.

I'm not exactly on the cutting edge of the fast life, but I'm not completely out of it. What I'd just heard might have been the sound of a girl weeping in a rest room cubicle. It also might have been the sound of a girl snorting cocaine.

As soon as Jonquil left I emerged from hiding. I hadn't even combed my hair when Tricia walked through the door.

"I've been waiting for you," Ms. Granite-face said. "We've got to get upstairs. I don't want to miss Niki." She hustled me out the door with my hair uncombed.

The big room was packed and the party in full swing by the time we got there. What a spread! Grocery store cheese on Ritz crackers, cut-up weenies on toothpicks, and paper plates full of peanuts. Paper cups of champagne were being handed out by Elliott Pierce. He poured as if every drip trickled from his veins.

I was lucky. Niki had been cornered by a large middle-aged woman from Costumes who was not important enough to take up the great man's time. Spotting me, Niki waved and shoved past her. The next thing I knew he was kissing my fingers.

"Bonnie, my love."

What a ham! I thought hand-kissing had gone out with the Three Musketeers.

"Nikolai Koslov, I would like you to meet my boss, Tricia Van Rensselaer," I said.

Doubtless hoping for the touch of those hot Russian lips, Tricia extended her hand. Niki shook it lightly. Kissing was saved for those of us closest to him. He looked at her, at me, then around the room.

"So many beautiful women at one gathering I never knew possible."

In her own reserved way, Tricia ate this up. When he left us abruptly a second later she nodded approvingly. "What a gentleman. Breeding always shows."

Breeding? From what I'd heard, Niki had been born on a chicken farm in the Ukraine. Wherever he came from, though, he knew how to work a room. As I sipped my champagne I watched him make the rounds. Everyone got a little bit of the Prince. The men got smiles and hearty handshakes and the women, particularly the younger ballerinas, got lingering handshakes and what flirtatious banter he could manage with his broken English. When Abigail's turn came she looked as if she would swoon at his feet. Her wits returned soon enough, however. She reached for her daughter and all but shoved the girl at Niki. I didn't hear what passed between them, but a smile beamed across Abigail's face. Jonquil must have decided to play her mother's game.

The ringing of a fork against a champagne bottle made me turn to the front of the room, where Michael Devereux stood.

As I've said, he was a tall, dark, handsome devil. With his looks alone he could have dominated the room. As artistic director, he commanded it.

"Boys and girls."

The group quieted.

"I am proud to welcome our very esteemed new principal dancer, Nikolai Koslov."

We clapped enthusiastically.

"And I would also like to welcome our two new corps members, Carmen Garcia and Jonquil Jeffreys."

We'd all heard rumors that the two girls were joining the company, so Michael's announcement was no surprise. Still, it generated a burst of applause. Abigail was positively aglow.

"And last, but I hope not least . . ." Michael continued.

At this point I expected Michael to announce that Chris Lansing was being promoted to principal dancer. The rumor had been floating around for weeks.

". . . I would like to tell you all about something that is very dear to me. As many of you know, I have choreographed a new ballet. It will premiere in four weeks . . ."

I glanced at Chris. If he was upset he didn't show it.

". . . with Niki in the title role. The evening will begin with a pre-performance tour and champagne reception back-stage for our patrons. There will be reporters and photographers, and a television crew will film the preparations."

"They're going to show us getting dressed on television?" Jonquil squealed.

Michael smiled at the girl. "The corps' dressing rooms on the main floor will be filmed, but we'll make sure you're all decent before the cameras roll. The champagne reception itself will be held in a practice room. I don't have to tell you how important it is that all of you are on your best behavior," he added.

"They will be," Madame interjected.

"A gala banquet will follow the premiere," Michael said. "All of you—including those who do not dance in the premiere—are expected to attend."

A wave of excited whispers swept the gathering. "What is the ballet?" "Whose music?" And the dancers' unspoken question that was so obvious you could almost hear it reverberating through the room: "Is there a role for me?"

"I expect my two-act *Icarus* to set a new standard for contemporary interpretations of the classics. I will return to the stage to dance the role of Daedalus."

"Who?" Jonquil's squeal, again. She had to be high.

"The music," Devereux went on, "will be a combination of traditional Greek folk music and a piece commissioned by me."

Tricia whispered, "Another old Greek turkey to drag across the stage. But we'll make a bundle from the filming and dinner."

Someone behind me said softly, "You would think that after the reception his God-awful *Hercules* got he'd leave the Greeks alone."

Niki didn't bother hiding his feelings. "If I am correct, there was *Icarus* done for Bolshoi some years ago. Was not successful." He motioned toward Galena Semenova. "You remember?"

"My *Icarus* will be more than successful," Michael said. "It will be unforgettable."

At this point Devereux gave a brief rundown of his ballet. If I remembered the myth correctly, he was taking some artistic liberty with it. Icarus had been quite young when his father, Daedalus, fashioned feather wings set in beeswax so the two could make their escape from the palace of King Minos. In Devereux's version, Icarus was old enough to have a love interest.

"That role," Michael explained, "will be danced by Galena."

Niki's eyebrows arched. "Will not audience laugh at age difference?"

"Laugh?" Galena said, clearly surprised. Then her expression softened. "But you joke. Always such a kidder."

"What is joke? I do not joke."

"Oh, I doubt they'll laugh . . ." Michael began.

"I do not doubt!" Niki shot back.

All the little rustlings of feet around the room stopped. All eyes shifted to Galena Semenova. She had moved a step or two closer to Niki.

"Surely, my darling Niki, you are not suggesting that I am too old to dance the role of your lover," she said, smiling at this naughty boy.

Niki smiled back. "I suggest merely that more suitable partners exist. Since Michael takes license with myth, perhaps he adds different role for you, role of mother . . ."

"You suggest I should dance your mother? In stage makeup, dearest Niki, I am any age I wish to be. Age makes little difference in ballet. If it does, I am hardly old enough to be your mother?"

By the end of that sentence, her voice had risen several octaves. Niki was unperturbed.

"Can that be?" For a moment he looked puzzled. "You leave Soviet Union twelve years ago; you are thirty-three years old. I am student at Bolshoi school. Fourteen years old. Surely a woman of thirty-three can have child of fourteen."

"I was not thirty-three, my darling boy! I was twenty-seven."

"But my dearest Galena. I attend birthday party when you become thirty. My first year at Bolshoi when I am mere child of eleven. You defect in Paris when you are thirty-three, and that is twelve years past . . . excuse me, but my English . . . very difficult."

Why the bastard had to look at me then is beyond me. But look at me he did. "Thirty-three and twelve?"

From across the room Galena turned and searched me out.

I shook my head. Frankly, I couldn't imagine why the six years made any difference, one way or another. Galena was right. In stage makeup, she could pass for fourteen.

"This is neither the time nor the place . . ." Michael began. Something had happened, though. This tall, dark, and handsome man with the beautifully modulated voice no longer dominated the room. Control had shifted from the twentieth-century Lord Byron to the short, messy-looking Russian with the heavy accent.

Niki wasn't about to drop the subject. He was counting on his fingers, articulating each syllable. "Thirty-four, thirty-five . . ."

"That was my twenty-fifth birthday party you attended," Galena said, equally clear. "I defected before I was twenty-eight."

"Forty-five," Niki countered, gleeful as a child who had come up with the answer to a difficult problem. "Is correct, Bonnie? Thirty-three and twelve make forty-five years?"

Every eye in the room turned to me. I looked at my feet.

"Thirty-nine," Galena shouted. "I am thirty-nine. Only last month!"

Niki smiled broadly. "Ah! You have embarrassment for your age. No big deal, my darling Galena. What are five, six years? Many fine roles for older women. Character roles. But for my partner I think someone younger." There was a note of finality in Niki's voice. He had no intention of partnering Galena and that was that.

"Animal! I will put a dagger through your filthy heart." Snatching the cheese knife from Elliott's hand, Galena advanced across the room. The little knife could hardly make it through the cheese, much less flesh and bone, but there was such fury in Galena's eyes that the crowd parted instantly.

"Please!" Michael's shout fell on deaf ears.

When she got to her tormentor, Galena lunged. She was almost as tall as Niki, but he was stronger. He grabbed her wrist, grinning all the while.

"Such fire! Is why Russian women make great dancers."

Michael finally reached his stars. He forced the knife from Galena's fingers, then pulled her away from Niki and toward the door. She went willingly enough, but when she got there, she spun and screamed at Niki.

"Thirty-nine!"

He answered with a smile. "As you wish, my darling."

I don't have to tell you that the festivities were over. Tricia and I were among the first to leave.

"God," I said, "am I ever glad to get out of there."

Tricia looked around to make sure no one could hear. "I absolutely adore him."

"You do?" I was surprised. Even if what Niki said was true, his performance had been anything but adorable. "You know what may have been behind that? Height," I said. "On her toes Galena would tower over Niki. When I saw him in class he chose the shortest girl to partner."

"Who cares what's behind it? That woman has had Michael eating out of her hand for years. It's about time someone around here had the guts to take her down a few pegs.

"Bonnie," she said when we reached my office, "your friend Niki is going to be a real boon to this company. You just watch. Things around here are going to change. Oh—and Bonnie? You're going to follow up on your uncle?"

"Certainly!"

I worked late that evening. I remember, because it was the night I met Bertha Wozniak.

The door to my office flew open at about seven-thirty, taking me by such surprise that I jumped. The party on the other side of it, a stout woman with a fringe of auburn curls around her forehead, gasped.

"Am sorry, misses," she said in accented but clear English. "I thought this was janitor's closet." She was armed with a bottle of ammonia and pulling an industrial-size vacuum cleaner.

"That's okay," I said. "You're new, aren't you? It's an easy mistake to make. You want to clean in here now? I'm about ready to leave."

"Thank you." She moved around the cramped space like

a pro, explaining as she did that she had only started that afternoon.

"I am thrilled to be here," she said as she pulled Abigail's trash can from under her desk.

"You enjoy your work that much?"

"Ah! I enjoy my work, but is the ballet I love. And Nikolai Koslov. Seven years ago I see him dance in my native Poland. Only youth, but already wonderful. Three weeks ago I see him at the Metropolitan Opera House. Sixteen dollars for cheapest tickets, on the roof almost. But for Nikolai, is worth every penny."

"Now that you work here, you'll be able to get free tickets sometimes."

She shook her head. "No. Am with private contractor. Oh!" She set the trash can down and jerked her hand back. Blood welled on one of her knuckles.

"Such a clumsy cleaning lady," she said. "Already tonight two cuts."

"Here." I handed her a tissue.

As she dabbed at her finger, we introduced ourselves and then chatted for a few minutes about the ballet, about Niki and the other stars. She was a real pleasure to talk to, one of the nicest, sanest people I'd met on that job.

From the first I admired her. Came here with nothing, I figured. Making minimum wage and going to the Met.

"Listen," I said on my way out, "if I ever get hold of any free tickets I'll make sure you get one."

She stopped her cleaning and crossed her hands over her heart. "Oh, misses. You promise? I would be so grateful."

She looked dangerously close to tears so I hurried out, calling "I promise" behind me. That was a promise I should never have made.

The outcome of the war between Niki and Galena was still up in the air, but the first battle had gone to Niki. Two younger principals were rehearsing for the female lead in Devereux's *Icarus*. Was it coincidence that they were the two shortest principals in the company? I thought not.

Twice during the next week, Galena Semenova let me know that she considered me part of the enemy camp, one of Niki's spoilers. The first time, I came face to face with her on the elevator. She was with Madame. When the doors slid open they were speaking English. One look at me and Galena switched to a hot blast of Russian. I'm not being paranoid. Whatever she said, it was about me and it wasn't nice. The way she raised her chin, narrowed her eyes, and spat the words sent a cold chill up my spine.

If I had any doubts, our second run-in dispelled them. We met in one of the long corridors that run under the theater. Galena was alone. As we drew nearer she stared straight at me, her unblinking eyes drilling angry black rays into me. If there had been an open door in the hall I would have ducked into it. Instead, I had to keep walking toward her. We were a couple of feet apart when she veered into my path.

"I shall be here long after Niki and his friends have departed," she said softly.

God, was she formidable! I don't mean I thought she was going to hit me or anything like that. But those black eyes and that straight black hair belonged on a sorceress. When she continued on her way, my heart was pounding.

What made the situation even more intolerable for me was Galena's popularity. Everyone but Tricia liked her. The young ballerinas considered her a role model. As for the old guard, well, she was one of their own.

I've always felt that the old guard shouldn't be discounted until it receives the last rites. You don't get to be "old guard" by being politically dumb. For my own sake, though, I hoped the rumors that Galena was planning to retire were right. It is unpleasant, to say the least, when a popular woman in a powerful position hates you.

Speaking of rumors, a whirlwind of them were blowing around the company about Niki. Niki had plans to choreograph his own ballets. Niki's early choreography showed a prodigious talent. Niki was divorcing his scientist wife. Niki, Niki, Niki. I heard most of this from Jonquil and Carmen.

"He invited one of the girls for dinner at his apartment and she spent the night," Carmen whispered.

"That's how she got her role," Jonquil added knowingly.

"No. She deserves it," countered Carmen. "She's terrific."

"Sure she is. At you know what!"

"Oh yeah? So what did you do to get your solo?"

The mention of Jonquil's solo always got us giggling. Of the seven Athenian maidens sacrificed to the Minotaur, she was the only one who got to put up a struggle. It lasted about five seconds.

I liked both girls, different as they were. Carmen was open and optimistic. The stars deserved their good roles,

Michael was a genius, Madame the world's best teacher, and Niki a deity. For Carmen there was nothing better than being a ballerina.

Jonquil was more guarded than her friend, and far more cynical about the dance world. I was pretty sure she was using drugs. It wasn't only the incident in the ladies' room. Her behavior could be erratic, her highs and lows higher and lower than those of the other girls. There was also her occasional runny nose. It could have meant many things, cocaine use among them. For Jonquil practice was drudgery, the strict diet "a drag." She was even blasé about Niki. "He's nothing special," she would tell her smitten friend.

Carmen didn't go along with that for a minute. One day she showed me an album she'd gotten at a stationery store. She was keeping a scrapbook of clippings about Niki's exploits. I wouldn't have been surprised if she had started a fan club. She certainly wouldn't have had a problem finding other members, not at first.

Even Tricia was briefly swept up into the cult of Niki. Tricia, whose temperature had probably never risen above 98.6, the woman who wouldn't sweat in a sauna. I'm not suggesting that she started collecting Niki memorabilia or slinking around him with her tail airborne like a cat in heat, but one morning when Tricia stuck her head into my office to hand me my usual load of mail, I learned that Niki had done something guaranteed to make her blue blood pump a little faster.

"He put that rodent in his place," she said. "We were meeting—Niki, Michael, Elliott, and I. Elliott kept pulling his usual nonsense. Trying to pinch pennies on the costumes this time. He was trying to talk Michael into remaking old costumes. Can you imagine?"

I don't like getting involved in the little battles for territory that go on around offices. I shook my head but said nothing. Tricia didn't need encouragement.

"Our friend Niki knows how to handle himself, Bonnie.

I could tell by his expression that Elliott disgusted him. Finally Niki said, 'Why not ask us to dance nude? That way we spend no money on costumes.' And you know how Niki says things like that, with that innocent expression. He had that fool squirming."

"What did Michael decide?"

Tricia cocked an eyebrow. "If you were in Michael's situation, what would you do? Niki is his chance to move this company into the major leagues. In other words, we're getting the new costumes. You know, Bonnie, I think we can look forward to some much-needed changes around here." Then she smiled at me. A small smile, for sure, but a smile. "Niki is the kind of man I could be interested in."

Niki, it seemed, was the kind of man many women could be interested in. For some reason I was immune to his many charms. Only when they were displayed as part of a choreographed ballet did I appreciate them. I can't claim that my choices in men have always shown a lot of common sense. I've often chosen the guy on the motorcycle over the guy with the sedan, often found myself wishing for the company of some scoundrel while I had a Young Republican in hot pursuit. Niki, though, did less for my libido every time I had to deal with him.

"By the way," Tricia said, snapping out of her trance. "Here are more responses to our invitation. Wait until you see the yeses." She extracted one envelope from the stack. "This one's a pet project of mine. Be sure you respond right away. She wants a pass to the pre-performance reception."

I took the envelope. "Who is she?"

"It's 'they,' actually, but you'd never know it. Billy and Isabella Spencer. He provides the money; she dabbles in the arts." Tricia flicked her hand. "Dreadful bores, but I got a five-thousand-dollar donation out of them last year. It got the silly woman on the society page, among other things."

"Other things?"

Tricia hesitated. Just one corner of one lip tilted up. It

wasn't much, but it let me know those other things were juicy. "Mustn't gossip about the patrons," she said after a second. "But Isabella Spencer should be good for eight or ten now, at the least. Her husband"—she shook her head—"an absolute Neanderthal, just opened another restaurant. They throw a big party for the company in the fall," Tricia added. "This year they're inviting the staff."

She dropped the rest of the envelopes on my desk. It was amazing the number of people willing to pay a thousand dollars a plate just to eat in the same room with Niki.

The monumental amount of work involved with putting on the gala seemed to grow by the day. Just that morning I'd been handed our department's sacred allotment of pre-performance backstage passes. These were a hot item, offering special guests a rare peek at the reality of ballet rather than the illusion.

"Hopefully you won't go handing them out on street corners," Elliott had said. "Reporters, patrons, and VIPs only. And yourself, of course. Staff won't be able to get backstage without them."

I'd taken the passes with a smile. "And one for my mother the Avon lady, and one for my father the machinist, and one for my Aunt Gladys the waitress, and one . . ."

As I said, Elliott didn't bring out my best. Curiously, Tricia did. Despite my initial reservations I found her efficient, reasonably pleasant, and more than happy to share responsibility. She was heaping it on me.

We'd sent invitations to the premiere and banquet on heavy, cream-colored stationery with "A Gala Affair" embossed at its top. The stuff was unbelievably expensive. When you're asking for one thousand dollars a plate, you can't use scratch paper. I was responsible for entering the responses and making sure the "yeses" got their tickets. With the tickets I included handwritten notes—"We're so looking forward to seeing you"—on smaller Gala Affair notepads, also unbelievably expensive. A little pretentious and a lot of work for me, but Tricia insisted that the patrons loved this personalized attention.

Before she left my office that morning, Tricia asked me to be at a three o'clock meeting the next day. "We're getting together with Michael and Elliott to work out seating and menus. I think Niki's going to join us. Let's see Elliott try any of his nonsense then. Niki will chop him down to size."

As it turned out, Niki did a lot of chopping the next afternoon, but it wasn't Elliott he used his ax on. At what I've come to think of as the battle of the chicken coop, Tricia was pulverized.

Michael Devereux waved his arms, indicating the vast expanse of the second-level rotunda. It was a gymnasium-size space, with marble floors, fluted columns, and a high domed ceiling.

"I see eight rows, with six tables each. Seven patrons and one dancer at each table. That gives us three hundred and thirty-six patrons . . ."

"Three hundred and thirty-six thousand dollars," said Tricia.

"But," interjected Elliott, who was tapping figures into the calculator in his hand, "if we could put in one more row, and put nine sponsors at each table—"

"Impossible!" Tricia interrupted. "The kind of people who pay a thousand dollars for dinner don't want to feel as if they're riding the subway at rush hour."

Elliott hooted. "From the size of your taxi bills, you're the last person I'd expect to be an expert on the subway at rush hour." He poked some figures into his calculator. "That comes to one hundred and fifty thousand dollars more. Do you realize how many costumes that buys? Do you know that our budget for toe shoes is running over three hundred thousand dollars this year? What do you say, Uncle Mike? A hundred and fifty thousand dollars buys a lot of shoes."

At the "Uncle Mike," Tricia rolled her eyes. "I know the

figures, Elliott, but these are society people we're dealing with. If you try to skimp . . ."

With these two every point involved a skirmish. How many tables, who sat at each table, who got shuffled to the tables behind the columns with partial views, who got to eat with the "name" dancers, who would have to settle for members of the corps. Uncle Mike—Michael to the rest of us—would occasionally step between them and make a decision, but generally he stayed out of it. As Tricia and Elliott beat every point to a pulp he studied some menus Tricia and the caterer had put together.

Niki was leaning against the wall behind Michael, looking bored. From time to time he glanced down at his cowboy boots and rubbed one toe against his pants leg. So far this gift from the governor of Texas had held Niki's interest longer than anything else he'd run across in this country. Tricia's one try to get him into an argument on her side met with a shrug and a laconic "I dance; do not make parties."

So Tricia and Elliott had the arena to themselves. There was a practiced dynamic to their struggle. Elliott gave Tricia the seven sponsors per table; Tricia gave Elliott the extra row. Tricia won the fight for pale peach tablecloths. Elliott carried the round devoted to centerpieces. I took copious notes and spoke only when spoken to. Until the chicken entered the ring.

"Chicken," Tricia said when they got to the menu.

"Chicken," Elliott agreed at once. Chicken was a given.

"Chicken," they said to me almost in unison. Chicken, I wrote in my notebook. *Amandine en vol-au-vent*, chicken bordelaise, *flambé à l'ecu de France, sauté aux fines herbes*. There is no end to the things you can do to a chicken. "As long as it is not underdone," was Michael's only comment.

Elliott turned to the Prince of Ballet, still slouching indolently against the wall. "How about chicken Kiev?" he said. I could tell by Elliott's smug expression that he thought he'd scored a real coup. "What could be more appropriate to welcome our new Russian friend?"

"Bourgogne is always nice," Tricia said.

Stretching languorously, Niki pulled himself upright. He surveyed the room as if seeing it for the first time. He glanced at Elliott, at Michael, and right past Tricia to me. He looked once again at his shiny new cowboy boots. Then he gave me a quizzical smile, the exact same kind of smile he'd given me during his fight with Galena Semenova. I felt an awful foreboding.

"Why we must have chicken, Bonnie?"

What did I know about these things? I looked at Tricia. She answered for me.

"Niki, many people today avoid red meat. Chicken is a safe choice. It's almost universally liked. It's also inexpensive."

Niki walked forward a few paces until he stood at the top of the staircase. It put him in a terrific tactical position. Normally he wasn't much taller than Tricia, but now he towered over her so that he could look down his nose.

"As child I watch mother on farm, twist chickens' necks." He made a wringing movement with his fists. "I do not like."

"Niki," Tricia said with exaggerated patience, "you have to understand that people are going to be here to see you. They don't care what they eat. Chicken is . . ." Here she tried a new tactic: teach the foreigner something about life in the United States. ". . . customary at such dinners."

Niki looked at me, incredulous. "Is true, Bonnie? Chicken is American custom?"

Why did the bastard have to keep singling me out? I was so nervous I tried to make a joke. "Sure is," I said. "Right up there with Mom and apple pie."

Tricia had plastered on this pained smile. "Please understand, Niki, that we have a very strict budget. Veal is too expensive. As Elliott would confirm . . ." She looked toward Elliott for support.

Maybe Elliott was as dumb as Tricia said, but he'd had

the good sense to take himself out of the line of fire. He was on his way to the other side of the room, tape measure in hand, intent on measuring the width of a column. He became so involved with this column so quickly that when Tricia called his name louder—"Elliott!"—he ignored her. Tricia's fists clenched.

"Michael, perhaps you can explain to Niki. . . ."

Like me, Michael tried making a joke of the situation. "As long as no one gets ptomaine and sues us, I can't see what difference it makes."

Those were exactly my feelings. Unfortunately, neither Tricia nor Niki agreed.

Niki walked down the remaining three steps. Now he and Tricia were almost eyeball to eyeball, gladiators about to square off for the main event.

"Chicken is peasant food," he said.

"Nonsense! Why, a nicely prepared chicken could be served to a king."

Niki scratched his head. He looked from Tricia to me. "You would serve peasant food to king?"

I don't think I could have answered if someone put a gun to my head.

Niki smiled and moved closer. He put his hand on my shoulder. "Bonnie, my friend. Please explain to this . . . woman"—he said "woman" with a twist of his mouth that questioned Tricia's gender—"that good host does not serve chicken to important guests."

"Bonnie," Tricia snapped, "is not part of the decision-making process."

Niki dropped his hand from my shoulder and drew back, eyes widening. "Why Bonnie cannot speak? Is America. Democracy. Everybody speaks."

Tricia shook her head. "Michael," she called. "We need your help here."

Michael looked up from his papers. For a split second he glanced at Tricia. Then he sighed and looked back down. The man was in a dilemma. Did he go with his faithful, longtime employee or his superstar? The seconds dragged, until the quiet became as uncomfortable as the fight.

"What kind of food would you prefer, Niki?" Michael finally asked.

On one side of me, Tricia made a faint little noise of disgust: "Umph." That was all

On my other side, Niki bent at the waist and rubbed a speck of dust from one of his boots. With their overlapping bands of tooled leather, fringe, and silver ornaments, they were unbelievably garish.

Straightening, Niki smiled.

"What you think of cowboy food, Bonnie?"

Tricia stepped around me. "Cowboy food! Kindly explain to me what you mean by cowboy food? You're not suggesting we serve our patrons chili dogs are you?"

"Texas barbecue," answered Niki. "We serve Texas barbecue."

Mount Rushmore crumbled. I could hardly believe the contortions Tricia's face went through. Her eyebrows shot toward her hairline. Her lips widened until it looked as if her next sound would be a scream. It almost was.

"We serve Texas barbecue over my dead body," she shouted.

Niki pulled back as if appalled by her outburst

Michael must have realized he had to do something. He stepped around the table. "Tricia. Niki. Please. Let's discuss this in a civilized manner."

Niki raised his hands, a gesture of hopelessness. "Civilized? How we discuss civilized with crazy woman?" A quick glance at Tricia, then he looked at Michael. "I do not discuss with her. I discuss with Bonnie." He turned to me. "What you think of Texas barbecue?"

I shook my head. "Niki, I'm not qualified to choose a menu."

"Why not? You are adult; you eat. You choose."

This was terrible. Niki smiling in my face, Tricia glaring over his shoulder, Michael wanting to appease everybody, and Elliott by now completely mesmerized by his column measurements.

"I think barbecue would be too messy, Niki," I said cautiously.

He tilted his head. "Messy?"

"Greasy. Messy on the tables. Gets all over your guests' hands. Ruins their nice clothes."

He gave this some thought, then nodded. "Ah."

Now if Tricia had been able to control herself maybe everything would have been okay. I was already planning a careful, step-by-step route back to the chicken coop. If Niki still wouldn't go for the chicken, I figured that after this scene Michael would be willing to spring for veal. But Tricia just couldn't wait. For her this had become more than a menu. It was a matter of principle and, as the Van Rensselaer motto implied, principles were worth dying for.

"*Now* do you understand?" she said to Niki. "When you get back to your desk, Bonnie, call the caterer and tell him we're having chicken. I would prefer bordelaise or —"

"What you suggest, Bonnie?" Niki asked as if Tricia weren't there.

Well, Tricia was having none of that. She stepped right between me and Niki. "If anything other than chicken is served, it will be served without my assistance." Then she made a tactical error. I don't know why she did it, but she took hold of his arm above the elbow. The gesture could have been interpreted as friendly, seductive, or threatening. Niki assumed the last. He jerked his arm from her grasp and rubbed it.

"I am certain that is possible," he responded, his voice cold as ice.

"We could have Greek food," I said suddenly.

With those five words, I stuck my foot into my mouth

about up to the ankle. And I was only half serious. Mostly I wanted to defuse the battle.

The warriors tore their eyes from each other and turned them on me. The way things had been going, I expected both of them to attack me. Michael glanced up from his papers.

"That way," I said quickly, "we can stay with the theme of the Greek myth of Icarus."

Tricia frowned. "Greek food? That's almost as bad . . ."

Niki clapped his hands. "Wonderful idea!"

Niki's seal of approval was all it took to divert Elliott from his measurements. "Greek food. I love it." Leaving his measuring tape behind, he crossed the floor to our little group. "A bacchanalia."

I stared at him, shocked. I'd fully expected Elliott to trounce my idea.

"I see centerpieces of grapes," he said in all seriousness. "Maybe some vines."

Michael was noticeably relieved. "That would be lovely."

"And the room is perfect," Elliott continued. "Marble, these lovely Doric columns. The waiters can wear togas."

Tricia's composure was shot. One of her hands was in a fist at her side. The other hand tugged on a clump of hair. "Togas! I can't believe I'm hearing this. You've all gone crazy. The entire idea stinks!" Attempting one last time to appeal to reason, she turned to Niki. After taking a deep breath, she said, "Not everybody likes Greek food. Almost everybody eats chicken." Her voice held the exaggerated patience of a mother lecturing a sulky child. The tone did not sit well with the Prince of Ballet.

"Woman! What is your problem? You own chicken farm? Want to sell your chickens?"

Tricia's temporary cool disappeared. "You pompous ass!" she yelled. "You muscle-brained animal. You come in here and think you can run everything? Fine. It's all yours!" She turned to Michael in a fury. "If you go through with this Greek . . . orgy, you can do it without me."

"I'm sorry, Tricia, but—"

Michael didn't get a chance to finish. "I quit," Tricia said. Spinning on her heels, she stormed from the hall.

All three of the men immediately turned to me. Then, as if on signal, Elliott walked to the table where Michael was working. The two put their heads together. While they held a quiet conversation, Niki leaned against a column, regarding his boots with a little smile. How perfectly self-assured he was, and what a perfect jerk.

Finally, Michael and Elliott stopped their whispering and walked over to us.

"Do you feel you can handle this banquet?" Michael asked me.

"Is nothing but big party," Niki said. "Of course Bonnie can handle."

Sure. A party for four hundred and some people.

"I'm not terribly experienced, but I . . ."

"We *know* you're not terribly experienced," Elliott said. "Unfortunately, you're all we've got. It's either you or hire an outsider. The cost there would kill us."

Michael interrupted his nephew. "Please, Elliott, we've had enough unpleasantness. Now, what do you say, Bonnie? We'll give you all the support we can. If it's your salary you're thinking about, I'm sure Elliott will be able to come up with a bit more."

"Let's not get carried away!" Elliott said.

"I guess I can do it, but please remember that I've never run anything of this size before." Or half the size.

"But Bonnie, why you are worried?" Niki asked. "You will make Greek banquet no one ever forget."

"That's right," said Elliott. "It will be the talk of the social season."

I doubted that very much. With my limited experience of the fund-raising field, an uneventful, even blessedly dull Greek banquet was what I prayed for. Unfortunately, things didn't turn out that way. Talk of the social season is right! They're still talking about it.

That night, Bertha Wozniak found me in Tricia's office going through files. I had no intention of moving in there, at least not then. For one thing, I was too busy. For another, I would have felt kind of crummy after what had happened.

"And how is marvelous Niki?" Bertha asked as she squirted some cleaner on the Van Rensselaer coat of arms.

"Marvelous Niki isn't quite as marvelous as you think, Bertha." I told her what had happened with Tricia.

"But Niki is artist. Temperamental."

"Ha! You should have seen how he treated his fellow artist Galena Semenova."

She smiled, and then—bang! She confirmed what I'd suspected. "Galena Semenova is big woman. Even in Soviet Union Niki was reluctant to dance with taller ballerinas."

"But he shouldn't have done it the way he did."

"Niki is genius. The world will forgive many things from genius."

5

The third and last skirmish I witnessed was the briefest and, for me, the worst. Niki did something vile. I'm sure he did it to embarrass Michael Devereux in front of me.

The incident occurred the day before the performance, after a dress rehearsal.

During those frantic days before the opening my infatuation with Michael's looks faded and we developed a pleasant working relationship. He listened to the things I suggested, and if they made sense he let me do them. He was not the kind of boss to hover. His love was dancing and choreography, not fund-raising. Since I like working on my own, his attitude made my work a pleasure. All in all, it was a good job I had stumbled into—a job that might go somewhere.

Michael liked the fact that I had been a dancer. Several times he asked me about my background, about tap dancing and chorus line work. These were awkward conversations; I found Michael hard to talk to. Still, he was beginning to think of me as an insider, so much so that I almost got an invitation to a party at his apartment. Then Niki got involved and put an end to that.

I'd had a difficult day. The waiters didn't want to wear the togas that Elliott insisted would "make" the banquet. The top (and cheapest) supplier of stuffed grape leaves, which the caterer insisted were vital to any Greek banquet, had unexpectedly retired after thirty years in the business. The woman who was doing the flower arrangements doubled the price she originally quoted. The peach-colored tablecloths I'd rented clashed with the purple grapes Elliott wanted for the centerpieces. There were too many bigwigs for the head table. And on and on.

There were the personal things, too. I had nothing to wear to the banquet, no time to shop for anything, and no money to buy anything with. And, on top of that, I did not have a date! Staff had been assigned a table at the back of the room. I was one of the few staff members who could bring someone and I didn't have anyone to bring. I was going to be surrounded by the beautiful people in their beautiful clothes, all coupled up like passengers on Noah's ark, and I'd be sitting alone in a three-year-old flowered silk dress that recalled a skinnier time in my life.

That afternoon I had a particularly rough meeting with Elliott. I gave in on the peach tablecloths. We'd go with the white and the grapes. After quite an argument, Elliott finally let go of those wacky togas. The waiters would wear the usual black pants, white shirts, and black bow ties. "You want them in penguin suits, you get them in penguin suits," he sniffed.

It's no wonder I was in a daze that afternoon. A million things were on my mind. I was walking through the upper corridor paying no attention to where I was going when I turned a corner and ran, head-on, into Michael Devereux, causing him to drop sheet music all over the floor.

"Oh, I'm so sorry."

He brushed away my apology as we picked up the sheets of paper. "Think nothing of it." When he straightened up, he stared at me. "You look exhausted, Bonnie. I'm afraid we're not treating you very well."

I'm sure I did look exhausted, but I wasn't about to admit that my new job was too much for me.

"No, no. I love what I'm doing."

Michael smiled. "Do you really? How nice to meet a dancer who has made the transition to a completely different field."

Michael might not have found this transition so unusual if he had known that the monetary pinnacle of my dance career had occurred fifteen years before in San Francisco, when I'd averaged about thirty dollars a day as the tapping part of Tap & Tune, a three-person group that was booked on all the best street corners.

"Yes, it has been a change."

He fell into step beside me. "I admire the way you've jumped into this gala. Sometimes dancers don't know what to do with themselves when their careers have ended."

"But I'm enjoying it. I've always loved parties."

We started down the open stairwell.

"Have you? In that case, I'm having some members of the company up to my place this evening . . ."

We had reached the ornate metal railing along the landing when he paused. It was an area clearly visible from the rotunda as well as from the hall above. No one seeing us would have thought we were talking about anything but the banquet, but I realized I was about to be invited to Michael's apartment.

I'm not suggesting that this famous man was asking me out. Believe me, I know when my luscious form turns a man into the slobbering slave of his hormones. Quite the opposite. Michael gave off no sexual vibrations. He simply liked me enough to consider me an "insider." I was thrilled. I couldn't wait for the words to leave his lips so I could say yes.

A noise on the landing above interrupted him. We glanced up at the same time. A second later Niki came trotting down the steps.

"Michael, my friend. We must talk." He stared from

Michael to me, and back to Michael. "Oh, but I have interrupted something?"

The bastard had been listening.

"No," Michael said.

"I have to get back to my office," I said to Michael. "I'll be watching dress rehearsal later." I left it at that. If he wanted me at his party, he knew where to find me.

I'd heard that rehearsals were going well. Around the company, the feeling was that *Icarus* was Devereux's best ballet in years, possibly ever. With Niki in the lead, it was guaranteed to be a popular success.

I wasn't able to get to the dress rehearsal until it was almost over. Tiptoeing into the darkened theater, I took an aisle seat close to the stage.

The music, with its mesmerizing Greek rhythm, was gathering force as Daedalus and Icarus slipped into their wings. Rather than using real feathers, the costume designer had constructed wings of silken feathers that weighed next to nothing and swayed spectacularly whenever the dancers moved. The wings themselves were attached to a harness affair made to look like a vest. This vest was hooked down the dancers' chests with heavy-duty clamps. Sewn to this vest-harness were bands of clear nylon line, invisible from the audience, that rose up to a pair of hoists out of sight above the stage. The apparatus was similar to the one used in *Peter Pan*. Set in motion, these hoists would lift the two dancers off the stage and send them flying on their journey to Sicily..

The choreography called for Daedalus to become airborne almost immediately and disappear high into the wings at the left side of the stage. The Icarus character—Niki—remained onstage a moment longer to share a last embrace with the princess he was leaving behind.

How smoothly it went. I was only four rows back, almost on top of the orchestra pit, and I didn't even see the nylon lines when Niki suddenly took flight. The sequence had been worked out with such precision that he began one of his great leaps and rose from there.

I watched in awe as Niki soared forty feet above the stage, giving the perfect illusion of flight as he glided toward a huge ball that, when lighted, was to be the sun. When he reached this sun, his wings collapsed and feathers began to drift down through the air to the stage below. This wasn't magic. A stagehand up on the catwalk was throwing handfuls of silken feathers. And as the feathers dropped, so did Niki drift slowly back to the stage, where he suffered a painful and dramatic death right in front of his princess, who ended the performance with fifteen seconds of grief-stricken torment before collapsing over Niki's body.

Was it really dance? Critics and purists always ask that question when choreographers use props and machinery such as hoists or ladders. I don't know. I'm not an expert. But it was pure entertainment. When the curtain fell on the princess weeping over the still body of Icarus, those of us in the audience and the dancers and stagehands backstage burst into spontaneous applause.

The curtain rose again. In the actual performance, this was the point where Niki, Michael, and the princess would begin many bows. This time it didn't work like that. What the curtain revealed was a scowling, head-shaking Niki.

"Is not right, this . . . wire thing."

Michael walked to center stage. "The hoist is very effective, Niki. And very safe. You needn't worry."

"You suggest I have fear? I have no fear," Niki responded angrily. "Is embarrassment I feel. My leaps are highest in the world. Why I must be degraded by this"—he waved his hand skyward, his upper lip twisted into an insulting sneer—"circus stunt. Classical ballet company should not rely on cheap tricks."

There may have been something to what Niki was saying. But being Niki he said it the wrong way. Michael, who had coddled his superstar at every turn, wasn't about to give in where his own choreography was at stake.

"As I told you before, the wire stays."

"Audience will ridicule."

Michael put his hands on his hips. "The audience will love it. The subject is closed."

I could have hugged him. Whether or not he was right about the artistic merit of the hoist, he was standing up to Niki.

The theater lights came on and the dancers began wandering away. Looking into the rows, Michael spotted me.

"Bonnie, can you meet me backstage? There are a couple of things we have to discuss. Timing, for one. Allowing for curtain calls, you're going to have the first patrons walking into the rotunda seven minutes after the music ends. . . ."

We met backstage. It was chaotic. Stagehands were moving back the *Icarus* sets and bringing out the props for that evening's *Romeo and Juliet*. I stepped out of the way of a man carrying an armful of swords.

"I'm afraid we have too many people at the head table," Michael said. He was explaining that we would have to scatter a few bigwigs at the tables closest to the head table, when Niki walked through the parted curtain from front stage. His wing apparatus was in his hand. He glanced at me, a sly smile on his face. He put the harness on the floor and walked over to where the *Romeo and Juliet* props were stacked. Picking up a sword, he slashed the air, fencing with an imaginary opponent. The sword was constructed of a lightweight, rather flexible metal. As a lethal weapon it didn't amount to anything. Its tip was rounded, and even if it hadn't been, the sword would bend before it would puncture. In Niki's hands, however, the sword turned into another kind of weapon.

He leaped around backstage, jumping electrical wires and dodging props, expertly thrusting the sword. Up, down, sideways.

"In Soviet Union I study fencing," he called over his

shoulder. Niki leaped close to us, backed away, and leaped again, jumping around like a pesky gnat.

Michael looked at him. "Bonnie and I have some last-minute things to work out here. If you could excuse us for a few minutes."

Stopping abruptly, Niki lowered the sword. "Oh, but I have interrupted your talk once again. My apologies. I see you later, Michael." Looking like a chastised child, he started toward the side of the stage. The sword was still in his hand.

He was several feet past us when he spun and made his move. I saw the whole thing, yet it happened so quickly I can hardly describe it. One moment he was still, staring at the back of Michael's head, and the next second he was in the classic fencer's position, forward knee bent, the sword inches from Michael's scalp. I couldn't believe he was going to stab the choreographer, but that's exactly what it looked like. I reached for Michael's sleeve to pull him aside. Too late. The point of the sword moved, slow but steady, into what I thought was Michael's neck.

Michael, finally aware that something was wrong, turned quickly. Not quickly enough. With a sure twist of his wrist Niki pushed the sword in and up. There was a faint tearing noise, and then Michael's scalp of beautiful coal-black locks sat askew on the side of his head, held in place by a flesh-colored strip that pulled taut between his skin and his hair.

I gave a cry. I couldn't help it. For a split second I thought Michael had been scalped. By the time I realized that what I was seeing was a toupee held in place by adhesive strips, Michael was already straightening it.

Niki's eyes widened in feigned horror. "What have I done? I am so sorry. Am a fool." Dropping the stage sword, he moved toward Michael, hands extended as if he could somehow help. Michael flung his arm, brushing Niki away. With a shrug and a secretive wink at me, Niki left the stage.

"Bonnie," Michael said bruskly, "please see that the head

table has Reserved signs on either side of Niki. One for the mayor and one for our envoy to the UN. Also, be sure that the waiters understand that the blue Reserved signs signify kosher plates and the yellow are vegetarian. I don't want any slip-ups."

He walked away without another word. I felt absolutely sick. I'd had nothing to do with what had happened but I was afraid that my presence there, the fact that I'd witnessed Michael's embarrassment, implicated me.

Time would prove that my fear was justified. From that moment, I was no longer a candidate for Michael's inner circle.

How on earth do you make sure that, out of more than four hundred people, the half-dozen vegetarians don't get something on their plates that's going to insult them? How do you make sure that the food gets to the tables hot at the same time the patrons get there hungry? And that the patrons at each table get to eat with a dancer of the proper "stature"? What do you do if a run-of-the-mill thousand-dollar-a-plate patron plops himself down at a big-shot table? Beg him to move? How can you be sure that two feuding real estate moguls don't get near each other? That the speakers—Michael, Niki, and the mayor—don't go on talking forever? How could I be sure that Niki, jerk that he was, wouldn't say something awful to somebody important? The idea of managing one-tenth of what I had to manage was overwhelming.

With the details of the gala crushing me from all sides, and my supposed alliance with Niki weighing heavily, I felt crummy. It was after eight that evening and the hallway outside my office was quiet. I gave in to a nice, self-indulgent bout of tears.

Bertha found me weeping into my little stack of yellow vegetarian reservation cards.

"I can't understand," I sobbed, "why they can't leave the meat on their plates, just for this one night."

She tipped my wastebasket into the big can outside my

door, then set it back under my desk. "My dear, don't worry. Your gala will be huge success. You must make sure that you enjoy festivities. Look at bright side. You have the privilege of working with Nikolai Koslov."

"Privilege? It's a curse. Niki is . . . a creep!"

My outburst surprised Bertha. Laying her rag over her bucket, she sank into my side chair. "A creep? My Nikolai? You can't mean that."

I blew my nose, dried my eyes, and proceeded to give Bertha a rundown of Niki's behavior that afternoon. I expected her to defend him in that pragmatic way of hers. She'd done it before. What I didn't expect, though, was the bit of gossip she let me in on.

"But my dear, don't you understand? He is twenty-six, reaching peak of his power as dancer. The male dancers do not last so long as the women. In six, seven years, his leaps will not be so great, his speed will lessen. Niki is too proud a dancer to be less than perfect. He will stop dancing and pursue next love—choreography. To do that, he must find his own company."

"You're kidding? You don't think he'd try to take over here, do you?"

She smiled. "You are such nice person, Bonnie. You do not look for devious motivations. Think about this: the Bolshoi is mired in bureaucracy. It will be years before director steps down. His successor must please the Soviet government. Niki has no desire to please governments, so he comes here. He is invited to join every prestigious company in the United States, but he chooses company with mediocre reputation. If he wanted to dance with best, as he claims, why did he not go with New York City Ballet, or with his countryman Baryshnikov at American Ballet Theatre?"

I thought about this for a minute. "But if it's his own company Niki wants, why doesn't he start one?"

"Niki has no money; he has no experience in capitalist business matters, in fund-raising. How does he put together a troupe of trained dancers? From where does his repertoire come? You see, he finds everything he needs here at Gotham Ballet. He perfects what they have, he hand-picks some people"—here she gave me a meaningful look: I was one of the chosen—"and they need him. They need his popularity, his talent, his devotion to perfection."

Everything Bertha said made sense. It didn't make me like Niki any more, but it helped me understand what he was trying to accomplish by undermining Michael's power.

Bertha was already up and working, dusting the top of my file cabinet. "Bertha," I said, "you are one of the brightest, most likable people I know. Have you ever thought of doing another kind of work?"

She smiled down at me. "I enjoy my work, Bonnie. There is nothing I would rather do."

What a selfless person. Like a yogi or a guru. Made me feel like a whining idiot with my silly little white-collar complaints. I was worrying about nothing to wear and this woman, my superior in both brains and common sense, was dusting my office. On an impulse, I opened the drawer that held my sacred allotment of backstage passes, the passes I was supposed to give only to reporters and VIPs. I'd given most of them away already, but I could spare one. I signed my name on the back of the pass. "Bertha, I want you to have this."

"What is it?"

"It gets you backstage before the performance. Only three entrances will be open and they'll all have guards. You can watch the dancers warming up and maybe grab a glass of champagne. A television crew will be filming everything. You may end up on TV," I said with a smile.

Her eyes widened. "Bonnie, I thank you. Am not sure I can use this. My friend's birthday is tomorrow. But I try."

"You're welcome to it. If you do use it," I cautioned, "you must blend in with everyone else. Dress up and pretend you're a reporter from a Brooklyn newspaper."

One hand flew to the scarf covering her short curls. "If I

go, must get hair done. Possibly wear blue silk dress and pearls, and . . ." She stretched out her other hand. Her thumb had a makeshift bandage on it. A finger sported a fresh scrape. "Ugly, ugly," she said, shaking her head. "Maybe manicure—"

I interrupted her. "Just don't call any attention to yourself. That's all I ask. If you get bored you can sneak out whenever you want. The lower level exit to the subway can be opened from the inside."

"Bored? With Niki?"

"Just don't tell anybody I'm throwing these passes around."

"My lips are sealed," she assured me. "Under interrogation I will not betray you. Pins under fingernails, rubber hoses . . ."

We both got a good laugh over the idea of the rental guards we had hired for the evening beating anyone. By the time Bertha pulled her bucket apparatus out of my office, my spirits had lifted. I colored in my seating diagram: blue for the koshers, yellow for the veggies, red for the VIPs, green seats on opposite sides of the floor for the feuding realtors. I would use this diagram to color code Reserved cards on the tables in the rotunda. I would ask Elliott to be sure the speakers kept it short and sweet. I would wave tips in front of the waiters to keep them moving. And I would do my best to steer the patrons to the right seats. And that done, I would collapse into my own seat at the table farthest back and enjoy the festivities.

6

The big day began badly.

I should have guessed there was trouble when I got to work an hour early and found Madame coaching Carmen through Jonquil's short solo as they waited for the elevator.

"Did you hear?" one of the volunteers whispered as I dropped change into the coffee machine.

"Hear what?"

"Niki won't let Jonquil dance tonight."

"What!" I couldn't believe it. What could she possibly have done to offend him?

"Drugs!" the woman mouthed over her shoulder as she hurried off.

Drugs. During the next couple of hours I heard that word over and over. The wardrobe mistress told me, with much excitement, that it had happened in her domain. One of the maintenance men said he suspected the whole bunch of them were shooting up. "Where do you think they get all that energy?" Even the caterer knew about it.

"No problem on the stuffed dolmas, Miss Indermill. Hey, I hear you got troubles with junkies over there."

Nobody knew exactly what had happened, but Jonquil had been caught by Niki using or carrying or under the influence of drugs. Niki had promptly gone to Michael and told him, flat out, that he refused to jeopardize his opening by appearing with a drug user.

I got the tearful details when Abigail finally arrived. She was over an hour late. Her face was puffy, her eyes swollen and red. She went straight to her desk, pulled an envelope from her purse and crammed it into her top drawer. Then she hunched over her work.

"Abigail? Are you okay?"

Shaking her head, she muttered: "I'm fine." A second later tears started streaming from her eyes.

"Is there anything I can do?"

"I don't know." She looked down as a messenger walked in with some mail. As soon as he had gone, she sputtered, "Would you lock the door? I don't want anyone to see me like this. It's awful, the whole place gossiping about Jonquil. God knows what this is going to do to her career."

I kicked the door shut and locked it. The rest of the story came out between sobs. Niki's version was that the evening before he had walked into a costume room and caught Jonquil snorting a line of cocaine off a hand mirror. Jonquil, supposedly upset about being caught, had thrust the offending substance into her pocket and become abusive.

Not surprisingly, Jonquil's version was quite different. She had been trying on the headpiece she was to wear in her solo, adjusting it in a small mirror, when a fit of sinusitis overtook her. Pulling out a nasal inhaler, conveniently kept in her pocket for such occasions, she proceeded to take several big sniffs, unaware that Niki had sneaked up behind her. To her great distress, he started yelling. She couldn't understand what he was yelling about, but she yelled back, put the inhaler and mirror into her pocket, and left the wardrobe room.

Abigail had too much of herself invested in her daughter's career to believe Niki's story. "I don't understand why he would do something like this, Bonnie. Do you? How mean, to hurt a young girl's career with a lie. Do you suppose he's taken a dislike to Jonquil because she isn't interested in him romantically?"

No. I supposed that Niki had caught Jonquil using cocaine and didn't want to risk his opening with her, even in a small role. I was sure that, for once, Niki was right.

"What are you going to do?" What I meant was, What are you going to do about the possibility that your daughter is using drugs? Abigail misunderstood.

"I don't know. Everything in my life is going wrong." For a second she paused and seemed to withdraw into herself. "Maybe you could help," she finally said.

"Me? How could I help?"

"Niki likes you. You could talk to him. He's here. I saw him when I came in. Explain to him. Once he understands . . ."

"Niki won't listen to me. And I think you should consider his side of the story. What if Jonquil *is* using drugs?"

She pulled herself straight. "That's ridiculous! She would never jeopardize her career like that."

She purposefully turned back to her work. For a few minutes we didn't speak. Then her shoulders started shaking. "Please, Bonnie."

The male principals' dressing rooms were in a short, narrow corridor off the main hall of the lower level. As I knocked on Niki's door, I noticed that Chris Lansing's room was directly opposite. How was Chris dealing with his new neighbor, I wondered? He had to be resentful: a private dressing room may be nice but it's not like getting your name up there in the big letters.

"Come in," Niki called.

Niki's room was a pigpen. Practice clothes were dropped where he took them off. His makeup table was a swamp of oozing bottles and runny tubes, all of it covered by a layer of dusting powder.

The Prince of Ballet was slumped in a big easy chair, feet up on a hassock. He put down the book he was a couple of pages into, but he didn't stand.

"Bonnie, my angel." Taking his feet off the hassock, he nodded at it. "Sit."

I shook my head. I did not intend to sit at Niki's feet like the faithful hound. "Hi, Niki. I'm here to ask a favor."

"For you, anything. What you want? You ask, you have."

"Would you let Jonquil dance tonight?"

He sank back into the chair and raised his head to the heavens. "That is one thing I cannot do. Why you ask such a thing? You want to jeopardize my first performance?"

"No, of course not." I started to explain Jonquil's side of the story, but Niki waved his hand to silence me.

"That girl thinks I am stupid? She thinks I don't know cocaine from medicine? That I have not heard the whispers about the 'Old Man' who sells these kids drugs? Bonnie, what you think? You think I am being cruel? I tell you, if I allow Jonquil to dance and she ruins performance, I jeopardize the entire company, not just myself. If the girl was more experienced, strong dancer, I maybe not care so much. But she is kid. When I go onstage, must be sure to surround myself with best possible. You should not ask me to compromise performance."

I was relieved when a knock interrupted his lecture. I opened the door. A company messenger handed me a huge bundle of flowers.

"Look, Niki," I said. "They're beautiful."

They really were. A fortune in long-stemmed red and white roses. I reached to pick the card from their midst. Greenleaf Florists, the envelope read.

"Who sends that?" Niki shouted. He jumped out of his chair before I could answer. Snatching the envelope, he ripped it open.

"Merde." That was the only message on the card. There was no signature. He tore the roses from my hands and shoved them back at the messenger. "Take them away! I don't want."

"But what will I do . . . ?"

"Now!" Niki slammed the door in the messenger's face.

What a reaction to a bunch of flowers. My heart was pounding. "Are you allergic?" I asked. "Do flowers make you ill?"

Niki sank back into his chair. "Ill? No. Is bad luck."

I shook my head. "No, Niki. In American dance, 'merde' means good luck. Like 'break a leg' in the theater."

"Bonnie, 'merde' signifies good luck in Soviet Union also, but red and white flowers together signify death."

"But whoever sent these wouldn't know that."

"I would not be so sure," he responded. "Now, what I tell you is, Carmen will be fine soloist tonight. Jonquil I cannot take risk with."

Nasty as Niki could be, in this case he was right.

On my way out of the room I glanced down at the book he'd been reading. It was a Russian-to-English translation of business terms. Talk about dry! That had to be deadly. Under it were two other volumes: *The New Entrepreneur's Guide to Running Your Own Business* and a biography of Henry Ford. Niki noticed me looking at the titles.

"I check from library this morning, but find too difficult yet," he said with a shake of his head. He opened the bottom drawer of his dressing table and dropped all three books into it. "Soon enough I understand. Maybe I let you help me read."

He said it as if bestowing an honor. I got out of there fast.

Abigail didn't stick around once I delivered the bad news. Like a rat leaving a sinking ship, she deserted. She did it in tears.

"I wouldn't be a bit of use," she sobbed. "I'm simply too upset to deal with anything. I'm getting one of my sick headaches."

"What about this evening?" I opened the drawer where I

kept the backstage passes. "You still want a pass, don't you? I'll sign it for you."

"Why is Niki being so mean, Bonnie?" she asked, ignoring my question. "He has everything a dancer could dream of. Why would he want to hurt Jonquil's career?"

I didn't know what to say. I was embarrassed for Abigail, I pitied her, yet I knew she was wrong. I held the pass toward her. "Want me to sign this? You're going to need it to get backstage after four."

She paused, then shook her head. "I'm in no mood to celebrate Niki's debut. Now that Jonquil's not dancing I have no reason to be here tonight."

There was one: her job. Abigail was supposed to help at the banquet. Pity got the best of me and I didn't mention it.

Six-fifteen and counting down. The rotunda was pure madness.

"Bonnie! You've got to help me! I'm desperate!"

All day long variations on that phrase had assaulted me. This time the words came from the perfectly painted lips of my friend Amanda Paradise.

I'd invited Amanda to sit with me at the staff table, and had wrangled a fourth-balcony seat for her. She was getting a free meal and a close look at the beautiful people. She wanted more. With her yellow-and-white mini, high-heeled sandals, and elaborate hairdo, she didn't look particularly stafflike.

"There's a big party before the performance. It's going on now and the guard won't let me in. He said you could give me a pass."

"I left the passes in my desk, Amanda. Anyway, it's not really a party. A television crew is filming some VIPs milling around gawking at dancers doing warm-ups and putting on makeup. Why don't you skip it?"

She looked as if I'd suggested she help set the tables. "Bonnie, Niki likes me. You saw him at the café." She tightened her fists into balls. "Please! I'm frantic."

I wasn't far from frantic myself. Damned if they hadn't sent the peach-colored tablecloths after all. And those grape centerpieces! Clashing with the tablecloths was the least of their problems. Those grapes looked like they'd come from California the long way, by barge around the tip of Argentina. Honest to God, most of them were as shriveled as raisins. Some of them were so far gone they were sprouting white mold.

Those grapes had proven the last straw for Elliott. Afraid to be away from the TV crew for more than a few minutes, he'd given the offending centerpieces a five-second stare, shouted at me "We'll never live this down," and raced off to the comparative comfort of the bedlam backstage.

"What do you mean 'we'?" I'd shouted to his departing back. "The lousy grapes were your idea."

Something had to go. The tablecloths were all right without the grapes. The grapes hadn't been all right for a long time. I motioned to Fernando, the head waiter. "Ditch the grapes!"

"Ditch the grapes?" He straightened his shoulders, ready for battle. "We just put the grapes out."

"Well, you can put them back where they came from. Then take the baskets of fruit and put them on the tables."

"The fruit baskets? The fruit baskets are for after dinner."

"Not anymore. Now they're the centerpieces."

He rolled his eyes and I thought I just might end up collecting grapes and distributing fruit baskets by myself. Wouldn't that do a job on my already not-so-hot dress. Fernando finally stormed away. Moments later, to my relief, his men began dumping several hundred dollars' worth of grapes into plastic garbage bags.

"Bonnie," Amanda whined, "what about the pass?"

"Amanda, these waiters sit down and start smoking the second I turn my back."

"I'll watch them," she said. "Please, Bonnie. You know what this means to me."

"Okay. You stay here and be sure they get rid of every grape and I'll go get you a pass."

She nodded excitedly. "Hurry!"

I ran all the way, pounding on the elevator button with my fist when it didn't come quickly enough.

Things were still going strong in the subbasement, but not in my office.

Racing into the room, I opened my center drawer and grabbed for the remaining passes. I could have sworn there were two left, but I found only one. I rummaged quickly through the drawer but turned up nothing. I'd been upstairs all afternoon. Maybe Abigail had changed her mind and come back for one. Hurrying to her desk, I yanked open her drawer. It was crazy, I know. If Abigail had taken a pass she'd have it with her. I was frantic, though.

Her drawer was almost empty, which will give you an idea of what she did around there. Just a few pencils and supplies, and an envelope with a folded sheet of paper stuck carelessly under the flap. I shook the envelope, hoping to see a pass fall from it. Nothing. I was trying to refold the paper when I focused on the handwritten words.

. . . can no longer tolerate this lifestyle. You have pushed Jonquil as far as you can. If you have not returned home by the end of the month, I will be contacting a divorce lawyer.

Ned

Ned was Abigail's husband. I looked at the envelope. It was postmarked several weeks earlier. The month's end had passed. Abigail had made her choice.

I put the letter and envelope back in her desk. One pass had disappeared, but I didn't have time to worry about it. The way things were going in the rotunda I wouldn't get to the pre-performance activities anyway. I signed my name on the remaining pass. Turning off the lights, I raced upstairs.

Under the thousands of tiny bulbs hidden in the vines draped around the columns, the peach tablecloths with their fruit basket centerpieces looked beautiful. The china and silver glowed; the wineglasses sparkled. By the big double service doors, Fernando adjusted his cummerbund. On the other side of the doors his platoon of waiters smoked and played cards. Behind the rotunda in a kitchen that had been expanded for the occasion, the caterer was firing up the coals for the shish kebabs. "No problems," he had assured me.

Collapsing against one of the vine-covered Doric columns, I took a deep breath and looked around. Six weeks earlier I'd been a temp. Now I was a fund-raising professional putting on a banquet that wouldn't have looked bad in the White House.

I'd missed the pre-performance reception but it didn't matter. There would be plenty of time to mingle with the press later. A long, satisfying career stretched ahead of me, filled with banquets and beautiful people. A working woman's heaven.

From downstairs in the theater I heard the audience's applause greeting the conductor and first violinist. A moment later the music reached me, swelling until it filled the rotunda. It was all so glorious. I rubbed my aching feet, then rose and walked toward the fifth ring, where an empty aisle seat was waiting so that I could watch the first act. Thus began one of the most horrible work experiences of my life.

Chris Lansing walked into the rotunda during the last act and slid into a chair near me. "Is there anywhere a guy can get a drink around here?"

"Not yet, Chris. Wait for the patrons. Did you watch the performance?"

"No. I just got here. I spent the whole day filming a chewing gum ad." He grinned. "Bet you've never seen a stick of sugarless gum do the tango."

I smiled back. He was a cutie, with a smile that could

have come right off a southern California beach. "No. I didn't know you made commercials."

"It pays a lot more than a soloist's salary. I can live on the residuals for months."

A burst of applause came from the theater. "Sounds like they love the nasty son of a bitch," Chris said.

"Darlings! Have you seen that performance? The pig! He can dance."

Galena Semenova, a vision in red chiffon, came gliding across the rotunda floor. "I was watching from the wings. We may make a profit this season!"

Over the weeks, Galena had thawed toward me until we were on an amicable basis. I owed this to Jonquil and Carmen. Once they told Galena I idolized her, the change had been immediate.

"Bonnie, where am I sitting?" she asked.

I pointed to the front, right below the podium. "Table two, next to the one with Michael and Niki. You've got an ambassador and a senator."

"Any single men?"

"Not that I know of, but if you lean back you'll bump heads with ——" I mentioned an actor who had just finished with a noisy divorce. She nodded. "This may be bearable."

Again the audience burst into applause. Chris shrugged. "I wish it was for me."

"Someday it will be," Galena said graciously. The familiar strains of the finale reached us. Then the rotunda was swept by applause. Not just applause. Bravos and screams that went on and on until it seemed they would never end. Finally they faded. Niki's debut was over. Mine was about to begin. I signaled the head waiter to have his men bring out the wine that would be served with the salad. Then I picked up my seating chart so that I could direct people to their tables. Tricia had told me that, though all of them had been notified of their table numbers, some would forget.

Minutes later the first patrons walked between the columns into the rotunda. Galena spotted someone she knew and floated across the floor.

These people were glorious, all tuxed and gowned and jeweled, rosy-faced and happy. And the way they looked around the rotunda at my handiwork and gave little ooohs and aahs, the way they reached happily for their first glasses of wine. I have to tell you, I felt such a glow of satisfaction.

A rush of faces and questions came my way, so quickly that most of them were a blur. The questions were continual: "Where do I go?" "With whom am I sitting?" "Will I be able to see the podium with that column there?" "Couldn't I move closer?" "Who's at Niki's table?" "What? How did they manage that?" With so much happening it's a wonder I noticed the woman at all.

She was of average height, with pale skin and brown hair that glowed under the lights and was pulled back into a loose twist. Her gown was light blue, with short puffed sleeves and a high Empire waist. Its low, gathered bodice had royal blue satin trim. All this woman needed to complete the picture of a Jane Austen heroine were over-the-elbow gloves. She had them, but they were clutched in one hand. A pretty woman, though among the sequins and feathers not a memorable one. Until she passed Chris and flashed him a warm, sly smile, that is. I glanced at Chris. To my surprise, he turned away from the woman.

"A friend of yours?" I asked.

"Why do you say that?"

"She seemed to recognize you."

I watched the woman find her way to a table near the front. A man in a black tuxedo had hold of her elbow, but I never saw his face.

"You're wrong," Chris said, his tone so defensive it startled me. What he did next startled me more. He leaned toward me and gave me a peck on the cheek. "Sorry," he said. "You've done a hell of a job here. I'm just uptight. I'm flying to Germany in the morning. A week with the Stuttgart Ballet. Anything for a buck."

"You'll be great," I said. "You better get to your table now. Your patrons have arrived."

"I'll charm their socks off." He wandered away.

The audience had loved Niki. That was clear from the smatterings of excited conversation I picked up: ". . . the way he moves. I've never seen anything so beautiful." ". . . and when he fell, I don't see how he didn't break his neck. The man is a miracle."

What were they talking about? There was no fall where Niki could have broken his neck. The way some of the patrons were talking, it sounded as if they'd just watched a circus tumbling act.

The wait for the performers was endless. I hadn't expected them to show up within seconds; they had to rush to their dressing rooms and change. But ten minutes passed. Fifteen, twenty. When it edged up toward twenty-five, I started getting worried. The plan was that the waiters would put out the salad unobtrusively while Michael made his quick speech. Niki would have his few words between salad and main course. This had been so carefully choreographed by me, Francisco, and the caterer that we could have done it blindfolded. But we had to have Michael there to start.

This was some drinking audience! I couldn't believe how quickly our first wine disappeared. We'd had a bottle for every two patrons and this was only the first wine. Well, what did I expect? It was after 9:00 P.M. and these people had been given nothing to eat. At a few tables, the guests were making their way through the fruit baskets. I saw a well-known writer drop an apple core onto the floor. A society matron chewed on a banana, a dippy crocked grin on her face. How long could this go on? By the service door the caterer motioned frantically my way, tapping his watch. Skirting the tables, I rushed to his side.

"We put the shish kebab in five minutes ago. It's got to come out of those ovens. What's going on here?"

I glanced through the service doors. A forest of salad waited. Where was Michael?

A red-faced Francisco rushed through the doors, pausing only long enough to say: "They're asking for more wine. Should I open the red?"

Damn! The dinner wine, and we hadn't even served the salad. "Wait five minutes, then give them anything they want."

"After eleven o'clock my men are on double time," he added.

The caterer stepped between us.

"It's now or never with the shish kebab."

The patrons had been growing louder and louder. Suddenly they were clapping. Thank God! Michael Devereux was walking across the rotunda. "Now," I snapped to the caterer. "Take the lamb out now." I caught Francisco on his way out the service door. "Get those salads out there fast!" Then I rushed back to the side of the rotunda so I could catch Michael's speech.

Michael climbed slowly up the marble steps to the spot where he was to speak. When he reached the top he turned and faced our patrons. How awful he looked, glum and exhausted.

The patrons didn't notice. They were having a great time. The level of activity on the rotunda floor was close to frenzied, with some of the waiters racing around serving salads while others dashed from table to table opening the dinner wine.

"My dear friends," Michael began. At the back of the rotunda a tray crashed to the floor. "Oh, oh," somebody shouted. Michael rubbed his head. "If I could please have your attention. I'm afraid I have very bad news."

Those closest to the front were the first to see how serious Michael looked. Then there was a sort of snowball effect, with table after table quieting. At the moment when the entire room was still, a side door to the rotunda opened noisily.

You cannot imagine how shocked I was to see an

ex-boyfriend of mine, a plainclothes homicide detective, walk into the rotunda. Two uniformed cops followed him. Something awful had happened. Tony LaMarca was not a ballet fan. I leaned back against a column.

I hadn't realized Elliott was behind me. At the moment that Michael began to say something, Elliott whispered, "Niki's dead."

I was so astonished that I thought I'd misunderstood him. I turned my attention to Michael.

". . . great dancer and, I must add, fine human being and dear friend of mine, Nikolai Koslov, suffered a fall during this evening's performance. Several minutes ago, Nikolai passed away without regaining consciousness."

It is almost impossible to describe what happened next. First there was a moment of stunned silence. Then there was chaos. Amanda, looking like a million dollars at the staff table, gave a little squeal and fainted dead away onto the floor, dragging the peach-colored tablecloth, the fruit basket, and most of the glasses with her. People started to cry. A group of patrons in full evening dress stood tearfully at their table, then hurried toward the door, only to collide with one of the waiters. His tray of oil-drenched salads crashed onto the marble floor. For some reason that started a minor panic. Through it all, the waiters pressed on, getting those salads out.

Tears welled in my eyes. I'm ashamed to say they were probably as much for myself as for Niki, but what a horror this was! Inexplicably I thought of my career. Was it over? Would I be a temp in the morning?

Tony appeared at my side. "Bonnie? You working here? One of the waiters said you're responsible for this."

The next second the caterer rushed through the service door. "We're back on schedule in the kitchen, Miss Indermill. Ready with the lamb." He looked out into the rotunda. "The opera's patrons would never behave like this."

* * *

Tony LaMarca looked tired and unhappy. He always looks that way on a job. "So there were two, maybe three exits that weren't locked or guarded. The exit to the subway, one to the . . ."

If the situation hadn't been so awful I might have laughed. "We weren't trying to keep people from leaving," I said. "We were trying to keep them from entering and crashing the reception. The passes"—I shrugged—"they were almost as much for publicity as for security. Michael wanted the patrons to think they were seeing something special. It's not as if we were expecting assassins."

Tony shook his head. "Your patrons sure saw something special tonight." He closed the little black book he'd been writing in. "That nylon line was okay up on top where the hoist is. The problem was with the stitching in Koslov's harness."

It was after midnight. What I knew about Niki's death was that the nylon stitching in his vest apparatus had been cut, probably with a razor blade. The stitches hadn't been completely severed. A couple had remained intact, pulling loose when Niki was forty feet over the stage and took a great final lunge toward the sun. He'd landed hard on his back at the feet of his astonished princess, who had nonetheless proceeded with her mourning solo. The curtain had fallen as she draped herself over Niki's body. Fifteen minutes later a company physician had pronounced him dead.

The police were pretty sure the vest had been tampered with before it left the prop room. A prop person had checked Niki's wings at four o'clock; they were fine then. At five-thirty a stage assistant had taken them backstage. After that it would have been impossible for anyone to get to the vest unseen, at least for the amount of time it took to cut the nylon thread.

I was sitting across from Tony at one of the tables in the rotunda. The big room was a disaster. Dishes had been cleared away, but the wrinkled, sagging tablecloths remained, splattered with food and drink. I fit right in, wrinkled and sagging.

My flowered silk dress looked as if I'd pulled it from a rag bag. Frizzy curls that had started as neat waves hung over my forehead. My fists were covered with brown smudges from the mascara I'd rubbed off my eyes.

From my anxious high of a few hours before, I'd fallen into nervous exhaustion. Almost too tired to stay awake but much too jittery to think of sleeping.

"Sounds like he was a real unpleasant guy," Tony continued. "There's a lot of people who wouldn't have minded getting rid of him."

I had told Tony about Niki's fights with Galena, with Tricia, with Michael. "He had this talent for pinpointing your sensitive spot and then using it against you."

"Why do you think he did that?"

"I don't know. At first I thought he was simply spoiled, like a child. But there's this cleaning lady here, and she thinks . . ."

"A cleaning lady?" He reached for that little book.

"Bertha. She's from Poland. A real ballet fan. A Niki fan, actually. She's followed his career for years. What she thinks is that Niki eventually wants—wanted—to run his own company, and he'd decided that Gotham Ballet would be a good one to run."

"Sounds pretty sophisticated for a cleaning lady."

I nodded. A surge of exhaustion hit me. "She is. Tony, I've got to go. I need some sleep."

"I'll drive you home."

As we left the rotunda we passed that center table where the woman in the Jane Austen gown had been sitting. In the chaos she'd lost her gloves. They were rolled into a tight ball on her chair. I picked them up absently as I walked by. They were obviously expensive, of a very heavy silk embroidered with shiny royal blue thread that matched the trim on her dress. No wonder she hadn't been wearing them. They felt clammy. I unrolled them and found that the inner glove was damp from fingertip to elbow.

"The lost and found is on our way out," I said to Tony. "I'll drop these off."

My street was deserted when Tony pulled up in front of my building. "Hey, Bonnie," he said as I opened the car door. "Maybe we could get together sometime?"

This wasn't entirely unexpected. When we'd broken up the previous summer things had felt a bit unresolved. I was afraid, though, that he was more interested in resolving them than I was.

"Sure. That would be nice," I said, not sure whether it would be or not. At 2:00 A.M. I stumbled into my apartment and fell, fully dressed, into bed.

It was late that day when I finally got up, showered, and turned on the television to watch the news.

A grim-faced reporter was standing in the afternoon sun outside the courthouse in downtown Manhattan. "Zofia Wojdat has denied the charges, and claims that she was not near Lincoln Center last night, but otherwise she has refused to make any statement," he said into a hand-held microphone. "In a news conference a few minutes ago a spokesman for the FBI told reporters that the Bureau, working with the Central Intelligence Agency, has positively identified Ms. Wojdat as a mid-level KGB officer.

"In another late-breaking development on this story, authorities have confirmed that small amounts of cocaine and another illegal substance were discovered in Nikolai Koslov's dressing room. We have nothing else on that right now, but will keep—wait! Something is happening. Zofia Wojdat is being led out of the courthouse."

The camera panned to the courthouse door. There, flanked by half a dozen men and one woman in a police department uniform, stood the cleaning lady, Bertha Wozniak.

I couldn't get my breath. Within seconds my shock gave

way to despair. Her words rushed back at me: "I enjoy my work. There is nothing I would rather do." All along she'd been putting me on, laughing at me. And I'd played right into her hands. I'd given a backstage pass to a KGB agent.

Bertha Wozniak, or Zofia Wojdat or whoever she was, seemed unperturbed by the handcuffs on her wrists and the reporters shoving microphones at her. No sooner was she ushered into a waiting car than the broadcast switched to the oval office of the president of the United States.

"That a known KGB agent can operate in this country, can practice her insidious brand of terrorism on the immigrant community in general, and a wonderful young man like Nikolai Koslov in particular, is a national disgrace. My fellow Americans, I promise I will not rest until justice has been done in this horrible, horrible . . ." The president's voice broke. Forty million viewers saw their president flick away a tear with a starched white handkerchief.

No one but my cat, Moses, saw me crying into the sleeve of my fuzzy pink housecoat.

7

With the media's help, Niki died a hero of the American Way, at the same time dealing a kick in the seat to *glasnost*. The U.S. position was that the Soviets had silenced him because he knew too much about his wife's work at the supersecret nuclear facility. But governments being governments, Niki's martyrdom soon took a pragmatic turn. Three days after he was lowered into the ground, Zofia Wojdat was traded to the Soviets for two CIA operatives who were being held in East Germany.

The evening news showed Zofia as she was hustled through Kennedy Airport onto a waiting Aeroflot plane. To the end she denied guilt, denied being in the Lincoln Center area on the night of the gala. Needless to say, the Soviets took her side, insisting that the affair amounted to a sham and a cover-up by the United States. They pounced on the drugs found in Niki's dressing table, insisting that Niki fell because he was so full of cocaine he couldn't manage his harness apparatus. They denounced the autopsy that showed that Niki's system was free of drugs as a fake. When it was released to the papers that B-negative blood—Zofia's type—had been found on Niki's hitch, they deemed this discovery a fraud, a desperate ploy by a decadent society.

I watched Zofia's departure on my ancient TV, its fuzzy picture adding a somber note to the broadcast. As she boarded the plane she briefly stared into the cameras, giving the West a good look at the face of evil.

Tony was on the sofa with Moses stretched across his lap. During those first awful days after Niki's death I'd slipped back into a romance with Tony. *Romance* probably isn't the right word. I wasn't sure how Tony felt, but the romance I'd once felt for him had faded. Our relationship, though comfortable, was motivated on my part by a need to be around other people and a desire to get at the heart of what had happened. I'm not saying I traded my body for clues. It was a difficult time and it was nice to have someone kind to hold me. But there were also those snippets Tony gave me, which I grasped eagerly and clung to, mulling them over again and again.

Carmen Garcia was the only person who remembered seeing anything peculiar backstage. Too bad it was Carmen, for several reasons. Because of her last-minute solo, she had been in the grip of a pre-performance excitement that bordered on hysteria. More important, she hadn't had her "eyes" in. Every time she repeated her story it came out a little different.

Carmen had seen a woman leaving the prop room around five o'clock, about the time the reception and filming had begun on the other side of the theater one floor up. Though too far away to see the woman clearly, Carmen waved. The woman had turned briefly, then hurried around a corner.

Carmen followed, not out of curiosity but because she wanted to get to the stairs. Before she reached the corner, a door slammed. Rounding the corner, though, she saw a woman—she couldn't swear it was the same woman—at an exit leading to the subway and street. Her view of the woman was partially blocked by some trash cans. The woman, hearing Carmen, pushed through the door and left the theater.

Height? She was "about average," Carmen thought.

Weight? The same. Hair? "Short, or else up. Maybe kind of brownish." The woman had been wearing a loose shawl or jacket over her shoulders. Carmen wasn't even sure about the length of the woman's dress. "It was probably a regular dress, a light color, down to below her knees," she told the police. "That hall's pretty dim, though," she added, "and I didn't see the front of her. She could have been holding a long skirt off the floor." According to Tony, with each of these observations Carmen leaned her head back, squinted, and said "I think."

I was realistic enough to admit that the woman could have been Zofia, the KGB operative, but as I watched the newscast of her departure I saw my bright friend the cleaning lady and not a murderer.

"Seriously, Tony," I said. "Does that woman look dangerous?"

By then, Tony had grown tired of my questions. "The FBI says the case is closed," he said. "What does 'dangerous' look like, anyway, Bonnie? It would help me on the job if I knew."

I ignored that. "And you won't let me see the guards' lists?" Three entrances to the backstage area had been open and manned by guards who had kept lists of people going in. Most people had used the street-level stage door or the door off the theater. Some had come through the door next to the garage that led into the lower hall.

Tony shook his head. "I can't do that. The list isn't even accurate. One of the guards was drinking. Another one let in anybody who looked like a dancer. The only guard who half tried was the one near the garage."

"What about the drugs? And that note?"

The drugs and note were the oddest things in this odd case. A little box, wrapped in a velvety paper that defied the fingerprint experts, had been found in Niki's dressing table. It contained, in addition to a gram of cocaine, some capsules. "Methaqualone. A depressant, sometimes used to take the edge off a cocaine high," Tony had explained to me. "Used to be sold under the name Quaaludes. They haven't been manufactured legally in this country since 1983." Folded under this box had been a roughly penciled note: "Good Night, Sweet Prince," it read. That this note was on a Gala Affair cocktail napkin didn't mean much. The napkins for the reception had been laid out early in the day. Almost anyone could have filched one.

When Tony ignored my question I pressed my luck.

"Why would the KGB leave anything so—strange?"

"Why?" Straightening, he dumped Moses from his lap and started brushing cat hair off his pants. "The guys over at the Bureau think the Russians wanted to create a smoke screen, get in some licks about America corrupting a fine young man."

"But why the note?"

Tony groaned, exasperated. "Maybe the woman has a weird sense of humor. What's with you, Bonnie? You're making me crazy. She's a Soviet agent, she has cuts on her hands, she has the same blood type—"

"It's a common type. Bertha was an enthusiastic cleaner. She was always skinning herself. Anyway," I added, "her prints didn't show up on the hitch."

"Half a dozen people handled the damned thing after she did! Why can't you drop it? Because your gala was ruined?"

I couldn't tell him the truth. I told him nothing. When he left a little later I wondered if he knew I was hiding something. Tony is not stupid.

As you've probably gathered, I never confessed. Even during those first terrible hours after I'd seen Bertha handcuffed and led away by the police, confession had not been an attractive option for me. When, after a day or two, she hadn't told the authorities that a staff member had given her a backstage pass, confession ceased to be an option at all. Living with guilt might not be easy but it was a picnic compared to living as a national disgrace. The woman who abetted the KGB and killed the Prince of Ballet. You think I'd get hired for a fund-raising job with a reputation like that following me around?

There was something else, too, that would come to me in my saner, more clearheaded moments. Like a sweet, furry little animal, this notion would snuggle up and comfort me. To begin with—and I may have begun with this because it made me feel better—backstage wasn't exactly Fort Knox. Surely a trained foreign agent working in a theater, intent on killing a performer, could have done it in less than the month it had taken Bertha. And why would one of the world's most sophisticated spy organizations—the KGB—go about a murder in such a slipshod way? The hitch conceivably could have come undone when Niki was two feet off the floor. If Bertha wanted Niki dead, why not a bullet or some old-fashioned, foolproof poison? As for the drugs and that goofy note, I thought the FBI's theory absurd. The main thing holding it together was coincidence—Props was on the same floor as Niki's dressing room, and while the reception was going on one floor up Bertha/Zofia could have moved easily from one room to the other.

Common sense told me that if Bertha had wanted to kill Niki, she would have done it with considerably more finesse than this torn hitch–drug smoke screen foolishness. Too bad this same common sense didn't tell me who *had* cut Niki's hitch. It didn't take me long, though, to put together a mental list of motives and candidates.

Financial gain could be scrapped. Niki hadn't had two rubles to rub together. Romantic jealousy was probably out, too. He'd flirted with most of the ballerinas but as far as I knew hadn't had time to get into anything heavy.

Career jealousy was a possibility, and Chris Lansing a likely candidate. Although Carmen said she'd seen a woman, she hadn't been wearing her contacts. She could be wrong. Had superstar Niki not joined Gotham, Chris would be a principal dancer. Around the company, reliable gossip was that Michael hadn't felt a need for two new male principals.

Then there was good old hatred. Talk about a plausible motive! When it came to pure loathing, nobody could generate it like Niki.

There was Galena. "I shall be here long after Niki and his friends have departed," she had said. And how about Tricia? Didn't she have good reason to hate the man who disgraced her in public? And Jonquil, her big moment ruined? And Jonquil's mother, for the same reason? And who knew how many others there were? The way Niki operated he'd probably made enemies of half the people he met—stagehands, the people who worked in the canteen—the list could be endless. The problem was, nobody but me was interested in exploring it.

My demotion—it wasn't actually a demotion because I'd never been promoted—followed Niki's funeral by a few days.

Michael Devereux called me to his office one afternoon. This was unusual. Since the terrible scalping scene we hadn't exchanged ten words.

"It's not that you haven't done a good job, Bonnie. You have." As he said this he cupped his chin in his hand, stared over my head, and nodded. I nodded with him.

"A fine job. All things considered." Now his head was shaking the other way—back and forth.

"You must realize, however, that Tricia, with her years of experience . . ." His palms went up at his sides. "She has agreed to return. She'll be back the week after next."

My immediate reaction, knowing Tricia, was that she had somehow or other put the screws to Michael.

". . . handling the job, her particular brand of sensitivity to the company's fund-raising needs . . ."

Sensitivity was not a word I would generally have associated with Tricia. He was right about one thing, though: the Gotham Ballet Company needed all the expert help it could get.

". . . under the circumstances, if you're interested in

continuing as her assistant and possibly helping out in other areas . . ."

His head tilted down. He narrowed his eyes at a framed photograph on his desk—a ballerina in a glamorous studio pose.

Michael's office was a veritable museum of ballet, the walls covered with photographs of the greats and the near greats. There was Galena Semenova in the feather headpiece from her famous *Swan Lake* role. Above her was a photo of Michael and a famous ballerina of twenty years ago as Giselle and Albrecht. A vamping, bow-lipped ballerina in one yellowing photo might have been Madame in her youth.

". . . there's certainly enough work around here . . ." Michael's gaze settled onto his blotter. The man was having trouble looking me in the eye. Vanity? Just because I'd been witness to his "beheading"? Because I'd inadvertently gotten a peek at that strip-mined acreage under his waving black head of someone else's hair? No way. There was something more going on.

". . . under the circumstances, in addition to your fund-raising duties," Michael was saying. There was that key phrase again. "Under the circumstances." And I knew the circumstances. My reputation around the company was linked to Niki and the things he had done. Too bad most of the things he had done hadn't been nice, because I was doomed to dance a pas de deux with his corpse for a long time.

". . . the company performs for a week every September in the Berkshires. We need someone to help with the administrative end of our trip and generally take care of things up there. The girls . . . Our first performance is less than two weeks from now, so we have a lot to do."

The girls? What was he talking about? Well, whatever it was it wasn't nearly as bad as it could have been. In fact, the longer he talked the better it sounded: ten days in the country during Gotham Ballet's annual end-of-summer stint in the mountains. Me, some members of the company, free room and board, maybe some antique shops and blueberry picking. I was being handed a much-needed rest. For a moment I could almost taste the maple syrup.

"This sounds very nice," I said. "And after the Berkshires I'll be working mostly with Tricia again?"

Michael's scar twitched. No doubt about it—he would have been happier if I'd said no to the Berkshires and pretended that "after the Berkshires" was a million years off. I was a reminder of too many terrible things.

He nodded and mumbled something about administration, then said, "For now, you'll be working with Elliott on arrangements for the trip."

"Will Elliott be going?"

"Certainly. Elliott will be there for the entire time. It's quite nice. You will be staying at an old estate. There are separate houses for the boys and girls. You'll help out with the girls, of course. I'd . . ." He hesitated, then went on with his voice lowered. "What I'd like you to do is keep an eye on Jonquil, in particular, and report any . . . irregularities . . . directly and only to me. I have high hopes for that girl. She's what a Devereux ballerina should be. We don't want any rumors getting started."

Irregularities? Why couldn't he say what he meant: drugs.

"I'll be up there most of the time, but I'm staying at the Hawthorne Inn in Lowell." His eyes flickered toward the door, indicating that our talk was over.

What a depressing job I had that afternoon. I had to remove the fund-raising files from my cabinet so that I could cart them back to Tricia's office. I'd arranged them so efficiently. By merely spinning my chair I could lay my hands on anything within seconds. Returning them to Tricia's lair was darkening my mood by the second. Elliott's sudden appearance in my office door did nothing to lighten it. Since the Gala Affair he no longer dripped sarcasm. He rained it, poured it.

"So, you're to help me out with the Berkshires. In that case"—he raised his shoulders and turned his head to the side, the picture of scorn—"we haven't a thing to worry about. After the smashing success of that Greek bacchanalia you orchestrated . . ."

"*We* orchestrated. *We*." The fiasco of the Gala Affair was still a touchy subject for me. I mean, even beyond the tragedy of Niki's death. Months later I cringe when I think of the olive oil congealing in those trays of cold moussaka, the mountain of stuffed grape leaves clogging our garbage cans. And that horrible, sticky baklava! Uck! It never spoils! They could stock fallout shelters with it. For days following the gala the canteen offered it as dessert. At first I felt duty-bound to eat it, but there's a limit. I'll never be able to look at the nasty stuff again.

"I'm awfully busy, Elliott," I said, hoping to cut his visit short.

Elliott was not one to take a hint, even when the hint came by way of a steamroller. "You're awfully busy? Well, that's certainly a refreshing change." He slid himself into Abigail's chair and began flipping the files on my desk.

"I understand the wicked witch of the west corridor will soon be back among us, spreading joy, spending money . . ."

"Tricia does her job well," I managed to say.

Elliott arched his brows. "My, aren't you the good sport. I suppose you're right. In any event, our Tricia was never really far from us, was she?" His sly smile suggested he knew something I didn't.

"What do you mean?"

"She showed up backstage before the *Icarus* debut. Talk about nerve!"

"Tricia was backstage?"

"Isn't that what I just said? Mingling with those reporters as if she were running the gala."

"I don't think she took a pass from our supply. I wonder who gave her one?"

"Don't look at me. I suspect she rode her broom through a window."

"Did she speak to Niki?"

He shrugged. "I wouldn't think so. Forgive and forget doesn't strike me as a philosophy either of them would embrace."

No. Forgive and forget hadn't been Niki's style. One slip—or, more accurately, sniff—and Jonquil was banished from his debut. And Tricia, with her family motto: "We should prefer death to disgrace." No way would she have gone crawling to Niki.

"But back to business." Elliott plopped a file on my desk. "In here you'll find some of the information you'll be needing. As you can see, most of us stay at a place near Mount Greylock called Greylock Compound."

Compound? Michael had used the word *estate*. There is a world of difference between an estate and a compound, and I know where I'd rather be. *Compound* sounds like a fancy word for camp, complete with bugs, outdoor toilets, and teaspoons of instant coffee in lukewarm, ash-filled water. The company was short on money but surely it didn't intend for its dancers to tent it.

"You mean a camp?"

"Hardly! A millionaire built Greylock in the twenties as his summer home. There are barns better than most people's apartments. We rent some big cottages and several bungalows for couples. Since you'll be keeping an eye on the girls, you'll stay in the girls' house. Most of them will share rooms, but if you're willing to do without a private bath you can probably have one to yourself."

I opened the file. The first thing in it was a note from Michael to Elliott. "We do not want a repeat of last year's problem. Please keep on top of things this time so . . ."

Elliott snatched up the note before I finished it.

"Whoops! That one I'll handle."

"What happened last year?"

He shook his head. "Don't worry about it. There's plenty left for you to worry about. And oh, incidentally, one other thing." He shoved a piece of paper at me, a list. "I've got to get our staff members' names and addresses to a patron. Isabella Spencer. She wants to finish the invitations to the party she and her husband give for the company. Is your address right?"

I checked the list quickly. "Yes."

"Be sure when you get the invitation you respond right away. These new-money types are fickle. We wouldn't want to offend them."

"God forbid."

When he'd gone, a quick look through the Berkshires file told me that transportation arrangements hadn't been made. Not for people, not for costumes, not for anything. And one glance at the brochure from Greylock—assuming we still had our cottages—and I realized we had to order meals in advance. We had to reserve practice rooms, get hold of a piano, do the zillion things necessary to take a dance company on the road. I had less than two weeks to do them. And first I had to return Tricia's files. Temporarily putting Elliott's work aside, I went back to the patrons' records.

"Spencer, Isabella and Billy," the next folder in the stack was labeled. Elliott's new-money types, Tricia's social-climbing bores, my future host and hostess. Opening the file, I thumbed through it. The couple lived on the Upper East Side and had a summer home in the Berkshires.

Isabella Spencer had been born in Philadelphia in 1949. A little pedigree was listed after her name: father this, grandfather that, private elementary schools, public high school, and college. Had daddy run out of money? B.A. in English literature from a school I'd never heard of.

Billy Spencer's date of birth wasn't listed. He'd been born in Florida. His occupation was restaurateur and his place of business an address on Broadway. There was no pedigree. Billy

Spencer had come from the teeming masses. If there had been anything notable in his past, Tricia would have uncovered it.

At the back of the file I came across the clipping—the one from the *Post* that had me grinning when Abigail walked into the office.

"Take a look at this," I said.

She leaned over my shoulder. "Chris! Who is that he's hanging all over?"

"Looks more like she's hanging all over him. That's our patron, Mrs. Spencer. This picture was taken at the Spencers' party last year." I read the caption aloud: "Gotham soloist Chris Lansing and hostess Isabella Spencer enjoy a private joke by rooftop pool."

"Oh. It's got to be a publicity shot. A patron would never have anything to do with someone like Chris," said Abigail. "I hear they're wonderful, gracious hosts. They rent the pool on the roof of their condo and turn it over to the dancers. Staff's invited this year, you know."

I nodded. "I saw her at the gala but I didn't know who she was." Now I did. Mrs. Spencer, though I didn't mention this to Abigail, was the woman in the blue Jane Austen gown, the woman Chris had denied knowing. If I was right about her warm-eyed look, he knew her well. Was this what Tricia had hinted at? I hadn't thought about Mrs. Spencer's damp gloves since the gala. The notion that I could have given them to Chris to return made my smile broaden.

I put the Spencers' file onto the growing stack next to my desk.

"Elliott just told me that you'll be chaperoning the girls in the Berkshires," Abigail said.

A few hours earlier Michael had said "help out with." Elliott had used the term "keep an eye on." Now I was "chaperoning."

If you haven't already guessed, my background, my nature, does not make me a likely candidate for chaperoning.

"Not chaperoning, Abigail. Helping out with."

"Oh. After what happened last year I thought maybe they'd try to watch the kids more closely. Jonquil's sharing a room with Carmen. But you two get along so nicely, I just thought maybe you'd watch out for her."

"What did happen last year? Elliott wouldn't tell me."

"I'm not surprised," she said. "Michael was furious about it. One of our dancers was accused of selling marijuana to some local kids that he met in a bar—a seedy place called the Scarlet Letter. Michael's made it off-limits for the kids."

"Which dancer was it?"

"Chris," she said, giving her head a tsk-tsk shake. "The charges were dropped, but I haven't trusted that boy since."

Abigail busied herself with some correspondence, a rare occurrence. Since her daughter's "misunderstanding," as she called it, my officemate's work product had hit a new low. A monument to the work ethic, Abigail had called in sick for two days after the gala, leaving me with all of the clerical mop-up. These sick days had surprised me; Abigail did nothing, but she did it at the office, where she could watch out for Jonquil's career.

"Why aren't you going to the Berkshires?" I asked.

"Jonquil doesn't want me there," she admitted, a high-pitched whine creeping into her voice. "I suppose when girls reach a certain age all of them think their mothers are awful. And we're having a tiny problem."

An understatement if I ever heard one. "Really?"

"Jonquil's inheriting some money from my mother's estate in a few months. She's never home now. I'm afraid when she gets that money she's going to run wild."

I grinned. "That's what I would have done."

Abigail's shoulders tensed. "You don't understand. Her career comes first." Panic now edged the whine.

By then the subject of Jonquil's career bored me silly. "Don't worry," I said. "I'll watch out for Jonquil."

"Good!" she exclaimed, her expression brightening.

"Then I won't have to worry. I'm sure you'll be a fine role model for her."

Me, a role model for a seventeen-year-old girl? The idea almost made me laugh out loud.

8

"Bonnie, it's unbelievable! This is the worst thing ever. I mean, she has to be like—like the grossest person in the world."

Swinging a newspaper in one hand and her dance bag in the other, eyes alight with indignation, Carmen flung herself into Abigail's ever-vacant chair. "You won't believe it. It's so absolutely disgusting." She dropped her dance bag onto the floor. "You're not busy, are you?" she asked as an afterthought once she had settled herself.

I nodded at the heaps of paper around me. We were leaving for the Berkshires in a few days, and on top of that I had to contend with the boost in sponsor interest caused by Niki's dramatic onstage demise. For once, Gotham had lived up to its motto: The World's Most Exciting Ballet Company.

"A little," I said, "but I'm always willing to hear about gross people doing disgusting things."

"Well, this one is the worst. It's so awful I'm not sure I should put it in my Niki scrapbook." Reaching into her bag, she pulled out the scrapbook. "What do you think?"

"More about Niki? I thought the papers were finally through with him. Was he sighted getting on a UFO?"

"Shame on you. That's mean. It's actually about his wife. She's so totally . . ." Words failed her. The girl clamped her lips together and shook her head.

"Unbelievably gross?"

"Just look." Carmen spread the newspaper across the desk. Having become accustomed to headlines screaming Niki's name, I immediately scanned the top of the page. Carmen pointed to a small column at the bottom. "Here."

WIFE OF MURDERED BALLET STAR TO REMARRY

Soviet news sources report that Irena Koslova, wife of the late Nikolai Koslov, will marry fellow fission scientist Georgi Morozov. The couple, who declined to be interviewed, are rumored to be vacationing together on the Black Sea.

Niki's gushy sentiments about his wife always had struck me as sugar-coated rot. Carmen was right, though. I wouldn't necessarily have called this news gross, but it was unbelievable. Niki's body was hardly cold.

"Didn't take her long to find Georgi, did it?" I said.

"It's sickening. How could she even look at another man after someone like Niki? I'd love to see a picture of her. She's probably beautiful but really cold looking. You know the type I mean?"

I shrugged. Amazing, finding another husband so quickly. It was taking me forever. Was the Soviet Union teeming with bachelors desperate to marry the first available widow? No way. Irena must have had Georgi waiting in the wings.

Carmen looked at the clock. "I'm starving. You want to get some lunch?" she asked, folding the newspaper into the book. "I think there's some baklava left in the canteen," she added with a grin.

"You know what they can do with that baklava," I said. "No, there's something I want to do. Did you clip the piece that mentioned Niki's wife's cousin? The one in Brooklyn?"

"Sure. I've got it. She's a beautician." Carmen flipped through the scrapbook to the clipping. "She's not really a cousin," she explained. "She's like a third cousin or something. Maybe that's why Niki never went to see her."

I glanced up from the scrapbook. "Or maybe because she runs something called the Hello Dolly beauty salon." I jotted down the cousin's name, Dolly Babak, then dug the Brooklyn directory from the stack of phone books on the floor.

"Niki wasn't a snob. You just didn't understand him. Lots of people didn't. I suppose he was an acquired taste," Carmen said, all of a sudden quite adult.

"And when did you acquire a taste for Niki?"

"Remember that time in Madame's class when he picked me to dance with? When we were finished he kept his hand around me longer than he had to. And he sort of squeezed a little. Here." She clutched her waist. "It gives me goose bumps thinking about it. I'm sure he was lonely," she added, her voice going whispery.

I smiled at the girl. "That squeeze wasn't a sign of loneliness, Carmen."

"I know," she said dreamily, "but all he needed was a girlfriend who understood him. His wife wasn't even a dancer. I mean, what did they talk about? If he hadn't died maybe he would have aked me for a date."

Crimson blotches had burst across her cheeks. "Maybe you're right," I said.

"Just my luck. You know there's a special on television tonight about Niki. Are you going to watch it?"

"Possibly."

"What are you looking in the phone book for, anyway?"

There was no Hello Dolly beauty shop listed, but there was a D. Babak on Surf Court, a street with a Brighton Beach exchange.

"A place to get my hair trimmed." I pushed my chair away from my desk.

"In Brooklyn? You're kidding. Where are you going to eat?"

"Brighton Beach."

Through the windows of the elevated train, I watched street after street of neat brick row houses flash by on my right. On the left, past some apartment building roofs, was a boardwalk. Beyond that came a wide, sandy beach and then the churning Atlantic.

I felt as if I'd been halfway around the world. An hour of traveling had me glancing at my watch every thirty seconds. This was turning into an Abigail-type lunch hour. From one subway line to another, through southern Manhattan, across the East River, through Flatbush, Prospect Park, and on to Sheepshead Bay. "Brighton Beach," called the conductor finally.

On the platform I was hit by a damp wind that twisted my trenchcoat around me like a shroud. Hurrying down the stairs to Brighton Beach Avenue, I ducked into the first store I came to, a small delicatessen.

The neighborhood is called Little Odessa for good reason. An hour on the subway and I was a world away from Manhattan. Here were huge brown sacks of bread—round dark loaves, long light loaves, flat loaves, and puffy ones. Lithuanian and Estonian and Armenian loaves. Wooden barrels of pickles—pickled herring, tomatoes, carrots, onions. Spice-laden sausages hanging from the ceiling. This had to be what heaven smelled like. Behind the counter two middle-aged women bantered in Russian. I had planned to do nothing more than get directions to Surf Court, but the aroma of this place wiped out all good intentions. When I left the grocery ten minutes later, I had directions and a shopping bag of goodies.

BRIGHTON IS BACK, proclaimed yellow banners swinging

over Brighton Beach Avenue. It sure looked that way. The streets teemed with shoppers, almost all of them speaking Russian.

Brighton Beach Avenue had been sheltered from the main force of damp wind from the ocean. Surf Avenue was separated from the beach by only one row of houses. The wet wind sent my hair flying. Buttoning my coat, I crossed the street and started up the boardwalk.

Surf Court was a half block of attached two-story brick houses, their front porches shielded by orange awnings.

The little green sign in a basement-level window that read "Hello Dolly" was all but obscured by shrubs. Walking down a flight of steps, I pressed the buzzer. A stocky, middle-aged woman with an unbelievably intricate blond hairdo opened the door.

"Do you speak English?" I asked.

The woman responded in pure, belligerent Brooklynese. "Do I speak English? Whaddaya think?"

"You're Dolly?"

She blocked the door with an ample hip. "Who wants to know?"

I hadn't done anything to offend her, but she looked pretty hostile.

I raised my hand to my hair. The damp had turned my natural waves into fuzz. "I was wondering if you could do something with this. A trim, maybe."

She didn't thaw, not right away. "Ah!" She gave me a narrow-eyed stare. "You're not an inspector?"

I shook my head. Her scowl faded. A smile took its place.

"Come on in. I thought you were from the city. You got to get a license to breathe in New York. Call me Dolly."

The shop was small and cozy, with the usual beauty shop smells and the usual hairdo magazines and photos of elaborate "do's" taped to the wall. There were other pictures, too. A wall of family photos. That's how I first got Dolly talking.

A snapshot of Niki and a young woman was crowded in

among the others. The couple was bundled in overcoats, standing in front of a modern building, snow falling around them. Their smiles seemed as frozen as the day. In life Niki had never looked so uncomfortable.

"Wedding picture," Dolly told me. "They don't make much fuss over there."

Tucked over the corner of Niki's side of the photo was a black grosgrain ribbon.

"Out of honor for the dead," Dolly explained. "And that one's more honorable dead than alive, for sure."

"You didn't like Niki?"

"I never got to know him. Nobody in the family could stomach him, though. Irena hadn't lived with the creep for three, maybe four years. At least according to my aunt—that's Irena's mother—and she should know." Dolly rubbed a towel over my newly washed hair. Combing it straight, she said, "How short you want this?"

I was the only customer. Having never experienced Dolly's magic touch, I grew a little anxious when she picked up the scissors.

"I like it long. Maybe trim half an inch. Do you and your aunt write each other?"

"Nah. We've never met. Irena's mother is my mother's half sister. My mother—she's retired down in Florida now— she visited Moscow last year. Part of a two-week tour. Hadn't been back since forty-eight. Seems like she spent most of the time gossiping instead of sightseeing. Came back full of stories about Irena and that bum husband of hers. You want I should do something about this?" Dolly held a strand from the top of my head straight up.

"What's wrong with it?"

"There's gray there."

"Gray?" I leaned forward until my head was inches from the mirror. She wasn't kidding. Gray hairs poked like wire from my damp reddish blond waves. I twisted my neck, trying to get a look at the back. "Is there a lot?"

"There's enough. A few highlights would take care of it."
Spinning the chair, she gave me a critical look. "Golden
blond. That's how I'd go. It'll look natural, like you've been in
the sun."

Generally I'm not much for fooling around with Mother
Nature. It must have been the prospect of ten days in the
company of teenage girls that did it.

"Okay. I've got to call my office, though."

No problem there. Tricia wouldn't be back for another
week and Abigail's concerns did not include my whereabouts.

I settled into Dolly's chair. "So tell me about Irena and
Niki," I said. "I saw him dance. He was wonderful."

Dolly was busy mixing a potent-looking solution of
chemicals in a rubber bowl. "He was a jerk," she said without
looking up. "I could tell you stories . . ."

And she did. Dolly loved to talk.

The couple had married young, while Irena was a student
and Niki a fledgling dancer with the Bolshoi. After six or eight
months, they had separated, then reunited, then separated.
Eventually they separated for good.

"When he wasn't working hard, he couldn't keep his mitts
off the ballerinas," Dolly said. "And when he was working
hard, he was nothing you'd want to live with. Mean and
spoiled."

"Why didn't they get a divorce?" I asked. "It's supposed to
be easy in Russia."

Dolly was doing something to my hair with tinfoil and a
paintbrush. At this intermediate stage my appearance was
alarming. "I couldn't say, for sure," she said absently. "But
according to what my aunt told my mom, the government
over there is conservative about celebrities. They don't like any
scandal."

"So? Isn't a married celebrity screwing around a bigger
scandal than a divorced one?"

Dolly hooted. "Here it is, but you have to understand
how things are over there. The government controls the

newspapers. You're not going to find reporters and photographers snooping around, looking for scoops. Every year or so the party dresses the happy couple up and parades them out to some big function, sticks their picture on the front page of the newspaper, and that's it! A snow-white image for the public to look up to.

"Anyhow," she continued, "once Irena got out of school, she went to work at some nuclear place in Kiev. Niki stayed in Moscow. The way I hear it, they hadn't seen each other for a year before he came to New York. Hardly even spoke."

Even before talking to Dolly, I had been pretty sure that Niki's mind was a void where nuclear fission was concerned. "I read that the Russians killed him because he knew too much about his wife's work," I said. "Supposedly, they were afraid he was passing on secrets."

She shrugged. "I read that too. You want to hang your head over the sink? What I figure is, they wanted to keep an eye on him. You know, in case he suddenly starts hanging around with guys from the Defense Department. It's not unusual. They have a defector with a close relative doing secret work back in the Soviet Union, they follow him around for a while. Just to be sure."

I raised my voice to be heard over a cascade of warm water. "But watching somebody isn't the same thing as killing them," I said. "If he knew nothing about her work, he wouldn't have had secret meetings with our government. So why would the KGB kill him?"

She smiled. "Because he was a miserable son of a bitch. That's a good-enough reason."

A good-enough reason for Dolly, but not for me. I left Brighton Beach an hour later with golden blond highlights, a sack of groceries, and a strengthened belief that Bertha and her KGB employers hadn't cut Niki's hitch. During the long subway ride back, I ran my list of suspects over and over in my mind: Chris, Galena, Tricia, Jonquil, Abigail. What about Michael? Was Michael's vanity so fragile that he'd sabotage his own company? One thing I was almost sure of: Niki's murderer had worked in some capacity at Gotham Ballet. The murderer had known when the lower level would be most deserted, had known how to find the prop room and where to find Niki's harness. Which meant that in a couple of days I could be sharing a house in the Berkshires with a murderer.

It was four o'clock when I got back to Manhattan. And how was I supposed to go back to the office, with blond highlights and a shopping bag smelling to high heaven and proclaiming "Brighton Is Back"? Even Abigail might notice something odd. I went straight home, feasted on blintzes, shared a sausage with Moses, and got one of the few decent night's sleeps I was going to have for some time. I missed the special on Niki.

The next two days passed in a frenzy of phone calls. There were rental cars and meals to finalize and bills to pay. It was like the Gala Affair all over again. The evening before we were to leave I was so exhausted I almost fell asleep on the subway going home.

My phone was ringing as I walked into my apartment. As usual I'd left Lincoln Center late. That morning I'd dropped Moses off with a cat-sitting neighbor. Now I planned to spend the next couple of hours trying to restore sanity to my checkbook. My job left me no time for even the simplest things, and my finances, never good, were a disaster.

Two rings, three . . . I almost didn't answer it, figuring it was either Elliott in a dither about some last-minute detail or, in some ways worse, Tony. We'd made halfhearted plans to see each other that night, but if he wanted to come over, I was going to plead exhaustion. I picked up the phone, my excuse ready.

"Hey, Bonnie. Tony. I know this is your last night here, but I'm not going to be able to get away."

"Oh. That's too bad." I could have told him about my trip to Brighton Beach, but I knew what his reaction would be.

"You did *what!*" he'd say angrily. "Why can't you leave this alone?" So I didn't mention it.

"Maybe I can make it up to the Berkshires," he said. "What do you think? I could drive up on Wednesday."

"I'll be pretty busy, but—well, sure. If you want to." I gave him the phone number at the girls' house, the bucolic-sounding Primrose Cottage.

"Okay," he said. "See you soon."

The second I hung up I knew what I had to do. When Tony called Primrose Cottage I'd flat out say, "This isn't working, Tony." It's one thing to conduct a halfhearted affair with someone who lives five miles away, another when that person wants to drive four hours to get to you.

I'd no sooner spread my bills across my kitchen table and opened my checkbook when the phone rang again.

"Hello."

"Hello, Bonnie."

My heart flipped completely over in my chest. At least that's how it felt. I could hardly breathe. "Derek. Hi."

"I've missed you. I'd like to see you."

Oh, no. Not that. I wasn't going to see him, not under any circumstances. He didn't deserve me.

"I was wondering, if I took a drive, could I stop by your apartment?"

"Tonight?" Never! Not tonight, not any night!

"Yes. Now. My car hasn't been out all week. It could use a run."

His car needed a run? Well, I could have used a "run" too, but only a fool would see him again, after that fight we'd had and all these weeks apart.

"I'm busy," I said. "But maybe for a few minutes." Whoops! Where had that come from? That sentence should have been "But maybe some other time."

"I'll be there in half an hour."

What had I done? I cradled the phone, feeling almost faint. Now I had to deal with temptation in its all-too-appealing flesh. Well, he'd see how dispassionate I was. Faced with my haughty indifference, Derek would soon scurry back to his meaningless life.

I stared into the mirror in my hall. How strong I looked! Those clear blue eyes, not missing a trick. A straight, American-girl nose that could smell a rat a mile away. That determined, upward tilt to my chin. And my hair—shoulder length and naturally wavy, with a trace of brand-new golden blond highlights. I parted my bangs and scrutinized the roots. No gray there. Not anymore. Backing away from the mirror, I gave my dress a hard look. Navy linen, à la Tricia. But wasn't it a little *stern*? If I hurried, I could take a quick shower and change into something that didn't shout "office." The night was muggy—rain was predicted—and there was that red tank top Amanda had given me. It really looked pretty sexy . . .

Into the fridge went a bottle of good white wine. Out the window went my self-control.

9

The Rent-a-Wreck van rode like a Conestoga wagon, lurching through curves, groaning up hills. A little bit of gravel on the road and you'd have thought we were in the epicenter of an earthquake. Elliott was driving. I was in the seat behind him, supposedly navigating. In reality, the chaperone of the girls' house was a wreck. Time after time my head fell, my eyes closed, my mind began that slide from consciousness to sleep. Time after time a teenager's shout jolted me upright. You'd think these kids had never seen a hill the way they carried on.

"The mountains are just beautiful," one of them called from the back seat. "There's a rest stop up ahead, Elliott. Stop so we can take some pictures."

The girl next to me began rummaging through her tote bag. "I forgot film." She shook my shoulder. The hundred-pound darling had a grip like King Kong. "Bonnie? Are you awake? Did you pack extra film?"

Film? I wasn't even sure I'd packed clothes. I groaned something to let the girl know I had not packed film and was not interested in discussing film, then turned my face into the corner of the seat and pulled my sweater around my head to block out the sunlight. The plastic upholstery was clammy against my skin. It smelled funky, like stale cigarettes.

"Here's the turn-off, Elliott. Elliott, you're going too fast. Now we passed it!"

One of the boys—this skinny kid with jug ears—piped up: "We're starving! When do we eat?"

"We just had lunch," Elliott barked. "And we're not stopping again until we get there!"

After four hours in the van with nine members of the under-twenty-one crowd and a hungover navigator, Elliott's disposition, nothing to write home about at the best of times, was plain nasty. The trip was reminding me of those horrible junior high outings when every half hour or so the driver pulls over and threatens his passengers. Elliott's passengers were too old for spitballs. But they were not past screaming for a pit stop every five minutes and shouting "God, Elliott! Where did you learn to drive?" every time the gears failed to mesh. Which was every time Elliott shifted them.

The only quiet one in the bunch was Carmen. She'd seemed down when she climbed into the van that morning and she'd hardly spoken since. If I'd felt better, I might have said something to her. However, I had my own problems.

Whether what Derek and I had done the night before constituted a "reconciliation," I couldn't have said. That morning, when he'd suggested visiting me in the Berkshires, I'd said no, that I needed time to think, a "cooling off" period. Very *cool* of me. But we'd had a very nice time doing what we'd done. In the process, we'd taken care of the bottle of good white wine I'd stuck in the fridge and the bottle of good red wine he'd brought with him. Dinner had seemed beside the point. Now I felt hellish. The very thought of food disgusted me.

Looking back on that trip, I know it wouldn't have made any difference if I'd spent the night before in a convent. The drive was doomed from the start.

We'd been late getting out of the parking lot. So many

items had been forgotten, calling for so many last-minute trips into the shops along Broadway that you would have thought we were off on safari to Borneo.

"Wagons, ho!" one of the kids had yelled a good hour and a half after our scheduled departure time, and our wagon train to the Berkshires—three rented vans, a borrowed station wagon, and an assortment of cars in varying states of dilapidation—had pulled into traffic. We didn't even make the New England Thruway before we had our first of several overheated engines. By the time we hit the Connecticut–Massachusetts border several hours later, our little section of the wagon train consisted of two vehicles—our rental van and Chris's yellow Subaru. We had no idea where any of the other cars were or if they were still on the road. During the course of the trip at least one of every conceivable gizmo ever attached to an automobile had exploded, sprung a leak, or fallen off and rolled down the highway. Most of these gizmos had been part of the Subaru's rusting hulk. I could see sparks shooting from under the car. Chris had to be deaf. His tail pipe had been dragging since the Bronx.

Elliott was a real old maid once he got behind the wheel. Things had been all right in the speed department as long as Chris was driving the Subaru. Elliott could barely endure sixty miles an hour. At the last pit stop, though, Jonquil—against Elliott's orders—had deserted our van and jumped behind the Subaru's wheel. That was the beginning of the big trouble.

"Is that kid crazy? Bonnie? Bonnie! Wake up! Would you look at the way she's driving! Over seventy!"

I glanced over his his shoulder. He jabbed his finger at his speedometer. Sure enough, seventy-two and climbing.

The view out the windshield was frightening. We'd left the highway and were on a heavily traveled two-lane road. The Subaru was moving so fast that the sparks from under it looked like bolts of lightning.

"I'm glad I'm not riding up there," the jug-eared boy said. "That tin can's about to explode."

I 119 I

"How can Jonquil stand that rattletrap?" asked the girl next to me.

"She's out of it. Must have visited the Old Man last night."

There was that "Old Man" again. The boy's comment made the whole group snicker.

I lifted my head. "Who is this Old Man? Anybody I know?"

"Huh? I was just kidding."

Sure he was. For a few minutes only little giggles and whispers and "shushes" and the roar of wind past the windshield broke the quiet in the van.

"At least Jonquil has a boyfriend," one of the girls mused. "I wouldn't mind that. Chris is cute."

"He's such a flirt," the girl next to me said knowingly. "I heard there's even some older woman he's going out with. She's about thirty-five or forty!"

"Disgraceful," I muttered sarcastically.

"At least he's straight. The first time I saw him in class I thought he was a mirage."

One of the boys broke in. "We're not all gay. We just like girls who can talk about something besides whether Michael noticed them at practice."

The conversation went along like this for several minutes, until Carmen roused herself.

"Niki," she said, "was the perfect man."

"Niki?" The boy with the jug ears laughed. "He was as boring as anybody else. More boring. What kind of a guy spends his spare time reading Russian translations of English business words and junk about becoming an entrepreneur?"

"How do you know what he read?" Carmen asked, beating me to the question.

"Chris told me."

And how had Chris known what Niki read? The morning I visited Niki in his dressing room, he had tossed those books into his bottom drawer—coincidentally the drawer where the drugs were found. If, as Chris claimed, he hadn't been in the theater all day, how did he know about the books? Niki had taken them from the library only that morning. Chris couldn't have seen them after the murder because Niki's dressing room was padlocked. And when the room was opened and cleaned out, Chris was in Germany.

A blessed silence fell over the van. I was so groggy I couldn't keep Niki's murder on my mind. My eyes slid shut. I was at the edge of sleep when Elliott shouted: "I'm going to strangle that kid!"

I opened my eyes. What I saw was terrifying. We were going downhill and gaining speed by the second. Ahead of us Chris's car fishtailed through a curve. Our speedometer read seventy-eight. Elliott leaned forward until his chin was inches from the steering wheel. Only ten miles from our destination and we were all going to be killed.

"Blow the horn, Elliott. Wave her over." The words were no sooner out of my mouth when this hideous odor assaulted me, even worse than the funky cigarette smell. The girl next to me, oblivious to everything but her appetite, had pulled a peanut butter and jelly sandwich from her dance bag. It was squashed flat. Revolting! My stomach lurched. I quickly shut my eyes. Would this hell never end?

"A cop! A cop!" The cry went up in unison. The girl with the sandwich grabbed my arm again. "He's slowing down!" Someone else yelled, "Here comes another one from behind! Oh, no! He's put his lights on!"

I opened my eyes as Elliott hit the shoulder. And I mean hit. A Massachusetts state trooper flew past after the Subaru, lights flashing and siren wailing. Another trooper pulled up behind us. The back of Elliott's normally pasty neck had turned cherry red.

"Would you step out of the car please, sir, and show me your license and registration."

The trooper was huge. His shoulders filled the van's

window. He had a bullet-shaped head, a bulbous nose, and a mean little mouth. Everybody in the van shut up and sat still.

In the end, if Elliott hadn't gone nuts on us there would have been no problem other than the usual indignities of a traffic violation. Elliott must be the only person on earth who doesn't understand that when the police clock you at seventy-six miles per hour in a fifty-five-mile zone, the passengers sit quietly while the driver grovels out on the shoulder, repeating a mantra of "Yes Sir Yes Sir."

The trooper had walked around to the front of the van to check the license number. Elliott was right next to him, his mouth going like gangbusters. He kept waving his arms toward the yellow Subaru. The second state trooper had pulled it over about fifty feet up the road.

A minute later, when the trooper walked past our van to get to his car radio, one of the kids broke our silence: "Look at the face on that cop!"

"An animal! Bet he's dying to beat somebody up. Elliott better . . . Hey! Where's Elliott going? Bonnie, maybe you better do something."

There went Elliott, fists clenched, marching up the highway. The first trooper had parked in front of the Subaru so that I had an unobstructed view of the fracas that followed.

Jonquil had propped herself on one of the Subaru's rear fenders. As the trooper jotted down the license plate number, she slid off the fender and started strolling back and forth at the edge of the pavement. She was swinging her red straw purse and looking just cooler than cool. With her black high-top sneakers, skinny black pants, and tight sweater, she was hardly the picture of dewy-faced innocence we needed. Suddenly the handle on her purse let go and the red bag flew into some bushes at the side of the road. Jonquil scurried after it.

She was crouched, sort of digging through the bushes, when Elliott got to her. He was in some state, bellowing like a bull. Jonquil stood, straw bag in hand, and screeched back. Elliott reached out and took her arm. For all his faults, I don't think Elliott was given to violence. I imagine he planned to pull Jonquil aside and give her a stern talking to. It was only a matter of seconds, though, before Chris was out of the Subaru's passenger seat and into a full-out brawl with Elliott.

I don't have to tell you that when a muscular twenty-three-year-old who tosses women around for a living gets into it on the side of the road with a scrawny administrator, it's going to be the administrator whose facial features are imprinted in the dust. The only surprising thing about this fight was the sudden fury of Chris's attack.

The trooper —our trooper—flew past the van, one hand clutching his holstered gun. The other trooper reached the two men and was trying to pull Chris off Elliott. Jonquil howled like a banshee, "Don't shoot! Don't shoot!" At the moment when the kids in my van took up her chorus, two more police cars roared up, sirens screaming.

What a mess! If Niki's death hadn't finished off my career, this would. "Let me out of here!" Crawling over the girl with the sandwich, I pulled back the van's sliding door and scrambled onto the road.

Forty minutes later, when we'd seen our two gladiators driven off in the backs of two police cars on their way to one of those tiny Massachusetts border towns, the rest of us settled into the van. We were minus the Subaru. One of the kids had started it up and the smoke pouring from its innards had all but obliterated visibility for several hundred yards. If everything went well—meaning if someone from the company showed up with money—Elliott and Chris would be bailed out of jail and the Subaru out of a repair shop that evening.

I had no reason to think everything would go well. So far nothing had. I didn't care anymore. I didn't care if I never saw Elliott, Chris, or the Subaru again. I cared about only one thing: sleep. Clean white sheets—the way they would feel against my skin when I got out of a hot shower—a fluffy pillow against my face; these were the things that mattered. I could not get to that compound too soon.

Starting the engine, I shifted into gear and began rolling up the shoulder of the road. Traffic was heavy and I suppose my grogginess made me hyperalert. I had gotten up a lot of speed and just edged onto the pavement when Jonquil shouted into my ear: "Oh, no! Stop, Bonnie!"

I crashed my foot onto the brake. The van's tires screamed as we skidded up the asphalt and once again hit the shoulder. What had she seen? Had I almost rammed another car? A big tractor-trailer roared by, its driver leaning on his horn. My heart pounded.

"I must have dropped my makeup by the side of the road."

"What?"

"When my purse fell. I'm going to run back and look."

"Oh no you're not!" Before she could object I had slammed that accelerator to the floor.

"But my makeup. I need it."

"We know you need it," one of the boys snickered.

"Drop dead!"

I glanced at Jonquil through the rearview mirror. "There's a whole station wagon full of makeup on its way up. You can use that."

"That's stage makeup! Goop! I want my own things." Jonquil's lower lip poked out. I turned my attention to the road.

Even then, before my troubles with Jonquil really got rolling, I suspected the worst of her. The way that straw bag had sailed into the bushes had looked purely accidental, and if the bag had belonged to anyone but Jonquil I wouldn't have give it a second thought. But it was Jonquil's bag, and I was sure she was using drugs. Had her bag really fallen, or had she been afraid she was going to be arrested? Had she managed to temporarily "lose" her stash of cocaine, just in case?

She finished the trip glaring out the side window with her lower lip pushed out so far it threatened to swallow her turned-up nose. She ignored most of the other kids, and she ignored me. That wasn't especially surprising. What did surprise me was the way Carmen pointedly turned away when Jonquil leaned over the seat and tried whispering something to her. From friends to strangers, overnight.

We rolled into Greylock Compound at six-thirty. A two-hundred-mile, mostly highway car trip had taken us almost eight hours. Roughly, we had averaged about twenty-five miles an hour. I was comatose, hands paralyzed on the wheel, eyes frozen open. When I stepped out of the van to register us at the main house, my legs felt about as substantial as a couple of rubber bands.

After dropping the boys at their cottage, I followed a winding, rutted road around a lake. Rounding a curve, we passed a long, low structure that proved to be a garage. A little farther and there it was: Primrose Cottage, glowing in the twilight, beckoning through its cover of trees. It was a gothic stone monster, all ivy-laden and adorned with turrets and balconies and porches.

"Wow! That's what I call a cottage."

That was what I called a bed.

I pulled in next to Galena's white T-bird. She hadn't planned to leave New York until that afternoon and even she had beat us.

"At last!" Galena said when we trooped through the back door into a big kitchen. "We were beginning to worry."

My relationship with Galena had improved steadily since Niki's death. I hated to think the two things were related, but it was nice being on good terms with her.

As the girls ran around looking over the house, I took the cup of tea Galena offered.

"You look tired, Bonnie. Come join me in the living room."

I followed her down a long hallway, past a dining room where several dancers were working on a big picture puzzle, and into this lovely old-fashioned sitting room, full of antique oak furniture and flowered chintz cushions. In one corner was a stone fireplace. The night was chilly and a small fire burned.

I sank gratefully into a rocking chair, leaned back, and sipped the hot tea. "I thought we would never get here."

"I know. We had a call from Michael. He's driving over now to collect our bad boys." Galena settled into a window seat next to a pile of toe shoes. Taking a pair of scissors, she started snipping lengths from a spool of ribbon.

Toe shoes come without the ribbons and elastic that secure them. Ballerinas always sew the ribbons and elastics themselves, rather like parachutists packing their own chutes. Galena was an expert. Hardly looking, she measured with her thumb from the heel to the exact spot where the ribbon should be attached.

Slipping off my shoes, I wiggled my toes in front of the fire. Now that the ride was over, it suddenly struck me as funny: Chris's hunk-of-junk car, the fistfight.

Galena noticed my smile. "You're feeling better. It's the tea. Ah! And you had a call. A man. I put a note in your room. He'll call back."

"Tony?"

"You have more than one?"

I held up two fingers. Galena smiled. "How wonderful. Yes. This was Tony."

I groaned.

At that moment two of the younger girls thundered down the stairs. An unusually sedate Carmen followed, gripping the handrail.

"How totally fantastic! Look at the lake!"

"I can't believe it! There's a gazebo at the end of the dock."

It really was wonderful. The sitting room looked out onto a porch that ran the width of the house. The porch itself wasn't fifty feet away from the lake. In the moonlight it was incredibly romantic.

The girls had huddled at the screen door that led to the

porch. The romantic feel of the place didn't escape them, either. Carmen said, in almost a whisper, "Isn't it a shame Niki isn't here to enjoy this?"

"Niki would have loved it," another girl agreed. "It's too bad he never got to see anything in this country but New York City."

Would Niki have loved it? I'd never heard him express any interest in the great outdoors unless it involved cowboys. If Carmen had anything to say about it, though, the cult of Niki would live forever.

Galena made a noise at the back of her throat. "Niki! You girls and your infatuations. Niki cared no more for lakes than he cared for people. If Niki was here he would be in his room doing his barre exercises. Have you young ladies done barres today? There are sturdy chairs in the bedrooms."

The girls exchanged guilty looks. When traveling, dancers often do workouts in their rooms, using chairs or anything else available for support.

As usual, Carmen wasn't diverted for long from her favorite subject. "Niki liked some people," she said pointedly.

I glanced at Galena. She had laid her toe shoes aside and stretched out in her seat. Her head was thrown back and she was rolling it from side to side. A simple neck exercise, a tension reliever, but even in the soft light it was plain this was not the throat of a young woman. Still, whatever her age, she looked great.

"Do you miss him?" she said to me.

She had caught me staring at her. Like the rest of the company, Galena was still under the illusion that Niki and I had been close. To say no now would make me seem like a Judas. To say yes would be a flat-out lie. "Sometimes," I answered.

"So do I. I had planned a thousand revenges. Now they are wasted."

A thousand revenges? What a thing to say! The girls were shocked. "Galena, you don't mean that."

Galena tugged at the ribbons she had sewn onto a pair of pointe shoes, then slipped one shoe onto her foot. The shoes come from the manufacturer with no specific left or right designation. The ballerina decides which shoe is best for which foot. I watched Galena flex her ankle. "Not right," she said, removing the shoe. Taking a single-edged razor blade from her sewing kit, she peeled back the shoe's lining and slashed at the arch. "A strong enemy can be a fine thing," she said, slipping back into the shoe. "He can keep you on your toes." With that, she rose and executed a perfect pirouette. The spool of ribbon flew from around her wrist and sailed across the room. The girls broke into laughter. One of them caught the spool and the tension was broken.

"Bonnie, will you change rooms with me? Please."

It was about ten o'clock. Carmen had darted from a door into the second-floor hallway and grabbed my arm.

"Are you serious?"

"Yes. If I have to share with Jonquil, I'll go out and sleep in the van."

"What's the matter? What happened between you two?"

"Nothing. I don't want to be friends with her anymore, that's all. The room is huge. You wouldn't even have to see Jonquil. It has a view and its own bathroom and a fireplace. Your room is tiny and ugly. And you have to use the bathroom down the hall."

"My room is all mine."

Her soft brown eyes grew flinty. "Okay, then. Could I have the keys to the van? I'm sleeping out there."

"No you can't. If you want to suffer you can sleep on the sofa."

I started down the hall. "That's too public. Can I sleep on your floor?" she asked in a small voice.

Turning, I stared at the girl. She looked miserably unhappy.

I'd reached the state of fatigue where I didn't care where

I slept as long as I slept. "Okay," I said. "I'll switch with you for tonight. Tomorrow we switch back."

Twenty minutes and a hot shower later I was snuggled deep into my pillows. The sheets, the pillows, they were all I had hoped for. And the room was a joy. Jonquil and I were over the parlor. Our windows looked out onto the roof of the porch and through a stand of trees to the lake. The room was big, too, though not as big as Carmen had promised. Jonquil's bed by the far wall beyond our bathroom was partially hidden by an old-fashioned oak wardrobe. In the dark, I could just make out her legs under the blankets. I could also make out her straw bag propped carelessly against the wardrobe. If I looked through it and found her makeup, would that mean that what she had left on the side of the road was cocaine? How was that for trust? In the room less than half an hour and ready to search my roommate's purse.

My thoughts drifted to my other problem. My biggest problem, I thought at the time. There may be women who are suited to polygamy, but I'm not one of them. Even assuming I could maintain the superwoman energy it requires, guilt was going to get me. When Tony called back, I had to tell the truth. "Tony," I would say, "I care about you but there is someone else. I will always think of you as a friend."

"I understand completely, Bonnie," he would answer. His hurt would soon fade. But not too soon.

The lake was lapping softly against the shore and a cricket chirped near a window. Someone on the third floor was running a bath into a clawfoot bathtub. Sleep closed over me, a dark curtain falling on a stage.

—|10|—

Everything seemed fine in the morning. As I lay among my pillows with the soft quilt pulled to my chin, an aroma of brewing coffee drifted up from the kitchen, tantalizing me into the day. Outside the window a bird was singing. The screen door to the porch banged and a moment later I heard Galena and another woman admiring the lake.

Galena and her thousand revenges. How silly that seemed in the morning light. The evening before her words had sounded so ominous. A case of shot nerves on my part, I decided as I stretched and kicked off the quilt.

Jonquil was already up, singing in the shower behind our bathroom door. Rising on my elbows, I looked at her side of the room. Neat as a pin. She'd even made her bed. According to most mothers, mine included, bed making is one of those activities that separate the good girls from the slatterns. I'm not sure where that leaves me. I have my compulsions, but bed making isn't one of them.

Where had Jonquil put that red straw bag, anyway? Ah, there it was, tossed on the chair beside her bed, begging to be searched. What a temptation—as inviting as an ice-cream cone on an August afternoon.

But was it right to start a beautiful day off by doing something as rotten as searching my roommate's bag? After that bed-making job, didn't she deserve the benefit of the doubt?

After stretching, I swung my feet onto the floor. The morning sun shone through the lace curtains on our windows, making patterns of light play over the oak floorboards.

"Jonquil, are you going to be much longer?"

There was no answer. I knocked on the bathroom door. "Jonquil?"

"Be out in two minutes, Bonnie."

Two minutes. And there was that red straw bag, almost within touching distance of my itchy fingers. If there was cocaine, it probably was hidden in the bushes by the highway, but you never know. I grappled briefly with the temptation. As usual, it won. "Take your time."

In five seconds I had the whole thing dumped out on Jonquil's blanket. Wallet, scarf, address book, keys, pen. And makeup. Enough lipstick and eye shadow and blusher loose in the bag to paint up an entire chorus line. To her credit, there was no makeup case and no cocaine. Packets of cocaine are very small, so I quickly looked through her wallet. There was nothing in it that shouldn't have been, but I did find something that gave me pause: Jonquil had a medical identification card from the company physician. Her blood type was B-negative, the type found on Niki's torn hitch. A common blood type, but . . .

Putting the wallet back, I ran my hands through the depths of the straw bag. It was lined in bright striped cotton. I felt every corner, every edge. Nowhere was there a telltale bulge of something hidden away. I still didn't trust her.

The shower stopped abruptly. Stuffing everything back into the bag, I threw it on the chair and scurried across the floor to my own bed.

Not ten seconds later Jonquil opened the bathroom door and walked out in a pink robe with a towel wrapped, turban-style, around her head. "It's all yours."

I was pulling my robe from my suitcase when she asked, "Bonnie? How come Carmen doesn't want to share with me?"

"I was going to ask you that. Did you two have a fight?"

She shook her head. "She's just moody, I guess. Okay if I borrow the van for a few minutes?"

What a picture of innocence, all freckles and strawberry wisps of hair fighting their way from under the towel. She had tilted her head to one side. Her smile was sweet. I was reminded of her mother.

"What do you need the van for?"

"I want to see if Chris is okay," she said, glancing down.

"I'm sure he is. Michael went to get him last night. If you want to be certain, call the boys' house."

"There's no phone there. They go over to the main house to make calls."

"You'll have to wait, then. I need the van." I really didn't. There was plenty to keep me occupied around the compound. But she wanted to go back for the stash she'd left at the side of the road. I would have bet a week's salary on that.

"But Bonnie! It's just for a little while, and—"

"And right after breakfast you have to go to practice. Madame is going to drive you. Chris will probably be there. You can talk to him then."

She put on her sour face, but she didn't give me any more argument. The last thing I saw as I closed the bathroom door behind me was Jonquil running her hands over her blanket, straightening the spot where I'd been sitting minutes before.

Madame was in the kitchen door, hands on her hips. "So where is that young lady? She knows better than to be late for practice?"

The young lady in question was Carmen. Everyone else

was either in Galena's car or standing on the back porch ready to climb into a station wagon.

"I don't think she slept well," one of the girls said. "She was taking a bath in the middle of the night."

Madame looked at me. "Would you please get her up and drive her to the auditorium. We cannot wait."

"I'll be glad to," I said. "She'll be there in no time."

A minute later I watched them drive off. Jonquil was secured on one side by Madame, on the other by one of the soloists. I didn't have to worry about her for a while. Walking back through the house, I climbed the stairs.

"Carmen." I rapped on her door. There was no answer. "Carmen? Are you up?"

"Yes."

"May I come in?"

I turned the knob and pushed. The door cracked open an inch, then jammed. It was blocked on the opposite side.

"Just a second," Carmen said. There was a scraping sound, then her voice retreated. "Okay."

As I walked into the room, the door rammed into a ladder-back chair. I stared at it for a second.

"The old chair under the doorknob? Why did you barricade yourself in?"

"I like my privacy."

She was sitting on the edge of her bed looking down at the floor. She had draped the sheet modestly over her shoulder. A little too modestly. Above the sheet, her leotard showed.

In some ways, I found Carmen and the other young ballerinas unsophisticated for their age. They lived in a very insular world. Generally, though, they were uninhibited about their bodies. It's part of the job. I immediately suspected Carmen of hiding something.

"What's the matter?"

"Nothing." She wrapped the sheet tighter.

I said the first thing that came to mind. "Carmen, are you pregnant?"

| 133 |

She forced a smile. "Pregnant? I never even had a boyfriend. How would I get pregnant?"

"Then what's wrong? What's with the bath in the middle of the night, anyway?"

"You've got to swear you won't tell anybody," she said after a moment.

"Won't tell what? How can I make a promise like that?"

I was shocked to see tears fill the girl's eyes. "Swear it, Bonnie."

"I swear."

Dropping the sheet, she pulled her long-sleeved black leotard over her shoulder. As she did, she broke into sobs.

The sight of Carmen's left arm and shoulder made me gasp. She was covered with huge purple bruises.

"What on earth . . ."

Her voice quaked. "My leg is worse." She shoved the sheet aside. She hadn't put her tights on yet. An awful bruise went from hip to calf on her left leg. A couple of bandages couldn't cover the broken skin on her knee.

"What happened to you?"

"I got hit by a car."

"When?"

"The night before last. Thursday. Real late. It started raining just as I was leaving the theater. I went out the back and was going to run across Amsterdam in the middle of the block but there was traffic so I stopped next to this car and—"

Her words were tumbling out so fast I couldn't keep them straight. "Wait, wait. You were in the middle of Amsterdam Avenue . . ."

"No, no. I was between two cars parked along the curb. I didn't want to go to the corner because of the rain. I stepped out to look and . . . and then I was in the street and this taxi hit me."

"Did he stop?"

"Yeah," she said with a nod. "He was almost as scared as me. He wanted to take me to the hospital."

"You didn't go to the hospital?"

"I didn't want to. I made sure I could walk, then I told him I was okay." She grinned through her tears. "He gave me a ride home for free."

"So you haven't been to a doctor?"

She shook her head. "That's why I took that hot bath last night, for the stiffness. I feel better already. Every minute I feel better. Look." Jumping up, she clutched her ankle and raised her leg high above her head.

"That doesn't mean you are better. Get dressed. I'm taking you to the company doctor."

An expression of pure horror crossed the girl's face. "No! You promised, Bonnie! You swore! It hardly hurts at all. If they think I'm injured they'll take away my solos and give them to someone else. They might even give them to Jonquil."

I should have known. Carmen had two little solos coming up this week, one in a modern piece of Michael's and one in *Swan Lake*. Together the two didn't last more than ninety seconds, but for a girl in the corps those ninety seconds mean everything.

"This is why you wanted your own room, isn't it? So nobody could see you."

She shrugged. "That's part of the reason."

Carmen had it all worked out. For practice she planned to wear long-sleeved leotards and black tights. For her evening performances that required bare arms or pale tights she was going to pack on stage makeup. "By Saturday when I do *Swan Lake* the bruises will be gone."

"Fine," I said. "But you're not doing anything until you've been x-rayed. Do you have insurance?"

She nodded. "I'm covered on my daddy's policy."

"Then get dressed. We'll find a doctor somewhere in town."

While I waited for Carmen I made a few phone calls and discovered that there was an emergency room in Lenox where she could be x-rayed. They said if I got her there early she wouldn't have much of a wait.

On our way out of the compound I stopped at the boys' log house on the other side of the lake. There were a couple of cars in the driveway but the yellow Subaru wasn't among them.

Pulling into the driveway, I called to a boy on the porch: "Where's Chris's car?"

"Still in the repair shop. Chris got a ride to practice with one of the guys."

"I'll be right back," I said to Carmen. "Is Elliott around?" I asked the boy.

"He's in the kitchen. And you better watch it. He's not in a good mood."

When was he ever? "What happened with the police?" I asked.

"They decided they didn't have anything on Chris. Elliott's charged with assaulting an officer, but Michael thinks he can get it dropped. Hey, Bonnie . . ."

"Yes?"

"Better not say anything about the eye. It pisses him off."

I found Elliott up to his elbows in a sink full of dishwater. He didn't turn when I walked into the room.

"You're going to be driving to the auditorium, aren't you?" I asked.

"Of course."

"Then please tell Madame that one of Carmen's contacts is bothering her. We're driving into Lenox to get it replaced. She'll probably be at rehearsal this afternoon."

"No problem." He slammed around some dirty dishes as if they were iron.

"Elliott, why are you doing that? A housekeeper will be along to clean up."

Still keeping his back to me, he said, "Oh, no, she won't! Not if I have anything to say about it! I've ordered her away

| 136 |

from the boys' house permanently. Now, if you'll do your job, it might make my life easier."

"My job? What are you talking about?"

"Last night—after the day I had—I no sooner get to bed when I hear voices outside by the lake."

"And?"

"And? And I get back into my clothes, go out there, and what do you suppose I find?"

I didn't answer.

He pulled his arms out of the sink, shook off his hands, and turned. His eye was as purple as Carmen's leg. I was unable to stop myself. "My God!"

"That's what I like about you. Always something nice to say."

"Sorry. What did you find at the lake, Elliott?"

"One of the younger boys—he's only seventeen—was out there with our so-called housekeeper. Some local girl. And another couple. The other couple disappeared before I could get a good look at them. Ran right through the creek, clothes and all."

"What does that have to do with my job?"

He narrowed his eyes. "It was Chris and Jonquil. That squeal of hers—it's enough to raise the dead! I can't do anything about him. He's overage . . ."

"And strong, too."

"Funny! But Jonquil . . ."

I shook my head. I wasn't about to admit that as a chaperone I was already a failure. "It may have been Chris but it wasn't Jonquil. We shared a room last night. She was sound asleep when I went to bed at ten. What were these kids up to, anyway?"

Elliott threw some pots into the sink with such vigor that the water lapped over the edge. I braced myself for something ghastly. What had he caught this vile foursome doing? Shooting heroin, or maybe performing some unbelievably perverse sex act?

"They had a bottle of wine, and I smelled marijuana. I'll tell you one thing I've decided: from now on, it's Checkpoint Charlie around here. I'm sleeping downstairs. The boys want to get out, they'll have to get by me."

"Elliott, you've got to keep some perspective or you're going to drive yourself crazy. Weren't you ever seventeen? Don't you know what it's like? You get some boys and girls together, in the woods, near a lake . . . it happens."

"It never happened to me!"

"No," I said. "I suppose it didn't."

"For the next ten days," he continued, ignoring my wisecrack, "we both have a job to do, and that job is to keep the underage kids in line."

I looked around the kitchen. What a mess. The sink was still full of dishes. Someone had upset a glass of orange juice on the table and it was dripping onto one of the chairs. Picking up my tote, I walked to the kitchen door.

"You're wrong, Elliott. You've got two jobs to do during the next ten days. You're going to be chaperoning, and you're going to be housekeeping. Don't forget to give Madame my message."

One of the boys was leaning on the van talking to Carmen when I left the house. It was good to see her smiling.

During the drive into Lenox, I asked her if she'd been wearing her contact lenses when she was hit.

"No."

"That's why you didn't see the taxi."

"It is not," she said angrily. "I did see the taxi. But . . ." She was quiet for a few seconds. "Bonnie, if I tell you something, will you promise not to say I'm crazy?"

"Of course I'm not going to say you're crazy."

"Somebody pushed me."

"Into the street?"

"Yes." Her voice began to shake again. "There were these two cars, like I said. One of them was big—a station wagon or something. I was in the street but I kept stepping between them when traffic came too close. But then I thought there was somebody behind me. I started to turn and I got kicked hard in the back. I mean, real hard. It hurt so much I stumbled and fell in the street."

"Are you sure?"

She bent and yanked down the waistband of her jeans, exposing her lower back. "What do you think that is, if it isn't a footprint?"

Near the tip of her spine was a dark spot about three inches long and two wide. I couldn't have recognized it as a footprint, but there was no reason not to believe Carmen.

My imagination leapt. Niki's murderer, lurking around a dark theater, stalking the one person who might identify her—or him. What a frightening thought. I didn't want to scare Carmen with it.

"That's horrible," I said. "When we get back you should go to the police. There are some street people who sleep in the park behind the theater. Maybe . . ."

"It wasn't any bum. They hang out in the subway station when it rains. I know who it was."

"Who?"

She hesitated. "Well, I'm not positive so I'm not going to say, but it was a dancer."

Something dawned on me. "Does this have something to do with why you're not speaking to Jonquil?"

"I don't want to talk about it anymore. But if I could have your room, I could keep the door blocked . . ."

"You can have it," I said. I'd already decided that sharing with Jonquil would be the best way to keep an eye on her. Besides, though I didn't want to tell Carmen this, the chair under the doorknob was starting to seem like a good idea to me, too.

"Thanks. It could have been Jonquil that pushed me"— she gave me a sideways look—"or it could have been Galena."

Exactly what I'd been thinking. "Why do you say that?" I asked.

Carmen shrugged. "I have my reasons. Just maybe Galena isn't as wonderful as everybody thinks."

That was quite a change. Galena had always been Carmen's ideal.

I walked the girl into the emergency room and watched a starchy nurse register her before I went back to the van. Given the way hospital emergency rooms work, she was taken care of for at least an hour. Now I had to do something about Jonquil. More accurately, about her stash.

Traffic was lighter than it had been the day before, and it took me no more than ten minutes to get to the hill. As I approached the spot, I flicked on my right turn signal and edged off the road. I'd had enough of screaming brakes. Thank heavens I was going so slowly when I rounded the first curve. I was at the crest, with a full view of the curves below, when I spotted Galena Semenova's Thunderbird moving up the shoulder in the distance. Seconds later the white car sped away.

I was stunned. With the exception of Madame, Galena was the last person in the company I would have suspected of being involved with illegal drugs. Murder, maybe, but not drugs. She was so self-confident, so altogether above groveling through the bushes at the side of the road. The likeliest explanation was that Jonquil had borrowed her car, but Carmen's angry words ran through my mind: "Maybe Galena isn't as wonderful as everybody thinks." What did the girl suspect?

I waited on the hill for a few minutes, then released the hand brake and let the van roll down the shoulder. My search of the bushes was fruitless.

That evening, dinner in the compound dining room was as uncomfortable a meal as I'd sat through in a long time. The company was scheduled to perform at eight, and since most dancers don't like to perform immediately after finishing a meal, we ate shortly after five. It is a barbaric hour for dinner, even by my not-lofty standards. The time, however, was not the worst of it. Carmen had received a clean bill of health from the hospital, but that had done nothing to lift her mood. She made a point of getting up and leaving the table full of young ballerinas when Jonquil joined them. As Carmen walked away, the expression on Jonquil's face was heartbreaking. Tray in hand, Carmen stomped by the table where I was sitting with Elliott and a woman from Wardrobe, and past the next obvious table—the one where Galena, Madame, and a few soloists were eating. Carrying her tray to the far end of the dining room, she slammed it noisily onto an empty table and ate alone.

While this little drama was being played out, I kept receiving chilly glances from Madame. I even got the impression that Galena was miffed with me. The only explanation I could come up with was that it had been Galena at the roadside, that she had spotted me in the van and thought I was spying on her.

When we had finished our meal and were filing out the door, Madame suddenly blocked my path.

"It is against policy for staff to interfere with company practice. I hope it does not happen again!" With that her diminutive figure charged through the screen door behind Galena.

My first reaction was "Huh?" Although I didn't have to stretch my imagination too far to imagine Madame as a prime mover in some of the grisly aspects of the Spanish Inquisition, even in my wildest fantasies, when paranoia soared, I could not place the sixtyish, black-clad lady in a drug ring. And surely she didn't mean that hiding drugs in bushes was a company practice.

I caught up with the two women at Galena's car.

"I'm sorry, Madame, but I don't know what you're talking about. What have I done?"

Galena had already slid into the driver's seat. Tapping her fingernail on the car's gas meter, she said, "Almost empty! It is bad enough that you call that child out of class to pick you up, but then my car is returned to me without gasoline!"

"But I didn't. What do you mean?"

"You did not leave a message at the auditorium that the van had broken down and Jonquil should borrow a car to pick you up?"

I shook my head. "Absolutely not."

The two women exchanged glances. Finally Galena shook her head. "I apologize, Bonnie. I'm afraid that young lady is headed for a great deal of trouble. Do try to keep an eye on her."

As soon as the two women left I checked the cast sheet by the commissary door. Jonquil was not performing or covering that night. Chris was. That meant that I would have the pleasure of Jonquil's company for the evening.

I drove to the girls' house in such a state of fury it is a wonder I didn't wreck the van. My angelic roommate was in the stone cellar sorting her laundry. A real junior homemaker that one. Mud-splattered jeans in one pile, filthy sneakers in another.

"Hi, Bonnie," she said sweetly. "Do you have anything you want to throw in with my whites?"

"I'm furious, Jonquil," I said with no preliminaries.

She paled and quickly looked away.

"You lied. You told Galena a lie about me so you could get her car."

"I'm sorry, but I had to have a car. If you'd stopped yesterday when I asked you to let me get my makeup case, or else let me use the van . . ."

She bent to pick up a fallen sneaker.

"I know why you wanted a car. It didn't have anything to do with makeup. I saw you at the side of the road picking up your stash."

Refusing to look at me, she started shoving clothes into the washer.

I felt kind of sorry for the girl. In some ways I identified with her. At seventeen I'd been tugging at the reins myself.

"I understand what it's like to be seventeen," I began. "You want to try new things, you feel restrained—"

"You don't know what it's like to be me," she snapped back. "Restrained? I'm, like, in jail. All I ever do is practice and rehearse and make sure I get my sleep and make sure I don't gain any weight and don't ride a bike or play tennis because I might pull something. I can't even go to the beach because if I get a burn it will look crummy onstage."

"But think about what you've got. When I was your age, if I'd had half your talent, and your opportunities . . ."

She slammed the lid on the washer. "You sound just like my mother."

She was right, and if there was one thing I didn't want to be it was a surrogate Abigail.

"I turn eighteen pretty soon," she said, glaring at me. "Then you'll both see. My Granny Foote left me ten thousand dollars. The second I get that money I'm gone from this crummy life!"

"What you do when you're eighteen is your own business. Right now what you do is my business. I'd like you to promise me something."

"Maybe."

"You won't use any drugs while we are up here . . ."

"Who said there were any drugs?"

". . . and you won't sneak out at night."

She hadn't expected that. A guilty look crossed her face. It was followed, almost immediately, by a defiant one.

"It's not nice to spy on people."

"I know it's not," I answered. "Please tell me you're going to behave so I don't have to."

"I promise," she finally said.

I made a quick retreat up the basement steps. It hadn't been such a terrible scene as scenes go, but I'd started feeling headachy and crummy. Once upstairs I bolted myself in the bathroom and had a quiet little cry.

No sooner had I dried my eyes and unlocked the bathroom door than Tony called. The idea of another confrontation right then was too much. Cowardice, I know, but I didn't do what I had sworn. We had a strange conversation, loaded with uncomfortable pauses. Did I still want him to visit? Sure, if he wanted to, but he had to understand how busy I was, and it was an awfully long drive. Well, that was all right. He needed to talk to me.

Those were frightening words. I hung up hoping that he didn't want to talk about anything more serious than the scenery.

One A.M. in the Massachusetts countryside. What are the sounds you hear when you're fighting sleep? Dive-bombing insects, an owl, faint splashes on the lake. And your roommate creeping stealthily across the plank floor.

From the moment I'd crawled into bed an hour earlier and listened to her too-steady, too-loud breathing, I'd known she was faking sleep. For at least an hour she didn't move a muscle. I wasn't fooled. Dancers are trained to endure excruciating positions endlessly. Flat on a bed she could go on forever. She almost did. My own deep, loud, steady breathing threatened to turn into sleep several times before Jonquil's bedsprings gave their telltale squeak.

I waited until she closed the door behind her before I quietly got up, put on my robe and slippers, and grabbed a flashlight from my bedside table. I opened our bedroom door just as the screen door to the porch creaked.

I tiptoed quickly down the stairs. There she was, a slight, dim figure lit by a half-moon, trotting beneath the oak trees toward the garage. Stepping onto the porch, I held the screen door until it closed quietly. Then I crouched and made an almost silent run across the porch, down the stairs, and into the trees.

The garage, like Primrose Cottage, was made of field-stone. But unlike the house, that structure, built to house not only cars but farm machinery and snowplows as well, had been allowed to fall into disrepair. The side door was ajar. When I pulled it, I found that it was frozen half open. The space seemed impossibly small for anyone other than a ballerina. I was about to back out and look for another entrance when there was a sharp noise and a whispered curse from inside the building. I squeezed through the opening. Making sure I was away from the faint light that showed through the door, I straightened and peered over the top of an old farm wagon.

There was nothing. Then a shadow moved against a far wall. I closed my eyes for a moment to help my night vision. When I opened them, I could see Galena's white car across the garage. Hunching down, I made my way around the wagon and crept forward. As I drew closer there was another clang, metal against metal.

I inched through the dark, intent on sneaking up on Jonquil. I didn't realize there was an oil slick on the floor until I stepped into it. For a terrifying second my arms flailed wildly. My footing gone, I toppled sideways into the back bumper of a car, giving my head a good thwack in the process. I pulled myself up in a panic.

I had dropped my flashlight. There was a stirring by Galena's car, then a flash of light clothing as Jonquil raced around the front wall toward the door. As I hurried after her the garage suddenly grew darker.

I reached the door. She'd squeezed through and pulled it closed behind her. Either her arms were more powerful than they looked or else there was somebody with her, somebody strong. Yanking hard, I got the thing open about six inches and squeezed through. A ripping sound told me that I'd left part of my wardrobe in the door.

The night was still and cool. I paused, listening and shivering. A second later feet pounded down the wooden pier that led to the gazebo at the lake's edge. Whether two sets of feet or one, I couldn't tell. I moved quietly through the trees toward the water.

She was at the end of the pier under the arched roof of the gazebo. Her slender figure was plain against the starlit water. I stepped away from my cover under the trees and was about to walk onto the pier when another sound reached me. A canoe was moving up level with the gazebo.

"Hurry up," Jonquil called softly. "It won't take snoopy long to get here."

"Snoopy is right behind you," I said, not bothering to lower my voice.

An oar shot up from the canoe into the wood pilings of the gazebo. The paddler pushed off hard, and in no time the canoe was slicing through the water away from the girls' house. "Wait, wait," Jonquil called across the lake.

She turned when I stepped into the gazebo. Her fist was in a ball. It swung up and I pulled back, thinking she intended to hit me. Suddenly her arm struck out toward the lake in a clean sweep. Something dark and shiny left her hand and sailed through the air. There was a tiny splash.

"Who was that in the canoe? Chris?"

"I don't know what you're talking about. I didn't see any canoe. You're just a snoop, that's all." Pushing past me, she marched back to the house.

Our commotion on the dock had woken Madame. She had turned on the porch lights and was waiting in the living room when I stormed through the screen door.

"Why such a noise out there? What are you two doing? Do you know what time it is?"

I must have looked a sight, what with the oily smears on my leg and the rip in the side of my nightgown. I muttered something like "Couldn't sleep" before marching up the stairs. When I reached the bedroom Jonquil was already under the covers, breathing steadily.

"That was awfully expensive fish food you threw into the

lake, Jonquil. At that rate your Grandmother Foote's money won't last long."

If she had managed to choke out an apology, or even to say nothing, I might not have gone to Michael. Instead, she attacked. "You can't stand to see anybody having any fun. I hate you. I hate you as much as I hate my mother."

That hurt. I was trying to think of a response when a ferocious heat enveloped my body. I put my hand against my forehead. It was hot and damp. As I lay back on my pillow, Jonquil delivered one last broadside: "And don't bother saying that someday I'll thank you for this, because I won't."

So ended my second evening in the Berkshires.

I woke with one of those horrible warm-weather colds. When I put my hand to the pounding sore spot on my head a painful lump reminded me of the night I'd spent.

Leaning over, I picked up my watch from the bedside table. The bright morning light glittering off its face made my eyes water until I couldn't read it. A sneezing fit started inching up from wherever they come from. I looked across the room through tearing eyes. Jonquil had already made her bed and disappeared.

I closed my eyes against the light. What a mess things were. Apart from my fears that Niki's murderer was stalking Carmen—fears the police, not to mention the U.S. government, would pooh-pooh—I'd blown my sensible adult telephone talk with Tony and I was at war with my roommate.

The first thing I had to do was tell Michael about Jonquil's midnight madness. Since there was no such thing as privacy around this place, I had to go to a pay phone. Rolling to my side, I pulled the watch under the sheet to block the sun. Ten till eight. If I hurried I could reach Michael before he left for practice, give him the news, and then drive back. With any luck most of the girls would be gone and I could get some sleep.

I found Galena holding court down in the kitchen, a circle of wide-eyed girls surrounding her. Carmen was at the table doing her best to act above it all, but I could tell she was listening. Galena waved her hands wildly as she spoke. Her eyes were shining, full of excitement.

"He intended to steal it, I'm sure. Can you imagine? I keep a car in New York for years. No problems. Here I am now, only two days in the country, and what happens? A thief in the night. My car—for me it is like a child." Reaching to the stove behind her, she grabbed the coffeepot and extended it to me. "Good morning, Bonnie. You heard about the excitement?"

"No." I took one of the heavy china cups from the shelf and held it while Galena poured my coffee.

"We had a sneak thief last night trying to steal my car."

"What?" That's how groggy I was. The part Galena's car had played in the midnight follies had slipped my mind until that moment.

"A thief broke into the garage and vandalized my car. I found the trunk open and a hubcap on the ground."

Madame snapped a finger. "Ah. It may have been Bonnie who frightened him away. She was out there late. She and Jonquil."

Galena slammed the pot back onto the stove. Hot coffee splattered from the spout. "You were near the garage? You saw this thief?"

Having been sworn to silence by Michael about keeping an eye on Jonquil, I couldn't very well tell everyone I'd been following her. A lie seemed easiest.

"No, no. I wasn't near the garage. I only walked down to the gazebo. Where is Jonquil, anyway?"

"On the porch," someone said.

"Girls," Galena continued, "from now on we must keep vigilant. How I would love to catch the thief. What I would do to him . . ." Snatching a knife from the counter, she gave a graphic demonstration. The blackguard who dared touch that big white boat could look for his vital parts on the floor.

I leaned against the wall, sipping my coffee. "Maybe the hubcap fell off, Galena."

She raised her eyebrows. Clearly I was not sophisticated in the ways of cars and thieves. "A hubcap simply falls off a car! A trunk springs open by itself? Never! There is a thief. I will speak to Michael. Perhaps he can get me a gun."

I almost choked on my coffee.

"Yes, a gun. I will sit in my window and wait. When I see him move . . . boom!"

Boom! That was all we needed—Galena blasting at shadows from her bedroom window. The way the kids were sneaking around at night there would soon be no troupe left.

"Please, Galena, no gun," I said.

She shrugged and seemed to weigh the idea. "Well, maybe not. Maybe a dog. A big, vicious dog. Tear the thief into shreds . . ."

When I left she was illustrating with her hands what a dog would do to that thief. It was not pretty. I liked Galena but she sure had a wild sense of proportion. If a hubcap on the ground called for guns and dogs, what retribution had Niki's public insult demanded?

I was piloting the van through the ruts on the way to the main road when I ran into Chris. Figuratively, that is. I was driving slowly, concentrating on not losing the oil pan, when he stepped from the trees on the roadside and stuck out his thumb. His California surfer face wore that big smile the younger ballerinas adored. It didn't do a heck of a lot for me that morning but I couldn't very well ignore him. I pressed my foot on the brake.

"Good morning," he said, climbing into the passenger seat. "Am I glad to run into you. I was afraid I'd have to hoof it."

"Good morning. Where are you off to so early?"

"Lenox. I'm meeting somebody." He glanced at his watch. "It's not really that early. Got a cold? You sound like hell."

I nodded. "Probably from running around half dressed in the middle of the night chasing Jonquil and her friends. How do you like canoeing at midnight, Chris? Pretty dark on that lake, isn't it?"

He didn't pretend innocence. Quite the opposite. "Caught again." He shook his head ruefully.

I glanced across the seat. He was all smiles.

"What did she do? Hide the coke in Galena's wheel and leave the trunk unlocked so she could get at the tools to pry off the hubcap?"

No answer; only that smile.

"You're old enough to do what you want," I said, "but you're going to get that girl into trouble."

"Aw, give me a break. We work like mules. If we want to let loose and take a little something every now and then, what the hell! Everybody does it."

"Everybody doesn't. Do me a favor and keep away from Jonquil for the next week, or else . . ."

Chris laughed. "Or else? Come on, Bonnie. You're too pretty to be a heavy. Tell you what, though. I'll do it for you, 'cause you asked." He paused. "I hear you're friends with that cop," he said, abruptly changing the subject. "The guy who was asking questions about Niki's murder."

What a strange topic for Chris to bring up. "Tony? Yes, we're friends," I said.

"Is he the kind of cop who's conservative about drugs and things? I've met some who were pretty cool."

"I guess Tony's medium cool. Why?"

"He didn't talk to everybody who was backstage, you know," Chris said. "There are people he missed."

"The case was closed before he got to everybody."

"Oh. So I guess it's all sewn up. I mean about that Polish woman. Like, they won't be talking to anybody else?"

He was leading to something but I couldn't tell what. "Not that I know of," I answered. "Where should I drop you?"

"There's supposed to be a Universalist church somewhere around here. Past the town square."

"A church?"

"Don't get the wrong idea. I'm meeting someone there. What would happen," he asked, his voice quieter, "if the cops missed somebody important? You know what I mean? Maybe somebody saw something but never got questioned?"

We were at a light. I stared across the seat at him. "Why are you asking these questions, Chris? Is there something you know? You said you weren't backstage."

"I wasn't, but . . ." He shrugged. "I was just wondering, that's all. Forget it. Hey, I heard you used to dance. Why don't you go out with us on Friday night? There's this place with live music. Most of us are going. I'll teach you some new moves."

"I don't care for social dancing."

Oh, brother! What a prude I sounded like. The truth is I love social dancing. There are few things I like more than dancing with a good partner. But there was something about Chris that . . . I don't know if the right word is *scared* . . . that unnerved me. He was cute and he could lay on the charm, sure. But psychopaths are often attractive on the surface. Pick up any newspaper and you'll find a story about another one who charmed several women to their graves.

I dropped Chris near the town square next to one of the town's several white, shingled churches. As I pulled away he was walking toward the front entrance. When I reached the corner and glanced in my mirror, he had veered off the sidewalk toward the back of the building.

I may not be much of a heavy, but as snoops go I'm all right. Instead of driving straight I turned at the corner. Behind the church was a parking lot that hadn't been visible from the main street. As I passed it I slowed, just in time to glimpse Chris climbing into the passenger seat of a silver-gray BMW.

The car had New York license plates and a small dent in its passenger door.

How he had done it I couldn't guess, but I was sure Chris had managed to hook up with a drug dealer. And in a church parking lot in a New England village so pristine you could almost have eaten off the sidewalks. When I thought of drug connections, I envisioned sun-beaten Central American border towns or dark Manhattan alleys. There were no lurid, flyblown cantinas around here, no sinister men whispering in doorways. This was a place of crisp white buildings and stately shade trees, a place where you might wander onto a quilting bee or somebody tapping for maple syrup.

Something funny was going on with Chris. Or maybe not funny. It wasn't that he fooled around with drugs; that he didn't try to hide. It was those other things. How had Chris known about the books in Niki's dressing table? And why his questions? Maybe he was "just wondering," but I doubted it. Did he know something about Niki's murder? Was he feeling me out to find out how Tony would react to his information? Or to be sure the police investigation was finished?

I found a phone booth and reached Michael in his room at the inn. There was more than a hint of impatience in his voice as he listened to my story. He kept hurrying me along, interrupting with "Yes, yes? And?" while I explained about Jonquil's misadventure. At one point a man's voice broke through the background. Michael's hand over the receiver stopped the conversation for what seemed like an hour.

I was starting to feel truly rotten. Though the day was cool, my skin was hot. I rubbed the sore spot on my head. Maybe I had a concussion.

"Yes? What was that you were saying, Bonnie?"

I sniffled. "I think the package Jonquil threw in the lake was drugs, and I'm sure Chris is involved. He was the one in the canoe."

"But you didn't see anything, did you? No drugs?"

"No, but why else throw whatever it was in the lake? And

there was Galena's hubcap. And don't forget that Niki caught Jonquil using drugs."

"That may be so, but we wouldn't want to get any unfounded rumors started, would we? You didn't mention any of this business to Galena or the other girls, I hope."

"No, of course I didn't. Galena thinks a thief is after her car, but—"

Michael didn't let me finish. "Now, listen. You didn't see Jonquil with drugs. You didn't actually see her fooling around with Galena's car. All of this is just speculation. Perhaps it's nothing more than a case of youthful high spirits on her part. She wanted to meet one of the boys and you interrupted. How was Jonquil this morning?"

"I didn't see her. Apparently she was fine." Which was a lot more than I could say for myself.

"Good. That's what we want. I have great hopes for that girl. I'll keep an eye on her today but I can't foresee any problems. But you sound terrible. You may have been in pretty rocky shape last night. Sometimes, Bonnie, when we're coming down with a cold, we can't be sure what we're seeing. The imagination is a powerful thing. When we're not well it can play tricks on us."

The man's voice interrupted him. This time I welcomed it. Talk about somebody with blinders on! This was the man who had forced me into the role of guardian of teenage virtue. Snoopy, as Jonquil so nicely had put it. And here he was trying to convince me I'd imagined the episode.

"I've got to get moving, Bonnie. You take care of yourself. Try some hot tea with lemon. And get some sleep!"

I intended to do just that. If Michael could ignore Jonquil's problems, so could I.

Driving down the rutted road to Primrose Cottage, I passed Galena and her carload of ballerinas. Jonquil was in the back seat. She didn't look at me.

I maneuvered down the steep drive and pulled up next to the house. The rest of the girls were waiting, dance bags piled by their feet. Madame would be driving them to practice in the van. I glanced around for her. There she was, that tiny tyrant in black, standing at the side door to the garage, the one that stuck and squeaked so badly. She was stooped over, examining something. When she stood up she was holding a foot-long strip of blue-and-white cotton, the cloth that had torn from my nightgown.

She hurried across the lawn, waving the cloth. "A clue. Torn from our prowler's clothing."

Isn't it always the way with little lies: they get bigger and bigger. I took the white-and-blue-flowered cotton from her. The print positively screamed "woman's nightie." Nodding thoughtfully, I said, "Could be from a man's shirt."

One of the girls giggled. "Our prowler is gay."

As soon as Madame and the girls drove off I went inside. In the kitchen the teenage housekeeper was washing dishes. Now that she wasn't working at the boys' house, she had lots of time for us. She was chubby, with a pleasant, round face and a lopsided smile. Elliott's femme fatale.

I went to my bedroom and lit a fire in the corner fireplace using the rest of my nightgown as kindling. As I watched the pretty print turn to ash and fly up the chimney, the absurdity of the situation struck me. Here I was trying to hide my part in the midnight attack on Galena's car when all I was guilty of was doing my job. I had a boss—not only a boss but a famous boss—who wanted me to do my job just enough to keep his company's reputation pure, who had literally ordered me to keep things quiet, to report to no one but him. And he intended to keep things quiet.

I was already sick of this chaperone business. Give me a banquet to run any day. My relationship with Jonquil had disintegrated into warfare. Cheerful, outgoing Carmen was now secretive and unhappy and possibly in danger. Sinking back onto my bed, I thought about that first day I'd seen these girls, these ethereal puffs of dandelion dancing with Niki. I remembered how charming and funny both of them had been at the café the night Niki joined our table, how Jonquil and I had giggled over Carmen's "I'm in love," and all three of us over Amanda's "I'd do it with him in a minute." There was no giggling anymore.

I started to push myself up. Maybe Michael was right. A cup of tea . . . The futility of trying to go anywhere hit me the second my feet hit the floor. The room swam and once again a great heat swept over me. I fell back on my pillow, into a sweaty, restless sleep.

I dreamed of a terrible woman/monster. She was huge—built like a dumpster. She wore a brown skirt that fell well below her knees and a white blouse buttoned at the throat. Her hair was pulled into a tight ballerina pincushion that stretched her coarse features into a scowl. This woman patrolled a long cinder-block hall, stomping her brown oxfords as she moved from one iron-gray door to the next. Behind these doors girls whispered: "Watch out. The matron is coming. The old snoop is going to catch you." The woman stopped and stared through a barred window in one of the doors. Beautiful young ballerinas in white tutus cowered on bunk beds. The matron's eyes flicked from one to the next. The matron's hideous face—Oh, God! It was my face, but it was distorted and cruel. I began shouting at the ballerinas, ugly words I couldn't understand. . . .

"Bonnie! Wake up! You're having a nightmare."

Galena was standing over me, her hand on my shoulder.

"I came to get you at dinner and found you asleep. Now you must eat. I brought you something."

My unlikely angel of mercy had put a cup of tea and a plate of cookies on my bedside table. Sitting on the foot of my bed, she winked. "It must be those two men of yours. They've worn you out and given you bad dreams. I hope they're worth it."

I sat up tentatively, expecting to explode in sneezes or collapse in a fever. Surprisingly what I felt most was hunger. "It's not the men," I said. "It's the job." I reached for a cookie.

She laughed. "The job! Who dreams about jobs?"

Except for the lamp on my dresser the room was in darkness. My fire had died and sun no longer shone through the lace curtains. I had slept all day.

"What time is it, anyway?" I asked.

"It's after eleven." She groaned. "Thank God I'm off tomorrow night! My Achilles tendons are murderous. I must get to the therapist." Lifting her feet to my bed, she began rubbing one of them.

Ballerinas' feet take terrible abuse. Even the young girls' looked bad. Galena's were horrible. Through the dim light I could see bruises, swellings, bunions, calluses.

"Awful, aren't they?" she said. "But serviceable so far."

I sipped my tea. "How was Chris tonight? I noticed on the cast sheet he was partnering you."

"He was excellent. A fine partner. Your roommate was also good."

I glanced toward Jonquil's bed. "Where is she? Did she come back with you?"

"Yes. She and some others are watching television. But you must tell me about these two men of yours. I adore a triangle. I once had a marvelous triangle."

I smiled. "This triangle isn't so marvelous. Tony is short, dark, kind of cute . . ."

She sniffed. "Basset hounds are kind of cute."

I started to giggle. ". . . faithful, loyal, honest, hard-working, has a good pension plan . . ."

Galena stretched her arms and faked a yawn. "You're putting me to sleep. The other one?"

"And the other one—Derek—is tall, blond, self-indulgent, flirtatious, sexy—"

Galena interrupted. "My kind of man!"

"—has little sense of responsibility to anybody but himself, doesn't know what commitment means, and . . ."

This litany of complaints sounded silly even to me. To Galena, it was ridiculous. When I ended with "His money's not going to last forever," she shrugged. "Maybe he'll get some more. My advice is, go for that one, the jungle cat. Save the basset hounds for when you're older. You're too young to worry about pension plans. I, on the other hand . . . well, who knows?"

I wasn't about to get into an age thing with Galena, but I was curious. "What would you do if you retired?"

"It is not if, Bonnie. It is when. I'll teach for Michael, or open my own ballet school, maybe. Or perhaps I'll be lucky. A White Knight will rescue me."

I smiled at her. "I remember that's what you called Michael when you got married: 'My White Knight.'"

She tossed her head. "So he was, briefly. We had quite a time of it," she said as she stood.

"I know. I read the gossip columns."

"The gossip columns? Then you know nothing! It was savage. You see that small scar under his eye?" She pointed her finger at her chest. "Mine," she said proudly. "A knitting needle."

"You stabbed Michael? And now you work with him?"

She waved her hand. "Bah. A mere scratch. I believe in forgive and forget."

"Why did you do it?"

"I discovered him with someone else," she said after a moment.

It was hard to imagine a man married to Galena looking at another woman. A brief smile crossed her face when I told her that.

"It was another man. A young man."

Wow! Rumor-crazy as the press is, this was one tidbit I'd never heard. "I had no idea Michael was bisexual."

"Few people do. Michael is very discreet, very image-conscious about himself and the company."

That I had discovered.

"By the way," she said, "I need a favor from you. Are you feeling better? Do you think you'll be up tomorrow?"

"I imagine so. What do you need?"

Reaching to my dresser, she picked up a two-inch-thick pile of envelopes and a five-dollar bill. "Could you get some stamps and mail these? Half of my bills are late."

"Gladly. I have the same problem myself."

She started to leave. At my door she paused. "In my heart I'll always be too lively for the basset hounds. I expect I'll end up with one, but I'll always be looking for a jungle cat."

Galena was really something. Life was a great wild adventure, filled with huge, savage emotions, and she was going to grip it in her teeth and tear off every bit she could. The more I saw of her the more I liked her. Forgive and forget, she said, and she certainly had forgiven my earlier relationship with Niki. At the same time, though, she had that uncontrolled violent streak. Better to be her friend than her enemy, I thought as I got out of bed.

My head was still stuffy but I felt better than I had. Maybe I'd slept through the worst of my cold, or maybe Galena's tea had chased it away. After I washed my face and brushed my teeth, I felt almost alive.

Jonquil was sitting on her bed when I came out of the bathroom. Her hair was down and she looked especially young and vulnerable.

I couldn't ignore her. If I was going to stay in this room the silent treatment would be miserable. "Hi. I hear you were good tonight."

"I was all right," she said with a shrug. She looked down. "Bonnie? I'm sorry about those things I said. I don't hate you."

From where I stood I could see tears welling in her eyes. I took a tissue from the box on my dresser and handed it to her. "I know you don't hate me."

She sniffled. "I'm still not going to thank you for this when I'm older," she said, blowing her nose.

"I never said you would. Those were your words."

"They're my mother's, if you want to know the truth.

That's what she always says. That and 'If I'd had your opportunities, blah blah blah.'"

"She wants you to do the best you can. That's not so unusual for a parent."

"Sure, but the way she does it. You know what else she says? She says, 'I'm reliving my dance career through you, but this time I'm doing it right.' Can you imagine how crummy that makes me feel? Especially when I screw up."

I could, but how could I tell Jonquil that? It wasn't for me to drive the wedge between Jonquil and her mother farther. I smiled at her. "Why don't you explain to your mom that you're grateful but you're not sure you like being a ballerina?"

"I've tried, but she gets upset and then I get upset and pretty soon we're both crying and screaming at each other. When we get back to New York maybe . . . would you talk to her for me?"

"I doubt if she'd listen, but I'll think about it."

When she'd gone into the bathroom and closed the door, I took Galena's bills from the dresser. There were so many of them they hardly fit into my purse. Con Edison, New York Telephone, all the regulars. I was shoving them in one by one when an address caught my eye. Greenleaf Florists, 1901 Broadway. That was the florist who had delivered the red and white roses to Niki.

Galena, with her public life, probably sent lots of flowers. She was generous to her friends, an openhearted person. There was no reason to think that she had sent the red and white roses, the roses that to a Russian signified death. On the other hand . . .

Jonquil was running bathwater. She would be a while. I slid the envelope from my bag. It wasn't a nice thing to do, drink tea Galena had brought me and snoop through her mail, but I did it. I held the envelope to the lamp. The detailed statement inside wasn't clear. Next I tried slitting the thing along the glued edge so I could seal it again. That made such a mess that I finally gave up, stuck my finger under the flap, and ripped it up.

A lot of flowers, to a lot of people. I ran my finger down the entries. A sinking feeling hit the pit of my stomach. She'd ordered flowers on the day of the gala. I followed the entry across. "One doz. roses, white, and one doz. roses, red, to Nikolai Koslov, State Theater, w/card. Message: 'Merde.'"

Merde. The literal translation is "shit," but in the ballet world it means "good luck!"

A thousand revenges! Galena had planned a thousand revenges, but just possibly the torn hitch had done the job. Stuffing the envelope into my purse, I climbed into bed and switched off my table lamp. I was half asleep when Jonquil came out of the bathroom. She opened and closed the oak cupboard. Her bedsprings squeaked.

"Bonnie, are you still awake?"

"No."

"You wouldn't have some money you could loan me until we get paid, would you? I'm really broke. I hardly have enough to go out with the other kids."

I half believed her. Poor girl. Stuck up here with no spending money. The half of me that didn't believe her prevailed.

"I'm sorry, but I need everything I have. Why don't you talk to Elliott? He'll give you an advance."

"Maybe." She clicked her light off and the room darkened. "Sweet dreams, Bonnie," she said softly.

"Sweet dreams to you, Jonquil."

12

Tony called from the Thrifty Inn before ten the next morning. That meant he'd left New York around 6:00 A.M. What could he possibly have to say to me that couldn't wait until he'd had a decent night's sleep? What if he'd been rehearsing a marriage proposal as he drove up?

My cold was much better. I felt clearheaded enough to practice my speech as I dressed. First I would tell Tony about my trip to Brighton Beach, that Niki hadn't known anything about his wife's work at the secret nuclear facility, and that the KGB had no reason to kill him. Then I'd tell him that Carmen's life might be in danger from Niki's murderer. As I spoke his lips would compress into a thin line. I'd finish and he'd tell me to mind my own business. Then the real pleasantries would start. I'd say, "Tony, you mean a lot to me . . ." No—that sounded like a greeting card message. Maybe, "I like you a lot, but . . ." One way or another I intended to do it and get rid of at least one problem.

I took two cold pills. Madame needed the van so I hitched a ride to the Thrifty with Elliott. A last resort, believe me. His performance as chaperone was no better than mine. The difference was, Elliott couldn't stop talking about it. Checkpoint Charlie wasn't working. "They march past me," he said, his fists going rigid on the steering wheel, "go to their rooms, and climb straight out their windows. Last night I heard three of them talking about this bar outside of town—the Scarlet Letter. Michael put it off-limits to the company, but you better watch those girls of yours."

"Don't worry, Elliott. The girls like the disco at the inn. They wouldn't go near the Scarlet Letter."

"I hope you're right. Last year that punk Chris . . . I'd appreciate it if you didn't spread this around."

Nodding absently, I glanced at Elliott. There were dark half circles under both eyes, one of them blending into the remains of the shiner. I almost felt sorry for him.

"Chris got involved with some of the locals at that place and the next thing we know a girl's father accused him of selling marijuana. Not that the girl was any angel. There's a bad element in that bar. We barely managed to keep it quiet."

Little did Elliott know: the story of Chris and the Scarlet Letter was common knowledge around the company. Another absent nod from me. Compared to New York City's bad element, Lenox's had to be a bunch of pussycats.

I'd expected to meet Tony in his room, but when I walked into the motel lobby there he was, perched uncomfortably in an orange plastic chair. Now's your chance, Bonnie. Do it. Sit down and get it over with. I walked past the reception desk, where a field of plastic daisies bloomed, the words forming on my lips. "You're very special to me, but . . ."

When Tony stood, the way he looked disturbed me enough to keep me quiet. There were worry lines on his forehead. His expression was guarded. "Hi, Bonnie. How are you? Let's get out of this place. It's depressing." Taking my elbow, he promptly steered me from the lobby.

The control I'd planned to muster wasn't working. You can't very well start to say "You're very special to me" when you're being hustled into a car.

"I hear there's a nice inn in town. The Hawthorne," he said. "We can get some lunch."

No way! There were too many company people—including Michael—staying there. What I had to do was going to be hard enough. With an audience it would be an ordeal. "It's not good at all," I said, "and it's terribly expensive."

We settled on a place near the center of town, Ye Olde Colony Public House. I'd heard it was kind of touristy, but I didn't think there was much chance of anyone from the company watching me do the dirty deed.

During the short ride our conversation was awkward, or nonexistent. Whenever I looked over the seat at Tony, he was intent on the road.

Like everything else in town, Ye Olde Colony was done up to look as if it hadn't been touched for two hundred years. Rather than the formal Federal look, it was rustic, sort of an eighteenth-century pub with unsanded wood floors and plank tables. The walls, with their carefully haphazard coat of whitewash, were hung with copper bed warmers and iron weather vanes. Everything had a tiny white price tag tastefully affixed.

Tony looked around slowly. He's a plain person, with ordinary tastes. "Sure is old-fashioned," he finally said. While we waited for a crowd of tourists to be seated, I glanced at the menu posted on the wall. The prices weren't old-fashioned.

A rosy-cheeked waitress seated us at a corner table next to the ever-popular spinning wheel. For some inexplicable reason, her outfit—a colonial cap, gown, and apron—caused a fleeting vision of waiters dressed in togas to flash through my mind. Thank God I'd been spared that.

"A drink while you decide?"

It was barely noon. "A diet soda for me," I said.

"Scotch, straight up," said Tony.

I'd never seen Tony drink anything but beer and wine. He was going to propose. A tremor of anxiety shook me.

"How have you . . ."

Both of us started at once. Then we both stopped abruptly. I looked down at my hands. When I glanced up at Tony, he was studying the menu and rubbing his forehead.

I struggled with myself. Blurt it out. Say "You're wonderful and I'm a fool for doing this, but there is someone else and I'm not sure what's going to happen . . ."

Tony took his drink right out of the waitress's hand. It disappeared in one long gulp. "Bonnie." He stopped and stared at me across the table. There was the strangest look on his face, so unhappy.

"What is it?"

"Well . . ." He hesitated. "Here. I got you this." He reached into his jacket pocket. Oh, no, I thought. Not a ring. I stopped breathing until his hand reappeared holding a few folded pieces of paper. "It's confidential, but since the case is closed it won't hurt to let you see it."

I unfolded the sheets. There were four of them: poor, sometimes illegible copies of a handwritten list. "What are these?"

"The lists of people who were backstage the evening of the gala. I knew you wanted to get a look at this so—you know . . ." His voice trailed off.

No, I didn't know. Everyone with any authority, including the president, insisted that Bertha was guilty and that the matter of Niki's murder was closed. As far as I knew I was the only person on earth who thought it wasn't, except possibly Carmen. And now I was being handed a list of people who had been backstage by the very man who had told me to mind my own business, in almost those words. Tony was a by-the-book kind of policeman, not one to sneak copies of evidence to a nosy girlfriend.

"Why are you giving me this? You told me to drop it."

He stared into his empty glass. "You asked for it."

I looked at the first page. The copy was faint. Even where I could make it out, the guards had scrawled guests' names so hurriedly that they could have been almost anything.

"It's pretty hard to read."

"I suppose so. It's not very accurate. When groups went backstage, the guards just wrote one name and put 'plus three' or whatever after it."

I turned to the next sheet. "Look at this," I said, flipping quickly back to the first page. "Isabella Spencer—she's a patron—is on the list twice. She went through the main theater door at a quarter to five, then through the stage door at ten minutes after five."

Tony shrugged. "Maybe she forgot something. Don't take that list too seriously. It's a mess. While we're talking about backstage, though, how's that Garcia girl?"

"Carmen? Why do you ask? I want to talk to you about her anyway."

"Oh, yeah? Well, last Wednesday afternoon she left a message for me at the precinct. When I got back to her she sort of hedged around. Said she'd called 'to chat.'" He arched an eyebrow. "My own kids don't call 'to chat.'"

"Wednesday? That's strange. Last Thursday night she was hit by a car. She thinks someone pushed her into traffic. You sure she didn't call Thursday night?"

He shook his head. "It was Wednesday afternoon a week ago. Is she okay?"

I nodded. "She thinks it was a dancer who pushed her."

"Any idea why she suspects that?"

"She wouldn't tell me. She's been secretive lately."

"Kids get that way. Where is she now?"

"Now? In class, I guess."

He glanced at his watch. "I don't have time to see her. Tell her to call me."

"Aren't you staying over?" I asked, surprised.

He shook his head. "I've got to be at the DA's office this evening. A big case. This is the only time we can get one of the witnesses there."

He'd driven all that way to have lunch with me?

Impossible! My anxious tremor returned, joined by a sinking feeling in the pit of my stomach.

"Bonnie, there's something I've got to say to you." He reached across the table and took my hand.

Here it came. Why hadn't I stopped this?

"I've met someone I'm serious about."

At first I thought I'd misunderstood. For days I'd been rehearsing variations on that line. It was supposed to be mine but it had come from the other side of the table. Tony had delivered my words.

"You mean a woman?"

He blinked. "Of course it's a woman. What do you think? I'd mess around with another guy?"

"I'm sorry. I'm . . . surprised." To cover my confusion I glanced around the restaurant. Wouldn't you know! One of the big booths was filling up with dancers from the company. A couple of them waved as they slid into their seats. Smiling weakly, I looked away.

My immediate reaction to Tony's announcement—my reaction once I got over the fact that he was saying my lines—was ridiculous. My emotions completely disconnected from reality. I saw my last chance at a solid relationship slipping away. Even worse, I soon discovered that my last chance was about to march down the aisle with someone else.

"We've only known each other a few weeks," he was saying. "It wasn't like I planned it or anything, Bonnie. I met her and . . ." He smiled, a guilty half smile. "It sounds corny, but we got swept away with each other. We figure a small wedding. Family, a few friends. We'd like you to be there."

He'd gone crazy for sure, dumping me and inviting me to his wedding in the same breath. I nodded at his empty glass. "Do you think I could have one of those?"

"Of course." He signaled for the waitress. He was feeling better already. The tense lines on his forehead had magically faded. Lugging around the heavy baggage of that secret had been a strain.

Maybe I would have felt better if I'd unloaded my secret too, but right then Derek didn't seem to have anything to do with what was going on.

The waitress placed my drink on a coaster in front of me. I took a long swallow. I'm not a scotch drinker. It tasted terrible.

"I wanted you to hear it from me, before you heard it from someone else."

Someone else? Who would I hear it from? Tony and I didn't have the same friends. "What do you mean? Who else would tell me?"

He sighed. "It all started with that Niki business."

Niki? A non-ballet person calling Nikolai Koslov "Niki"? I caught my breath. My last chance at stability was going to marry someone from Gotham Ballet.

"I met her when I was investigating his death. Some of the people around the ballet might know about us. I kind of doubt it, but . . ."

"You're telling me I know this woman. Who is she?"

He shook his head. "She feels guilty. She wants to tell you herself."

I finished the rest of the drink in two gulps. It went roaring to my head. The room started to spin. This solid brick of a man was casting me afloat. A script of soap opera lines rolled through my head: "How could you?" and "After all we've been to each other." Thank goodness I didn't say any of them.

I glanced down at the table. The security guards' lists were tucked neatly under my place mat. "So you brought me a consolation prize?"

"Come on, Bonnie. I remembered how you were interested in the case, and . . . yeah, you're right." He paused. "I wanted to give you something to make you feel better." He looked at his watch. "I guess I should get moving. It's a long drive back to New York." Clenching his fist, he tapped my shoulder softly. "I'm glad you're taking this okay. You're a real brick, Bonnie. Be sure that Garcia girl calls me."

"Sure," I said, giving him an absent nod. He'd driven all the way up there that morning to break up with me. How awful. I'd been his albatross. I picked up the papers and tucked them into my bag, right next to Galena's florist bill. Whoopie! So I had a couple of useless clues in a closed case. Big deal. Someone else was getting a husband.

There is no explaining why I felt so bereft as I stood in the town center and watched Tony's car disappear toward the highway. I don't think Sigmund Freud could explain it. It was not the proverbial "used" feeling of the scorned woman. Tony was too decent a person to use anyone and I knew that. Perhaps at the bottom of it was the possibility that Tony had seen something frivolous and unanchored in me, something that made me too insubstantial for the long run.

I stopped in the dime store to buy a roll of tape so that I could repair Galena's damaged florist bill. That done, I crossed the street to the post office, bought stamps, and mailed everything. Then I started walking. The afternoon was lovely. The sun was bright and a cool breeze made the trees sway gently. It was three miles to Greylock, and as I strolled down the country roads past manicured fields and abandoned apple orchards, I had a lot of time to think.

I'd gotten exactly what I wanted. My problem was, I hadn't gotten it the way I wanted it. After a mile or so my thoughts became riveted on one thing: who was this other woman, the one who for weeks must have looked at me as an object of pity?

The worst had to be considered: Tricia. I could just picture her with my job and my last chance at stability. All those nice outfits, too. Tricia was solid enough for a police lieutenant. She was solid enough for the president. The only person who'd ever ruffled her was Niki. But she was such a snob. Would she settle for a second-generation Italian cop whose idea of great art was the Mets' infield in action?

And how about that Galena? Hours earlier she'd told me to stick with the jungle cat. Was it because she'd already latched on to my basset hound? Or—and this was a real heart-stopper—what if it was one of the baby ballerinas? What if Tony had actually found me less substantial than one of those bits of fluff?

Looking back on these thoughts now, I realize that they were a by-product of the two cold pills and that glass of scotch I'd slugged down. They sure seemed real at the time, though. My mind was a daze of ballerinas' faces. The one with the space between her teeth, the one who skipped class a lot . . .

Tony had met this woman while investigating Niki's death. Chances were she'd been backstage. I walked into the girls' house, took two more cold pills, climbed into bed, and spread the guards' lists on the blanket.

Tony was right; the lists were a mess. Half the names were illegible, half were misspelled. From what I could make out, in addition to the members of the company there had been a couple of dozen female patrons backstage, along with a small mob of female reporters and politicians. Some of these had my initials after their names, some Michael's, some Elliott's, and some none. Tricia's name was there, with no initials. Galena had gone through the stage door using her company identification. There was Amanda's name on the theater door list. The guard hadn't bothered writing my initials. A reporter for the *Village Voice* did have my initials, as did one from the *Daily News*. I flipped the pages. No Bertha Wozniak, thank heavens.

Only the television crew and a few others had come through the back door near the public garage, far from where the pre-performance brouhaha was taking place. The television crew had signed in as a group under one name using a pass from Elliott. There were a few other names, most of them unfamiliar. But who was this? Paige Davenport, using a card I'd signed, had passed through the garage entrance. Paige? How dramatic! Was Paige a woman or a man? Probably a woman. That woman from *Dance Magazine* I'd sent a pass to—what was her name? And the one from the New York Arts Council?

I yawned. This was ridiculous. Maybe I'd meet Paige Davenport at Tony's wedding. The cold pills were working. The names disappeared into a haze. I closed my eyes and slept for sixteen hours, straight through until morning.

13

"Wow! That color is great on you!"

"It is?"

I squinted and backed away from the mirror. Four feet, five, six feet. I still looked like a giant butternut squash.

"Yellow is hot this season," the salesgirl said.

She was about sixteen. She was hot this season. Her black hair was highlighted with a couple of magenta streaks and she was wearing a leopard-print tunic over black tights. She tapped her booted foot to the beat of rock and roll blaring through the tiny shop.

Phoebe's was one of the few dress shops in town that catered to the young disco crowd. I'd heard some younger ballerinas talking about it. As I turned slowly, startling myself with the rear view of this yellow number, I thought that perhaps I belonged somewhere else.

I didn't need a yellow peasant dress. Most of us who live beyond a hundred-mile radius of the Andes don't. I didn't even want one. What it came down to was, I wanted a lift. This dress was having the opposite effect.

The low-slung ruffle called more attention to my hips

than they deserved. The high lace neckline called attention away from my bosom, which could have tolerated it quite nicely.

From the shop's window a haughty mannequin mocked me. On it was a red, glittery dress with no front to speak of and no back, period. Only a degree of modesty about displaying my all to the world kept me from pouring myself into it. Did I dare?

Dragging the peasant flounce behind me, I walked to the window and looked at the tag tucked into the sleeve. Wow! Forget that. I was tucking the tag back in when something on the street outside caught my eye. A silver-gray BMW with New York plates had pulled up across the street. It looked like the car Chris had climbed into in the church parking lot, the one I figured belonged to a drug dealer.

I backed away from the window. The driver's door opened and out stepped a slender woman with brown hair. She was simply dressed in black slacks and a black-checked jacket, but there was this look about her—an expensive look. And a familiar look. As she walked into the drugstore I got a good look at her face. Tiny features, pale skin. It was our patron, Chris's good friend, Mrs. Spencer.

"You want to try that red one?" the clerk asked. "I'll take it out of the window."

"No. I'll just take that." I nodded at a cotton sweater I'd tried on moments earlier. "Can't go wrong with black."

The salesgirl shrugged. "That's what my mother always says."

As she wrapped the sweater I tugged off that bilious yellow nonsense and got back into my jeans.

"Cash or charge?"

"Cash." Digging into my bag, I pulled out my wallet and opened the pocket where I kept my bills. I thumbed rapidly through the ones and tens. I'd had four fifties. They'd been in my wallet when I bought the adhesive tape the day before. A quick look in the secret compartment revealed the folded twenty I kept for emergencies. And that was it! No fifty-dollar bills. I rifled through the rest of my bag. The grand total, counting tokens, loose change, and emergency money, came to less than forty dollars.

The clerk was writing up my receipt. "Can you make that MasterCard? I don't have quite as much cash as I thought."

I don't think the Concorde could have covered the distance between central Lenox and Primrose Cottage any faster than I did. Screeching into the driveway, I leaped out, raced into the house, took the stairs two at a time, and flung open the bedroom door.

In five minutes everything I had brought with me—bottles of shampoo, books, every sock, every slip of paper—was spread across the floor. My duffel bag was inside out, my underwear scattered from one end of the room to the other. I did everything but unravel my sweaters and rip the seams from my jacket. Nothing! Exhausted, I sank down on my bed and stared at Jonquil's side of the room. As usual, you could have bounced a quarter off Miss Neatness's bed. Hospital corners yet. The kid could have been in the marines. Unlike my mother, though, I'm not convinced that bed making is a sign of virtue. Quite the reverse.

I started with her bottom dresser drawer—leotards, tights, leg warmers—and moved up drawer by drawer through jeans and T-shirts and underclothes. I found her cocaine tools—single-edged razor blades, a mirror, and some straws—folded into a sweatshirt. I pocketed them and kept looking. There was no way my search was going to go unnoticed. The kid was compulsively, perversely neat. Getting her socks back into those tiny balls defeated me and I didn't care.

Next I went through the big oak wardrobe, item by item, every pocket, every hem. Nothing more damning than a couple of bottles of Dristan. Your nose tends to act up when you're always shoving stuff in it.

Under the bed was last. Her shoes yielded nothing. Dragging out her suitcase, I gave every inch of it a going-over.

Not one thing, except for one of those leftover Gala Affair notepads.

I leaned against Jonquil's bedframe, slamming that pad of paper into my leg and staring at the fireplace. Was it possible? My blue-flowered nightie had had a deep pocket on the right side. In my fever-induced daze could I have put the money in the pocket and then burned it? Burned my own money? No. I'd burned the nightgown two days ago. I'd had the money yesterday.

I had not the slightest bit of real evidence against Jonquil, but I knew she'd taken my four fifties. This was too soon after she'd hit me for a loan to be coincidence.

On hands and knees I started straightening the mess I'd made. Shoes back into their neat line under the bed, hospital corners in the sheets. I grabbed the pad of paper and tossed it toward the open suitcase. It missed and flopped open on the floor. When I stretched to get it, the pages flipped rapidly, and for a split second black pen marks flashed in front of me. I picked up the tablet.

Only the last sheet in the pad had been written on. I gazed down at the open tablet, stunned. The sheet was covered with my name. Bonnie Indermill, again and again. I ran my finger across the page, counting them. There must have been a dozen Bonnie Indermills. Some of them, the ones at the bottom of the page, were strangely familiar. How creepy! They looked like my own signature. My writing is legible, with a neat forward slant and no particular curlicues or loops. Someone had been practicing my signature. I couldn't have told the last two or three Bonnie Indermills from my own.

Until that moment I'd never considered my signature a part of my being that could be violated. Looking down at that sheet, though, I experienced this strange fear. It was like being in one of those "body takeover" science fiction movies, except that instead of trying to take over my body, something was taking my name.

Why would Jonquil, for that matter anybody, be writing

"Bonnie Indermill" all over this page? There aren't a lot of reasons to practice someone else's name. Right then I could think of only two. One, a dancer planned to use my name for the stage. That was absurd. In the first place, her Bonnie Indermill wouldn't have to look like mine. In the second, when I'd been trying to make it as a dancer I'd considered using another name because mine didn't have one iota of class or one dollop of sex appeal. No ballerina in her right mind wanted to get out there and strut her stuff with a name like Bonnie Indermill.

That left just one other option that I could see: somebody wanted to be able to sign my name in a way that wouldn't be questioned, and judging from where I'd found this pad that somebody was Jonquil. My two hundred dollars wasn't enough for her. She planned to hit my credit cards, or maybe my checkbook.

I thumbed through my checks, making sure none were missing. My credit cards were tucked into one of my wallet's leather pockets. I don't have that many, and they were all there. It was possible she'd taken one and then returned it, but there was no proof. All I could do was wait for a bill.

When I cleaned Jonquil's side of the room, I didn't return the pad of paper to her suitcase. That went into my own duffel bag, along with the list of people who had been backstage the night of the gala. It was my evidence—of what, I wasn't sure—but since I had it I might as well keep it.

The afternoon's events had killed my appetite. I ate a real ballerina dinner that evening—green salad, slice of cantaloupe, scoop of low-fat cottage cheese, glass of skim milk. The conversation went with the meal: tendu, arabesque, elevation, who had done what with whom to get what role, who hurt where and what they were doing for the pain. I'd had enough meals with the company to find this dull going. It's hard to drop in and out of the insular world of ballet and I was feeling more and more out. As I picked through my salad I studied the ballerinas around me. Those animated, sparkling faces.

Which one was it whose elevation, whose pas de chat had swept a New York City police detective off his tired feet? And which of them had been so enchanted by his house in Queens, his pension plan, and his season tickets to the Mets?

And what was it to me, anyhow? My immediate financial affairs were more important than my affairs of the heart.

I cornered Michael Devereux outside the canteen after dinner. It was not easy for me, but I couldn't let my money simply disappear and not say a word to anyone.

"May I please have a second with you?"

He grimaced. "Only a second. I'm on my way to the theater."

"Of course." Even before I told Michael my problem he was irritated. By then I was firmly rooted in the category of people he'd rather avoid. Everything I had anything to do with turned out, at best, unpleasantly. Because of this, I told him about my missing money without mentioning Jonquil's name. That kind of problem was something he didn't want to hear about. Unless he saw it for himself, my suspicion was mine alone.

When I was through he nodded that handsome head. His black curls—whoever's black curls they were—sprang softly against his neck. "A thief." He gave me a thoughtful look. "You've been sick. You're certain you haven't misplaced the money? It may turn up, you know. This is a serious accusation."

I shook my head vigorously, relieved he was paying attention. "No. It was in my wallet yesterday. Now it's gone."

Across the driveway Madame waved. "Are you coming, Michael?"

"In a minute," Michael called. "I believe you, Bonnie," he said, his voice low. "I'm going to talk to Elliott about this. There was a girl he told to keep away from the boys' house the first night we were here. I understand she's still working at Primrose Cottage. She undoubtedly got into your wallet yesterday while you were asleep. We'll see about reimbursing you and taking care of her, too. Now I've got to get going."

Damn! This was all wrong. Michael was already walking toward the car where Madame was waiting. I couldn't allow that poor girl to be fired over my lousy two hundred dollars. "Wait."

Michael Devereux spun. "Yes? What is it?" His voice was sharp.

"I'm sorry. I just remembered where I put the money."

His expression hardened. "May I assume that I have heard the last of this subject?"

"Yes, you have."

He left without another word. In Michael Devereux's book I was no longer a minor irritant he had to put up with in memory of dear departed Niki. I was a mess and so was everything I touched. In my book he was no prize either, but the problem was I needed him; he didn't need me.

My conversation with him had accomplished exactly nothing. All week I'd accomplished nothing. I'd been spinning my wheels like mad, going nowhere. Chaperoning Jonquil was a disaster, I'd lost what might have been my last chance at wedded bliss, and I was out two hundred dollars! Some rotten frolic in the woods this was.

I was walking down the road toward Primrose Cottage when Chris skidded up next to me, his Subaru wheezing.

"You going to the performance? Want a ride?"

"No, thanks. Not tonight."

"Then how about meeting us later? We're going to a disco out on the highway. Arnie's. Live music. The Screaming Green Mountain Boys in their limited engagement. One night only."

"Maybe," I said.

"These guys are classics. You'll never get to hear them in Manhattan."

My *no* was already forming on my lips. But how appealing Chris looked in the late afternoon sunlight, with those blond curls and that surfer smile. It wasn't my intellect he was appealing to, either. It was those good old prurient interests, the ones that get you in trouble.

"I'll teach you how to dance," he said.

"I know how."

"I'll teach you better."

A couple of ballerinas walked by on the other side of the road, but he kept that big surfer smile coming straight at me. It was a real zinger. Maybe I was particularly vulnerable. Despite my reservations about Chris, I was flattered. This cute twenty-three-year-old was flirting with me. And I deserved some fun. What harm could there be in dancing?

"Maybe," I repeated.

"I'll be waiting for you."

It was almost seven when I got back to the girls' house. When I walked into the living room, I found Jonquil staring intently at a slip of paper in one hand and dialing the phone with the other. Her dance bag was on the floor. The second she realized I was behind her she slammed down the receiver. This was a conversation she didn't want me to hear.

"Who were you calling?" I asked.

"My mother."

"You're not a good liar."

"What's that supposed to mean?"

"Let's have a talk." I sat down across from her.

She glared at me. I braced for Jonquil at her worst.

"What about? I have to get to the theater."

"Money. The night before last you asked for a loan. I told you I couldn't spare anything and today I'm missing two hundred dollars. . . ."

"I don't know what you're talking about. I didn't touch your wallet," she snapped.

"Did I say it was in my wallet?"

Her eyes narrowed. "You're just like my mother. Always accusing me of things. Now if you don't mind I have to make a personal call before Madame gets back to pick me up. I'd like privacy, if that's not too much to ask."

She settled back into the chair. Her fist was clenched around the slip of paper.

I don't think I've ever been that angry. My heart was slamming into my ribs so hard it hurt.

I nodded at the paper she clutched. "You don't know your mother's phone number? You live with her."

She stood up. "I'll make my call from the theater."

As she made her way past me, I snatched the paper from her hand. There was a phone number scrawled on it. A Manhattan prefix: 212.

"Make the call right now. I'll dial it for you. I wouldn't mind chatting with your mom."

She lunged for the paper but I was already dialing. I got a recording of a man's voice: "At the tone, leave your name and number. Someone will get back to you as soon as possible."

I held the phone toward Jonquil. "You want to leave a message?"

Outside the girls' house a car horn blew.

Shaking her head angrily, she grabbed the piece of paper from me.

"Then I'll leave one." I lifted the receiver. "This is Bonnie Jean Indermill," I shouted into it. "I know what you are and I know who you are, and if I hear of you selling anything to any of these kids again I'm going straight to the cops." I slammed the phone down.

Jonquil marched to the living room door, dance bag in her hand. "You're such a bitch. As bad as my mother. Why can't you let me lead my own life?" Spinning, she stormed from the house.

A big scarlet A in neon lights illuminated the highway. That was the sign for Arnie's. The second I saw it I knew the kids had duped me. This was the infamous Scarlet Letter. I could hear the Screaming Green Mountain Boys all the way out in the parking lot as I pulled up next to Chris's Subaru. Red lights flashed through the bar's open windows, and from my seat in the van Arnie's wood walls seemed to pulse to the music. The parking lot was filled with motorcycles and Jeeps. A different side of the Berkshires, for sure.

My hair was down and I'd changed into black stockings, my short red leather skirt, and that new black sweater. There were little rhinestones around the scooped-out neck. Slightly punk and more than a little tacky for my usual hangouts in New York, but perfect for the Screaming Green Mountain Boys.

My entrance caused a sensation with the men along the bar. This was not the champagne brunch–antique shoppe crowd. These were the men who worked on the road crews and phone lines. They whistled; they pounded their fists on the bar. I had three invitations to dance and one to join some guy out in his Jeep for what I will describe here as *unnatural sex* by the time I got to an empty bar stool. I leaned against the bar and watched, sipping a low-cal beer and tapping my feet to the music. It was fast and loud. The bar vibrated against my back.

Jonquil was nowhere in sight. I spotted Carmen on the dance floor with one of the locals. The poor guy hadn't known what he was getting himself into. He looked clumsy and exhausted; she looked as if she could go on all night.

"You from around here?" The man with the Jeep was next to me.

"No."

"You want to dance?"

I glanced at him. He had the requisite beard, tattoo, and beer belly.

"No, thanks. I'm waiting for someone."

He stayed put. "Nice sweater. Are those diamonds?" He reached a bear-size hand toward me. When I pulled back he smiled and asked, "You want another beer?"

I shook my head. Maybe my outfit hadn't been such a good idea.

"What are you, stuck-up or something?"

All at once a hand was resting on my back. I spun. It was Chris.

"You finally made it! I was starting to think I'd never get you out. You look good enough to eat."

Laughing, I swung my stool purposely away from the man with the tattoo.

"How was tonight?" I asked. "Terrific as always?"

Chris leaned closer. "I'm always terrific at night."

"Where's Jonquil? She's supposed to be here."

"That's what I thought too. Rumor is she took off with an older man." He wrapped his arm around my waist and pulled me away from the bar. "Come on. Let's dance. I'll show you how a pro does it."

"An older man? Are you serious?"

He grinned. "That's what Carmen told me. Right after the performance Jonquil got in a car with some old guy."

"You mean *the* Old Man?"

Chris dropped his arm from my waist and looked at me a long time. "What do you mean, *the* Old Man?" he finally asked. "I don't know who you're talking about."

"Sure you do, Chris. The Old Man with the drugs."

Even in the flashing lights, I could tell that his stare had become hostile. "You've been listening to too many rumors, Bonnie. There is no Old Man."

He was lying. I visualized Jonquil parked in a dark alley with this Old Man. He was a nasty-looking older man, the kind who wore gold chains and had a big pot hanging over his belt. He was handing her a black plastic packet of cocaine. She was handing him my money. How much cocaine did you get for two hundred dollars? I'd heard of five-hundred-dollar-a-day habits, but I didn't think Jonquil had one of those. Not yet, anyway. Two hundred dollars might last her a while.

A lot of things I could do flashed through my mind. I

could hit every restaurant and bar and—God help me—motel in town searching for her. I could ring Michael's room and tell him. If I really wanted to be rotten I could call Abigail and let her deal with her child.

I looked out onto the dance floor again. Carmen spun by. Her local had disappeared and she was dancing with one of Elliott's truants, the kid with the jug ears. When she saw me, she leaned toward him and said something. Carmen liked me, but I still imagined her saying, "Hey, we better behave. The Matron is here." Stepping over to the bar, I put down my beer. "Let's dance, Chris!"

There are men who dance when they have to, and there are men who dance because they like to. And then there are men who are born dancers, men who dance almost as naturally as they walk. The moment Chris and I stepped onto the dance floor, I knew I was lucky enough to be with the third kind of man.

I'm good on the dance floor. Years of tap and jazz dancing lessons, even if my study was sometimes halfhearted, have had their effect. With Chris, I was better than good. I was intoxicated by the music and the movement. I was part of it; it was part of me. I danced until the bar closed—with Chris, with some of the other boys from the company, with the local guys. The only one I didn't dance with was Tattoo. From time to time I saw him staring at me from the bar, looking drunker and drunker.

The Matron showed them all that night. I deflected more passes than I could count, everything from moonlight motor-cycle rides to an out-and-out proposition from Chris. "We could get a room at the Thrifty Inn," he said during the last dance, a slow number.

"Chris, you're a little young for me."

"I like older women." He pulled me closer. "What is it? You're hung up on that cop?"

"No! Where did you get that idea?"

"A couple of the kids saw you having lunch with him. If he drove up here just to see you, it must be serious."

I shook my head. "Not at all."

"Oh?" He nodded. "So I guess the cops are still interested in Niki, still sniffing around. Anything new going on?"

There it was again—Chris's peculiar curiosity about the murder investigation. "Not that I know of." I stopped moving and looked him in the eye. "Why do you ask these questions? Is there something you know about Niki's death?"

He hesitated until I actually thought he was going to reveal something. "Of course not," he finally said. Tightening his arm around my waist, he started swaying to the music. "Now, what do you say to the Thrifty?"

Never for a moment did I seriously consider topping off my stint as chaperone by spending a night in the Thrifty with the company bad boy. For just an instant, though, I played with the idea. But that's not quite right. What really happened was, the idea played with me. Like the proverbial forbidden fruit, that wild young man was awfully attractive.

"I could lay my hands on some coke," he whispered, "if you're interested."

I pushed away from him. "I've got to get the kids together. Tomorrow night's the big one."

Chris grinned. "Michael's *Swan Lake?* We could all do it in our sleep. Why don't you run them back? I'll go ahead to the Thrifty and get a room. No one ever has to know."

"Good night, Chris."

It wasn't. Not yet. When Chris was around things had a way of boiling over.

I had gathered everybody from the company and steered them out of the bar. We were on our way to the van when Tattoo spotted me. Stumbling from his Jeep, he staggered across the parking lot.

"Hey, honey. Where you staying?"

He was really drunk and his words slurred. A couple of

my kids giggled. As I unlocked the van he leaned against the door, blocking it. "You coming back here tomorrow night?"

I shook my head. "No. Please excuse me. I have to get everybody in the van."

"You sure?" He swayed away from the door.

Chris already had the engine of his Subaru running. I was surprised when he got out of the car and walked to the van. The situation was not out of my control.

"It's all right, Chris," I said.

Tattoo took a few steps forward, stared at Chris then back at me. "What are you messing with a faggot dancer for? Good-looking woman like you." Raising his hands in a circle over his head and rising on his toes as well as he could under the circumstances, he began a grotesque drunken parody of a ballet dancer. He didn't make it through the first pirouette. Chris grabbed Tattoo's arm and twisted it hard behind his back.

"You want to see a faggot dancer? I'll show you one."

"Forget it, Chris. It's not impor——"

Chris dropped Tattoo's arm. Lifting his foot, he lashed out with it into the other man's stomach. Tattoo doubled over and fell to his knees, retching.

Carmen gasped. "God," said the boy next to her.

"All of you into the van, now!"

Chris was standing over Tattoo, waiting for the other man to get up. "Chris," I said. "I think you should leave your car here and come with me."

He shook his head. "I'm going to wait around for a few minutes. This guy might want to learn some more about ballet." Glancing up, he smiled. "Unless you've changed your mind. You could let one of them drive back."

I shook my head. What I'd just seen had taken care of any lingering lust. "Absolutely not."

I drove straight back to the compound, virtue, such as it was, still intact.

My night didn't end when I collapsed into bed. It went on, and on.

I stirred sometime after 2:00 A.M. Jonquil was rummaging through her drawers. In my half sleep I mumbled, "Who was the older man you went out with?"

"Nobody," she whispered.

Sometime later I woke to the sound of weeping. That time I got up and crossed the room. Jonquil was on her stomach, hugging her pillow.

I sat on the edge of her bed. "I'm sorry we had such a terrible fight. What can I do to help you?"

"Nothing. I'm all right."

I started to get up, and she rolled over and wrapped her arms around my waist.

"I'm sorry too," she sobbed. "I'll give you back your money as soon as I can. You shouldn't have made that call, though."

"Too late," I said. "It's done. And it's not the money I'm worried about. It's you."

"Don't worry. I don't want to say anything because it might get back to my mom, but there's somebody who's going to help me with . . . everything."

"I hope you're not doing something you'll regret."

"I'm not. I promise."

Another promise. How many was that? I'd lost count. I sat with Jonquil until she slept. All the while my imagination ran wild. She had found a mentor in the filthy Old Man. She was going to be shot full of drugs, raped; she was one step away from the street. When I finally slept again, the gray gloom of early dawn was filtering through our windows.

─|14|─

Terrible specters threatened me. Obscene images crawled from darkness into the morning light. A foot lashed out; there was a body, a scream. For a moment the murky shadows became crystal clear. They clouded as I woke, leaving me groggy and troubled.

Jonquil was doing warm-up exercises when I opened my eyes. Sitting on the floor, legs stretched, she leaned forward until her chin touched the floor between her knees. Then she turned onto her stomach and reversed the maneuver, bending her back until the soles of her feet rested against her head.

She was fresh-faced and, apart from a little puffiness around her eyes, looked fine. How nice to be seventeen—crying at 2:00 A.M. and ready for action five hours later.

When she noticed me watching, she grimaced. "I'm stiff as a board. I'm going to use the shower first. Okay?"

"Sure."

What was it I'd been dreaming? Murder, drugs, filthy old men, young girls bruised from vicious kicks. As I gradually came to life I tried to put these things in order. They didn't lend themselves to it, but bubbled in my mind like a half-done stew. The ingredients were all in the pot but they didn't taste right together.

If there was a constant it was Chris. As I lay there, I put together a rough theory.

Niki had discovered the Chris–Old Man drug connection and had threatened it. Though Chris said he hadn't been in the theater the day Niki died, he knew his way around backstage well enough to sneak into both the prop room and Niki's dressing room while the reception was going on upstairs. He planted the drugs in Niki's room to discredit Niki, then he snuck into the prop room and cut Niki's harness. Carmen spotted Chris on his way out of the theater. Fearing she might eventually realize it wasn't a woman she had seen, he decided to get rid of her. Thus the kick into traffic.

This theory had big problems, not the least of them Chris's personality. I wouldn't have put it past him, driven into a sudden rage, to grab Niki by the throat and beat the Prince of Ballet to a pulp, but I couldn't see Chris sneaking into a prop room and meticulously cutting threads. And if he had, what had he been wearing to make Carmen mistake him for a woman? Chris looked totally, aggressively male. As for the drugs, even assuming Chris would willingly part with a nice stash on the flimsy chance that Niki might be discredited, the "Good Night, Sweet Prince" didn't go with the Chris I knew.

Another problem with this theory was Niki's attitude about drugs. It had hardly been a moral issue with him. I doubt if many things were. What he cared about was the quality of the performance. Jonquil's drug use, *combined* with her inexperience, was what he couldn't tolerate. How, then, had he posed a danger to Chris's drug connection?

First things first. As soon as I could drag myself out of bed, I went to Carmen's room.

"Carmen?" I knocked hard. "Are you up? I have to talk to you."

The girls' house was stirring. Voices from the kitchen, the smell of coffee—these were the things I'd miss when we left.

The sound of Carmen sliding the chair from under her doorknob was a part of the morning routine that I could do without. I waited patiently until she opened the door. When I walked past her into the room, her eyes widened.

"You look tired, Bonnie. Like my mom when she stays out late. You should see her! Can't move the next day."

I had grown tired of hearing young women tell me I reminded them of their moms. "I feel fine."

This one looked fresh as a daisy too. Her little room, though. What a wreck! Kindred souls, she and Niki—at least in the housekeeping department. Clothes were piled everywhere—jeans on the floor, sweaters on doorknobs, drying tights on the iron bedframe. I shuddered. "You couldn't find an elephant in here, Carmen."

"I didn't lose an elephant. Want to sit down?" With a sweep of her arm she dumped a pile of clothes from her bed onto the floor.

"Thanks. Please close the door. This is private."

"Sure. What's the matter? Whatever it is, I didn't do it." When she had slammed the door, she regarded the chair for a second.

"I don't think the chair is necessary now."

"You're probably right. Nobody's going to try anything with a witness." Crossing the tiny room, she dug a brush from the junk on her dresser and went to work on her hair.

"You know that policeman, Lieutenant LaMarca?"

The brush stopped mid-stroke. "Sure. What about him?"

"He tells me you called him last Wednesday. When he got back to you, you didn't have anything to say. Why did you call him?"

"When did you see Lieutenant LaMarca?"

"A couple of days ago. He's a friend of mine."

"A boyfriend? Did you notice that guy I was dancing with a lot last night?"

"The one with the—" I'd started to say "jug ears," but I

noticed her hopeful expression staring back through the mirror. "The one with the nice smile?"

She nodded. "That's him. Joey. I think he likes me."

"I wouldn't be surprised. You're a likable girl. But let's not change the subject. What did you want to tell Lieutenant LaMarca?"

"It wasn't anything. I thought I remembered something, that's all."

"About the person you saw leaving the prop room?"

She nodded.

"Could it be that the person might not have been a woman?"

"Huh?"

"Could it have been a man, maybe in costume or tights? People run around backstage in all kinds of outfits."

"I don't think so. I can't see, but I can see better than that. Just because I never had a boyfriend, that doesn't mean I can't tell them from girls."

"It couldn't have been Chris?"

"Chris? Because of the way he kicked that guy last night, you're thinking he kicked me? No way. Chris likes me. He spent two afternoons coaching me when I joined the company." She turned to me, pensive. "He's not really as wild as he acts, Bonnie. I always thought if he wasn't going with Jonquil, maybe . . ." Her voice trailed off.

"Have you ever met the Old Man?"

My question surprised Carmen. "What's that got to do with anything?"

"I don't know. Have you met him?"

"No. I'm not sure there really is an Old Man. Whenever Chris goes to score some dope, he says he's going to see the Old Man. It could be a lot of different people."

"So when you got shoved into the street, that couldn't have had anything to do with drugs?"

She shook her head. "I don't see how. Why are you asking

me about drugs, anyway? Just because I'm Hispanic that doesn't mean I know about drugs."

"It was just an idea. So what was it you thought you remembered about the person coming out of the prop room?"

The girl shrugged. "I didn't know if I really saw it. I'm so used to seeing it that I thought maybe I imagined it. That's why I decided not to say anything to Lieutenant LaMarca. Then after I got shoved in the street, I figured I was right but I didn't have time to tell him."

I stretched. "Carmen, I had a long, hard night. Could you repeat that slowly?"

For a moment she stared at her arm in silence. The black-and-blue marks had faded to a sick yellow. She began squeezing foundation from a tube and rubbing it over them. "I told you they'd be gone in a week."

"Next time the taxi may be going too fast to stop," I said. "Or maybe you'll be standing next to an open window, or—"

She slammed the tube onto the dresser. "I've been thinking about those things, all the time. But I'm careful. You haven't seen me get in any more accidents, have you?"

"You're not going to be able to sleep with a chair under your door forever."

"I don't want to make trouble in the company," she said, turning back to the mirror. "Michael doesn't like troublemakers. What if I'm wrong? He might not give me any good roles to dance. He already likes Jonquil better than he likes me. She's got longer legs. And she's thinner."

"I'm sure he likes you just as much. But what's more important: dancing good roles or your life?"

This didn't take much thought. "They're the same thing," she said after a second.

"Dead girls don't get good roles." In her mirrored reflection I could see tears filling her eyes. "I'm not trying to frighten you," I went on. "I'm trying to make you understand you can't handle this yourself."

"I know. I'm . . . I'm scared, Bonnie. One of them is trying to . . ." She bit her lower lip.

Getting up, I put my arms around her shoulders. For a second this kid let down her defenses. Burying her face in my neck, she sputtered, "One of the girls wants to kill me."

My eyes started brimming. What a job chaperoning was! Tears in the morning, tears at night. "Lieutenant LaMarca wants to talk to you. Why don't I drive you to a phone booth now and you can call him."

She straightened and dried her eyes with her hand. "Can I wait till we get back to the city?"

"You tell me. You're the one who's scared."

Grabbing a tissue from the dresser, she blew her nose. "Yeah, but now that I know I was right and who I've got to look out for, I'll be okay. It's got to be someone who hated Niki. That's either Jonquil or Galena, and I'm almost positive it was Jonquil. As long as I watch out for her . . ."

"But lots of other people hated Niki. To tell you the truth, toward the end I didn't like Niki very much."

"How come?" She gave me a sly look. "Were you in love with him and he wasn't paying enough attention to you?"

I couldn't help grinning. "Carmen, you are obsessed with love. No, I was never in love with Niki."

"That's okay. You don't have to tell me. I know you didn't cut the hitch."

"How can you be sure? I could have gotten backstage."

"Yeah, but look." She walked rapidly across the floor. "Look at my feet, Bonnie. They're turning out. That's how we all walk. You don't have a turnout. I checked. I've been checking everybody. The woman I saw walking out of that room—I think she did."

The turnout—the ballerina's duck walk—is not simply a matter of forcing the toes out at will. When a young dancer's bones are still developing, repeated exercise molds the hips and thighs until the bone structure actually changes. The ballerina's muscles adjust until the femur in the thigh rotates in its socket. Carmen demonstrated once again, walking toward me with toes turned out at forty-five-degree angles from her legs.

"Lots of people who aren't dancers turn out their toes," I said. "It's called being slew footed. Besides, those halls are dim. You admitted that you weren't paying attention and you weren't wearing your contacts. You're not sure what the woman was wearing but you remember her feet?"

"That woman was probably a dancer," Carmen insisted. "One of the doors in the hall is glass and there was light shining through it. At the corner it hit the floor almost like a spotlight. When that woman heard me she spun left. I don't think her right foot moved. You do that."

I tried it and stumbled. "When you saw the woman a minute later at the door to the stairs, did she stand the same way?"

She shrugged. "She was only there for half a second, and the trash cans hid her legs. I wasn't even sure it was the same woman, because I heard a door slam before I got to the corner. I told that to the police."

"Why didn't you tell them about the woman's walk?"

She lifted her shoulders and rotated them. "I don't know. I didn't think about it. Not at first. It's, like, everybody I know is in the ballet. All my friends, my teachers. Even my sister is studying. Everybody I hang out with. It seems normal that everybody turns out. But then last week I watched the special about Niki's life. They showed that Polish woman getting off the airplane in Moscow. Her feet didn't turn out. They weren't even straight. They turned in! She had pigeon toes!"

A voice from the hall interrupted her. "Carmen? Why are you always late these mornings? We must leave now!"

Carmen cringed. "It's Madame," she whispered. "I'm coming, Madame." Rushing to a pile of clothes, she started stuffing them into her dance bag.

"What about calling Lieutenant LaMarca?"

"I can't. This is more important. Madame is coaching me

in my swan solo. Michael changed it. The second I get back to the city I'll call him. I promise."

"All right," I said, "but you've got to promise me something else. You don't wander off alone. You stay with the group all the time."

"That's what I've been doing. Don't worry, Bonnie. If I go off, I'll go with Joey." She raced out the door, dance bag swinging.

A late September Saturday night, warm enough to get away with a light jacket, clear enough to stretch out on your back and pick out the constellations. I spread my blanket—borrowed from Primrose Cottage for the occasion—near one of the oak trees that framed the lawn of the theater. I could have taken a spot in the wings or behind the orchestra, but this was the kind of evening for blankets on the grass.

The venerable *Swan Lake* was on the program for Gotham Ballet's final Berkshire performance. While many companies have the famous second act in their repertoire, Gotham's dancers were doing the entire four acts. Galena was dancing the dual role of Odette, the tragic swan queen, and her counterpart, Odile, with Chris as Prince Siegfried, Michael in a special appearance as Siegfried's friend Benno, and an older male dancer in the character role of the evil magician, Von Rothbart. Because the company was under-staffed, Jonquil and Carmen each were doing two roles: country girls in the first act, and swan maidens later.

That night was not only the company's last performance in the country; it marked the end of the theater's season. The rows of seats were filling rapidly and so were the grassy knolls beyond them. Soon people were wandering over to my spot by the trees, spreading blankets and popping wine corks. A couple behind me offered me a paper cup of wine, which I accepted happily. As daylight faded, I noticed our patron, Isabella Spencer, taking a reserved seat close to the stage. Looking at her in her buttery-looking leather pantsuit, my mind jumped to the Thrifty Inn. Hard to picture her in an orange Formica chair surrounded by plastic daisies.

I turned to the stage when Tchaikovsky's great overture began. First the soft romantic woodwinds, then the tentative strings, and finally the crash of the cymbals and the trumpets with their swanlike cries. The music soared, filling the night, and then it quieted. The curtain rose. It was Prince Siegfried's twenty-first birthday party. Dancing boys and girls filled the stage.

It was a while before I realized something was wrong with Chris. This was a party scene, with one of the characters running around handing out drinks. I'd never seen Chris dance Siegfried and at first thought his reckless, swaggering steps had been choreographed that way.

That wasn't the case with Jonquil. The second she blundered onto that stage I knew she was high. The country girl smile she was supposed to wear started as a dopy smirk and quickly became a grimace. Her normally graceful carriage was sloppy and every step a bounce. When she danced the pas de trois she lost count of the music so badly that the boy partnering her gripped her wrist and yanked her along. I watched in horror; that was my two hundred dollars at work. When the first act curtain fell my fists were clenched. All the promises I'd wrung from her—useless.

"The corps doesn't seem well rehearsed," the man behind me said.

"It's that second girl. The redhead," responded the woman. "She's throwing them all off."

In Act II, Siegfried meets the Swan Queen at the lake formed from her mother's tears. With a real lake shimmering in the background beyond the stage, the set was almost unnecessary. Everything was perfect, almost.

As a swan maiden Jonquil was a mess, missing the music, dancing a couple of steps behind and then ahead of the other maidens. When she passed close to my side of the stage I saw her lips moving. I knew enough about dance to realize she was trying to count the beat.

Chris wasn't much better, but he was experienced enough to make most of his swaggering look intentional. Once he stumbled, almost pulling Galena into the orchestra. I picked up my binoculars and focused on the couple. Her eyes were narrowed. It looked as if she hissed something at Chris through clenched teeth.

The third act was no better.

"I thought he was supposed to be good," said the man near me when the dancers left the stage.

"He is good!" the woman insisted. "I saw him with the Stuttgart Ballet less than a month ago. He danced Hamlet. He was terrific."

Hamlet? The woman's words stunned me.

I turned to her. "Chris Lansing danced *Hamlet* in Germany?"

She nodded. "Yes. I guess they all have their 'off' nights."

"This is certainly one of his," her husband said, but I was no longer listening. The words on the note in Niki's dressing table were running through my mind. Good night, Sweet Prince, from *Hamlet*. Chris had been on his way to Germany to dance *Hamlet*. The drugs and that strange note in Niki's dressing table had nothing to do with Niki! They weren't part of any Soviet subterfuge, either. They had been intended for Chris—a little wit, and a little something to speed him on his way. Somehow they had ended up in the wrong dressing room.

Soft violins, a harp, and the last act began. The pensive swan maidens had gathered at the side of the lake. Jonquil was not among them. Galena the Swan Queen appeared, a beautiful study in grief. Moments later Chris rushed onto the stage searching for Odette. It is a powerful scene with some of the most glorious music imaginable. Chris had pulled himself together, but his efforts came too late. I think it was a relief to everyone when the soaring trumpets announced that Siegfried had followed Odette into the lake and the ballet was over.

I went backstage immediately, intending to find Jonquil and drag her to the girls' house. It was pandemonium back there. The wings were crowded with stagehands packing up flats of scenery. Dancers were standing in little knots, whispering.

"Have you seen Jonquil?" I asked a ballerina.

"Who didn't?" the girl answered. "She's probably getting dressed."

I hurried down the hall and flung open the corps girls' dressing room door. Carmen and a few others were at the long bench in front of the mirror. Their chattering quieted the second I walked in.

"Where's Jonquil?"

Carmen shrugged. "She left a couple of seconds ago. Somebody was waiting for her."

"How are you getting back?" I asked Carmen.

She looked up, alarmed. "Pleeeze, Bonnie. I want to go to the disco with—you know. I can sleep late tomorrow."

"No way. You have to pack. Find Madame or Elliott and get a ride straight back!"

"Boy, is she ever getting bossy," one of the girls said as I left the room. "She used to be nice."

The parking lot behind the auditorium, reserved for theater people and their guests, was lit only by a few dim bulbs on the building and by the full moon. As I got into the van a beam of light swept across the lot. A silver BMW had pulled in. The driver stopped back by a clump of trees and turned off the headlights, leaving the engine running. In the faint light, I could just make out the dent in the passenger door.

The stage door opened. Chris came out and hurried across the pavement. When he opened the BMW's door, light filled the interior of the car. Before it dimmed I saw Isabella Spencer lean across the seat toward him. Couldn't even wait for the Thrifty.

I was at the edge of the lot when I glimpsed a thin girl with a red ponytail climbing into the passenger seat of a dark, late-model American car. Seconds later the car passed me and turned toward the main exit. It was Jonquil, sitting next to an older man. Gunning the engine, I tried squeezing in behind them. Several cars blocked my way.

Traffic was heavy leaving the theater and I could just keep the dark car with its two passengers in sight. At the road they turned left away from town. Ahead of me a line of cars waited their turn. I couldn't wait. I swung the van off the white gravel road into the grassy area where the spectators sat. There was a shout. One of the parking guards was heading toward me, his expression grim and his palm stretched out. "Hold it," he yelled. Speeding up, I cut in front of the line and onto the road.

I drove as fast as I dared. The van was anything but quick on the takeoff and I held my breath as I forced it past slower cars. Finally I spotted the dark car with its two passengers several cars ahead. At the crossroads for the highway they caught a yellow light and turned right, heading north. Swerving to the shoulder, I passed the other cars and made a quick right on a red light.

The dark car's driver did the speed limit all the way to Mount Wilcox. There he got off the highway and began the climb up the mountain road. I was no more than a hundred feet behind Jonquil and the Old Man. If I accomplished nothing else in the Berkshires, I would keep that kid out of the greasy clutches of that old pervert drug dealer for one night.

The road was steep and curved, with cliffs rising on one side and a sharp, wooded drop-off on the other. The drug dealer kept his speed low. From time to time a set of headlights flickered in my rearview mirror, but this third car stayed well back.

We reached the summit and began the abrupt drop down the other side of the mountain. Somewhere near the bottom the dark car pulled off the pavement onto a gravel road. He was going so slowly that I came to a complete stop and waited for him to round a curve. As soon as the red taillights faded I turned onto the gravel.

WILCOX HOUSE. ESTABLISHED 1834. The sign was white rimmed with gold and carved at its top in the shape of a crown. The lettering was an elegant dark green script.

A curving drive led up to the main house, a big colonial building nestled into the mountainside. An old double sled was on the perfectly kept lawn, and at either side of the front door candlelit bay windows twinkled. An attendant dressed in colonial livery was parking cars. He held the car door for Jonquil while the Old Man stepped around the dark car. As the attendant drove away, Jonquil took the Old Man's arm and leaned against it. They entered the inn together.

"Do you have a reservation?" the attendant asked when I pulled up at the door.

"I'm meeting someone. I'll only be a minute, though. I'd like to leave my van here."

The man told me I could park at the edge of the circle if I promised not to be long.

Brass lanterns lit my way up to the double oak doors with their etched-glass centers. Another uniformed man opened the door and I stepped into a lobby filled with overstuffed antique chairs and delicate walnut tables. The carpets were ankle-deep, the walls hand stenciled. A magnificent wood staircase rose along one wall. I walked up to a reception desk.

"I'm looking for a young girl and an older man who just arrived. She dropped her wallet. I found it."

"Oh, how kind of you," the clerk said. She told me to follow a long hall into the last dining room.

I counted four fireplaces in three rooms, and enough brass and copper to redo the plumbing and electricity in a good-size apartment building. There was a hush over the entire inn, somehow almost cumulative, as if no voice had ever been raised there. This was the kind of place I would always be too young for. At eighty, I'll be too young. Anyone who has ever choked on their dinner because they were laughing, or spilled a glass of red wine across a white damask tablecloth, or sent a fork clanging to the floor is forever too young for this inn. What a spot for a greasy old pervert and my stoned little charge.

I spotted them by a window at the far end of the last dining room, sitting on opposite sides of a round candlelit table against a background of heavy lace curtains. Jonquil's back was to me. I had a clear view of the man as I approached. He was not as old as I'd expected. His hair was light red, flecked with gray. He wasn't all that slimy-looking, either. In fact, in his plaid sports jacket, oxford shirt, and striped tie, he looked strangely suburban for a dirty old man from Manhattan. He also looked very stern and unhappy. When I was within a couple of feet of their table he glanced up. The way I was bearing down on them, I must have looked quite odd. As I got closer, Jonquil was saying ". . . but if you'll take me with you, I promise never to—"

"Hello, Jonquil," I said. "That was quite a performance you gave this evening. Why don't you introduce me to your friend?"

She looked at me, astonished. "I didn't know you were coming here. This is Bonnie Indermill from the company," she said to the man. "Bonnie's my roommate. The one I told you about."

The man rose, an uncomfortable smile on his face. As he extended his hand, I got the most terrible feeling. Red hair, pale blue eyes, a pug nose with a bridge of freckles. "I'm glad to meet you," he said. "I'm Ned Jeffreys, Jonquil's father. She told me last night how nice you've been to her. I understand you loaned her some money. I promise you'll get it back."

I will save myself the embarrassment of describing what followed, my bumbling "Nice to meet you" and my absurd excuse for being in that dining room. Walking back down the hall through that ankle-deep carpet, I caught a look at myself in an ornate mahogany-framed mirror hanging over a field-stone fireplace. My face was on fire, redder than Jonquil's hair.

The road was empty when I turned onto it and began the climb up the mountain. I'd gone only a few hundred feet when somewhere nearby an engine started. What I'd just done occupied so much of my thoughts that I didn't notice the car behind me until its headlights in my mirror almost blinded me. I glanced back as I came out of a curve. It was one of those macho-type Jeeps, the kind that had filled the parking lot of the Scarlet Letter. I could make out the roll bars over an open seat. There was a single passenger. Was it possible Tattoo had spotted me and thought he was being cute? Was this some kind of redneck foreplay? Tilting the rearview mirror to deflect the glare, I pressed down on the accelerator. The van, true to form, groaned and shuddered as its speedometer inched up to a roaring thirty miles an hour. The other car stayed on my tail. At one of the few straight spots in the road, I pulled to the right and waved my hand out the window, urging him to pass. He clung to my bumper.

We were approaching the crest now. That was where it got bad, where the right side of the road amounted to some big white rocks, a few straggly pine trees, and a drop of several hundred feet. I had just reached the sign that read ELEVATION 2,400 FT. when there was a dull thud. My head wrenched back sharply as the van lurched and skidded sideways. The Jeep had rammed me!

I turned the wheel to the right, urging the van as close to those rocks as I dared. Again I tried waving the Jeep past. It had fallen back. Then he hit me hard, a real "wham" that shook the old van to its frame and me to mine. An icy sweat broke out over my body. This creep was trying to push me over the cliff. I rolled up my window, pulled back onto the asphalt, and hit the accelerator. Forty-five, fifty miles an hour. The steep downhill was a series of hair-raising S turns. I faced a black abyss as the road curved and my headlights fell over the edge. Tires screamed as I rounded the nightmare curve at fifty-five.

The Jeep's headlights glared into the side mirror. He was trying to pass. Maybe he would leave me alone. No. A terrible scraping sound and I felt the van go into a sideways skid. The other car had broadsided me. I instinctively swung the wheel hard left. Another impact, crash, and shattering glass. His headlights dimmed. I'd pushed him into the mountain.

Straddling the white line, I kept one eye on the side mirror. The road behind me remained dark but for the round yellow moon. Slowing, I rolled down the window. Nothing broke the night's quiet but the crickets and cicadas and leaves shifting in the faint breeze.

Somewhere on the highway between Mount Wilcox and Lenox I experienced a delayed reaction. I couldn't get enough air into my lungs and my body shook so violently that, with the tears rolling down my face and my hands slick with sweat, I could hardly keep the van on the road. I was almost in Lenox before my knees stopped shaking and tears no longer clouded my vision.

Who had tried to run me off the road? Some random nut? That was the most comfortable notion. A random nut wasn't likely to pursue me. Or Tattoo. Maybe he'd decided to take out the humiliation of Chris's kick on me. But he'd been so drunk I doubted if he'd even remember the kind of van I drove. The likeliest possibility was the scariest. Was that threatening phone call to Jonquil's drug contact coming back to haunt me? Had some sleazy dealer come up from Manhattan, gotten hold of a Jeep, and tried to run me off the road? But how would he know how to find me? Wouldn't he be more likely to look me up in the New York City phone book, wait near my apartment, and cut my throat? I decided to call Tony when I got to the girls' house. He could get my key from my neighbor and check my apartment.

By the time I drove down the main street in town, any thoughts I'd had about going to the local police had vanished. I was leaving the next day, waving good-bye to the worst "vacation" ever. Jonquil was in her father's good hands. As soon as I got back to the city I'd make sure Carmen put herself into Tony's good hands, and that would be the end of that. If I told the local police it could have been Tattoo on that mountain, I might not be able to return to New York with the rest of the company. If I told them it could have been a drug dealer from New York City they'd never find him anyway.

When I pulled up at the girls' house I examined the back of the van carefully. The piece of junk had never looked good. The new dents in the back didn't actually hurt much, but people—Elliott in particular—were sure to notice the big scrape on the left side. I decided to let Lenox's bad element—the ones Elliott was so afraid of—take the blame. "Came up next to me in that parking lot last night and rammed me," I'd say.

Once inside, I went straight to the phone and dialed Tony's home number. His phone rang one, two, three times. I was ready to hang up when someone answered.

"Hello," said my dear friend Amanda Paradise.

I hung up.

15

Tuesday morning. I wasn't quite ready to kiss New York City's grubby sidewalks, but they sure looked good to me. As I walked to the subway savoring the witty signs in car windows—NO RADIO and EVERYTHING ALREADY STOLEN—I waved to a neighbor whose Doberman had just deposited a horse-size pile on the sidewalk. It felt great to be back. No ballerinas to chaperone, and so far no drug dealers lurking near my apartment.

In the office it was business as usual. When I found Abigail scanning a copy of the day's cast sheet, I figured she was looking for her daughter's name. Sure enough, her first words were not the customary "Good to have you back" or "Did you have a nice time?"

"Did you catch Jonquil's *Swan Lake?*" she asked, scarcely glancing up. "The poor thing had to leave after the third act. She got sick."

"Good morning, Abigail. Yes, I saw Jonquil's sick little swan." Unlocking my desk, I shoved my purse in, making as much noise as possible. The mess around me was infuriating. Unopened mail was piled everywhere. On the floor next to my desk a heap of address changes waited to be entered into the computer. On my desk lay a stack of unanswered phone calls.

"Really busy around here while I was gone? Tearing your hair out?"

That drew a blank. "No, not really." She looked back at the cast sheet. "Michael is starting to rehearse a Balanchine ballet this afternoon. Jonquil would be perfect for a pas de trois in the second movement but since she's out sick, she may be overlooked." Abigail sighed. "Why is it that whenever things are going well for us something bad happens?" She stared back at the cast sheet. "I'm so concerned."

I said exactly what popped into my head. "It's not Jonquil you're concerned about. It's yourself. If you concerned yourself more with this office, it—"

The ferocity of Abigail's response startled me. Crumpling the sheet, she threw it on the floor. "How dare you say that! Everything I do is for Jonquil. Since she was five I've had that child in the best classes available. I've devoted twelve years of my life to getting her onstage."

"Then why don't you devote fifteen minutes to opening last week's mail?" I shot back.

"Gladly," she snapped. "I was planning to do that."

We worked quietly for a few minutes, Abigail slitting envelopes, me at the computer. Then I heard—what else?— weeping.

"You don't understand, Bonnie," she sobbed.

When I looked up, she had buried her face in her hands. "Oh, Abigail," I said. "You're so right about that. Why don't you find someone you can talk to? Get some help for yourself."

"You mean a psychiatrist?" Dropping her hands, she shook her head. "There's nothing abnormal about helping your child along, Bonnie. But I suppose you wouldn't understand that. You have nobody but yourself to worry about." Abigail let out her breath. "You seemed like a nice person when you started here."

"I was a temp when I started here. The work didn't matter as much."

"It still doesn't matter." Pushing back her chair, she half stood, hands gripping the edge of her desk. Her knuckles were white and her tears made her eyes glint. "You're just like Tricia. Two of a kind."

For over a week this woman's daughter had accused me of being just like her mother. Now Abigail was accusing me of being like our boss. Under some circumstances the comparison might have upset me, but not then.

"I want to be like Tricia," I said. "She has great clothes and she opens the mail." I flicked my hand at the still-unopened envelopes.

"Did I hear my name?"

Tricia poked her head through the door, interrupting what was becoming quite a scene.

"Good morning," I said.

She nodded briskly. "Bonnie, can I see you in my office."

It was a command, not a question. My stomach gave a nervous flutter. This was, after all, the first time Tricia and I had spoken since the battle of the chicken coop. For all I knew she planned to tell me she no longer welcomed my assistance. I wasn't too nervous, though, to stare at her feet as I followed her down the hall. Her toes pointed out a little. Nothing particularly pronounced, but to be sure—

"Tricia!" I said suddenly. She spun. Her feet turned awkwardly.

"Sorry. I thought there was a mouse near your door."

"I wouldn't be surprised," she said, walking into her office. "This place is crawling. Now. Down to business." Sliding into her chair, she looked at me quizzically. "I expected you yesterday."

"We got in late Sunday evening. I called yesterday morning and told Abigail I was taking a vacation day."

For a moment Tricia looked so angry I thought her next words would be: "You're fired."

"I never got the message. I don't know where Abigail's mind is, but it's not on her work. That office is falling apart."

"The work is a little backed up," I said.

Tricia pounced. "A little backed up! The woman has done nothing for weeks. Not that she ever did much, but this is ridiculous. If Michael wasn't so crazy about her kid she would have been out of her a long time ago." Tricia rolled her eyes. "If it isn't 'One of my sick headaches,' it's 'That computer just defeats me.'"

Tricia could do a vicious wilting violet, complete with the back of her hand pressed to her forehead. I couldn't help grinning. She didn't smile back.

"Anyway, I've convinced Michael that I need you here full-time. If I can't get rid of Abigail I'm going to get her switched to Elliott's department. Do you think you can handle the office alone for a while? Maybe we'll be able to get a part-timer eventually."

"No problem," I said, and then, feeling bold, I added, "I'll put in ten hours a day."

My sarcasm was lost on Tricia. "That's how I would handle it," she said. "You know our routine. We want to get that new donation campaign started. And speaking of donations, you *will* be at the Spencers' party on Saturday night. I'm afraid it's a command performance."

"I'm looking forward to it."

"And dress! Casual but elegant," she said crisply. She must have expected me to turn up in pajamas and bunny slippers. With that, she turned to the papers on her desk.

As I've said, Tricia wasn't one for office niceties. I figured this for a dismissal and got to my feet. "I'll get started now."

I was at her office door when she called me back.

"Oh, Bonnie. I understand the gala was . . ." This kind of thing did not come easy to Tricia. She stumbled for words. ". . . professionally handled. You're a good worker."

A good worker. That's not necessarily something I want engraved on my headstone, but coming from Tricia it amounted to a rave.

"The gala went pretty well," I said modestly. "It would have been terrific, if only . . ."

She finished the sentence. ". . . Niki hadn't fallen. Such a shame," she added, but she sure didn't sound as if she meant it.

I nodded. "I'm glad I didn't see it. Were you there for his performance?"

"Third ring left. I wasn't about to be seen in the orchestra. I was eyeball to eyeball with Niki when his hitch let go. You should have seen that little cowboy's expression," she said, a small smile blossoming on her lips. "If his princess hadn't finished the performance the audience would have realized something was wrong."

"Did you get backstage before the performance?" I asked, knowing full well she had.

She nodded. "I couldn't bear not to. The company— well . . ." She looked down. "It means a lot to me. I convinced a guard that I was a ballerina. I'm sure Michael would have given me a pass but I refuse to crawl."

That was as close to vulnerability as I'd seen Tricia. The moment didn't last. As I left her office I could have sworn I heard a soft chuckle.

A bright Wednesday morning. Sun flooded Derek's loft. It warmed my back, making me feel lazy and slow.

"I could sleep all day," I said with a yawn.

Across the kitchen table Derek grinned. "Why don't we?"

I smiled back. "You're impossible."

Nothing had cooled off during our cooling-off period. Quite the opposite. I'd called him the second I got home Sunday evening. I'll skip the details; I assure you he was glad to have me back.

So far—not that three days is much time—I'd been the embodiment of composure. The big M word, the H word— what were they to me? Gibberish.

As for the Tony-Amanda business, Derek had gotten an

abbreviated version. I'd left out the things he didn't need to hear. There weren't all that many. My rekindled affair with Tony had burned on a low flame.

Now, as he sliced a banana into his cereal, he brought up the subject again. He knew Amanda long before I did. He'd always liked her.

"It would be a shame to lose a good friend over something so silly," he said. "You refuse to call her because she's marrying a man you didn't want." He cocked an eyebrow. "You didn't really want him, did you?"

"No, I didn't. The man is not the point. The point is, she . . . oh . . . I don't know what the point is. Maybe there isn't one. But I think it's her place to call me."

"Amanda's probably embarrassed," he said. "What a ridiculous situation. She's afraid to 'confess' to you and you're too stubborn to call her."

The situation was even more ridiculous than he knew. The Tony-Amanda business had shaken me until I wasn't eager to talk to Tony either. I'd given Carmen a sealed note for him. In it I'd explained my suspicions about Chris, and also described my trip to Brighton Beach.

I shrugged and poured myself some coffee. "Sometimes that's what life is: one ridiculous situation after another."

"You may be right."

He held out his hand. I motioned toward his cup, but he took the coffeepot from me, set it down, and took my hand in his. He looked so serious. Oh, no, I thought. Not again.

"I've been thinking about the discussion we were having right before we broke up," he said.

Discussion? My side of our discussion had been conducted at a shout and his mostly with confused silences. Just to be sure I didn't have the wrong discussion in mind I asked, "Which discussion was that?"

"You're not going to make this easy for me, are you?"

I didn't know how to answer.

"Okay," he said. "I'll do it myself." For a second he

looked perplexed, as if he had no idea how to proceed. I don't suppose he did.

He sighed, and then—some gritting of teeth surely went on—he began, bravely and formally. "You could possibly consider . . ." He hesitated and dropped my hand. His line of thought wavered, and I held my breath hoping he wouldn't lose it altogether.

"There's plenty of room here, if you were to move in." The way he nodded at the space around him, he could have been a real estate agent selling condos. "Moses would probably like it," he added, the romantic devil.

Moses isn't fussy. He likes where the food is. This sure wasn't moonlight and roses I was getting. And from a man whose voice on the telephone could curl my toes. A prospective buyer, I followed Derek's glance around the loft. Yes, there was plenty of room—a veritable tennis court of unbroken space. Lots of light, too. Given a choice, I'd want a few walls, and some of his furniture was a little *manly*, and . . .

I looked back at Derek. He was staring down, pushing some sliced banana around his bowl. Offbeat indeed, with that tiny blond ponytail and an apartment with no interior walls. Where I come from men who paint for a living wear white coveralls and carry ladders. Where I come from adult males don't eat and sleep in the same room. I come from the land where even breakfast has its own nook.

Derek strained to see the clock on his stove. "You want to call in sick today? I'm serious. We could talk, or"—he shrugged—"maybe bring Moses down here to look the place over."

Where I come from, thirty-five-year-old men don't call in sick at the drop of a hat. To call in sick so that a cat can inspect an apartment is unheard of.

And what was wrong with me, anyway? If I was so crazy about where I come from, why hadn't I stayed there? Why was it that every time I got what I wanted, I wasn't sure I wanted it? All this time I'd been wanting commitment and now the first whiff of commitment was giving me a blue-eyed smile from across the table.

"That's a good idea," I said. Tony and Amanda, Niki and my clues—they all slipped into the dark recesses of my mind.

I doubt if Tricia believed in sick days. Thursday morning she caught me at the coffee machine.

"You're back for good, I hope. That's two days this week you've called in."

I thought fast for someone who had more important things on her mind. "I realize that, Tricia. But I didn't feel good yesterday morning. Around noon, just when I started feeling well enough to come in, my uncle called. I told you about him. He's a vice president with ———."

Tricia's mouth rounded into a surprised little circle. "Oh! Wonderful! I was going to remind you. And?"

"He wanted to take me to a matinee. I thought that might be better in the long run than coming in here for a half day. Better for the company, I mean."

"It was," she said, nodding approval. "You're thinking like a real fund-raiser. What did you see? I didn't realize there were matinees on Wednesday."

"The Rockettes." This uncle has simple tastes for a zillionaire captain of industry.

"The Rockettes! If he's interested in dance I hope he plans to pay Gotham Ballet a visit."

I slipped my quarter into the machine and punched the BLACK, NO SUGAR button. The cup dropped through the slot, barely ahead of the coffee gusher that followed.

". . . invite him to a performance," Tricia was saying. "We'll get him house seats."

I nodded. Was I going to have to kill this guy off? Maybe a corporate transfer. Brazil's always nice.

Lucky for me the sudden appearance of my officemate diverted Tricia. It sent her, in fact, into a snit she didn't bother concealing. That was the one and only advantage of working with Abigail. Sick days and all, I looked good in comparison. Abigail was twenty minutes late, clutching her coffee change and well into wilting violet mode.

"Oh, my. That subway simply defeats me."

"A real jungle this morning, wasn't it?" I agreed.

Tricia's face was a study in disgust. "Don't you walk? You're not even a mile away."

"I usually do, but—"

"I'm going over to IBM now," Tricia interrupted. "Bonnie, be sure to keep me up to date on your uncle."

I could depend on Abigail not to grill me about my uncle. The minute Tricia's click-clicking heels faded down the hall, she smiled weakly. She seemed to have forgotten our tiff, which was fine with me.

"Did you happen to hear if Michael cast any roles yet for this new ballet?" she asked. "Jonquil's going to miss rehearsal again. That's four days. The poor child can't lift her head off the pillow."

"And a good morning to you," I said. "No, I haven't heard a thing about casting."

"Before I go to the office I'll just run upstairs. Maybe I can catch Michael. Oh, Jonquil's going to call you. She has something of yours."

She sure did. Two hundred dollars. "I'll save her the trouble." The minute I got to my desk I picked up the phone.

The fifth-floor walk-up Abigail and Jonquil shared on West Eighty-third Street wasn't the smallest one-bedroom apartment in Manhattan by any means. For one person it would have been fine. A couple who were wild about each other might have lived there in relative peace for a while, too. But the mother-daughter combination that I knew? How they had survived almost two years was hard to imagine.

At first glance the apartment looked fairly grand, a crumbling remnant of gentility. The ceiling in the small entrance foyer was tremendously high, with ornamental molding at its edges. The rickety modern table that held a telephone and some pens looked oddly out of place. At either side of the foyer were arches, one leading into a box of a kitchen, the other into a living room that was too small and poorly proportioned for its lofty ceilings and bricked-up rococo fireplace. There was a wall where there shouldn't have been one. A door at one end of it opened onto a sliver of a bedroom. And that was it—a chop job by a Manhattan landlord.

Jonquil had been up and around and far from death when I arrived. She was in jeans and a sweatshirt, with her hair in a neat braid.

"Look what I got," she said as I followed her into the living room. She held up a pair of college catalogs, one in either hand, as if they were trophies. New York University and Fordham.

"Good for you," I said, looking around the living room. The furniture was a haphazard mixture—some quite nice, some of dubious ancestry.

"We brought some stuff with us when we moved up here," Jonquil explained. "Mom picked up the rest of it at tag sales."

By then I'd turned and noticed the wall over a crumpled daybed. It was covered with battered dance shoes, their frayed ribbons and elastic bands draped over hooks that were mounted on a pegboard. There must have been a couple of dozen shoes, both pointe and soft.

Jonquil was rattling on about her catalogs and course offerings, oblivious to the collection that was fascinating me. "I picked them up yesterday while Mom was at work. I'm going to apply for next fall. Don't tell her. I haven't broken the bad news yet. Bonnie? You're not listening." She followed my gaze. "Oh. You noticed Mom's collection. Kind of disgusting for a living room wall, isn't it?"

"She collects dance shoes?"

"Yes. Most of them have autographs. Look at these."

Scooting around the daybed, Jonquil carefully removed a worn shoe from its hook. "Maria Tallchief's shoe from *Prodigal Son*. She wore them so soft. See how the shank bends almost in half."

I stared at the faded signature on the silk, captivated.

"She was married to George Balanchine, you know. And here's Suzanne Farrell"—pointing to a pink shoe—"and Natalia Makarova." She grabbed a pair of shoes that had been dyed black. "These are Galena's from her Odile role, and these"—she lifted a tattered soft shoe reverently—"Nureyev's. He wore them in *Afternoon of a Faun*."

I looked from the shoe into Jonquil's face. The cynic, the whiner, the liar—I couldn't see any of them. She was beaming.

"Jonquil," I said, interrupting her, "are you sure you're doing the right thing leaving the ballet? A part of you loves it."

Hanging Nureyev's shoe back on the wall, she sprawled into the cushions that turned the daybed into a sofa. "I don't know, Bonnie. Maybe I'll hate the real world and want to come back. Maybe I'll never get another chance like Michael is giving me. But I have to try it."

I knew Jonquil too well to lecture her, but I had to fight the urge. She had so much that I'd craved. You can't live other people's lives for them, though. And despite what her mother thought, you can't live your life through other people. "I know you have to try. Have you told Michael you're quitting?"

Straightening, she shook her head. "No, and if I go to practice he might cast me in this Balanchine ballet he's rehearsing. I'm afraid to answer the phone. I don't even want to go to the Spencers' party. I know what it's going to be: ballet this, ballet that, all night long." She groaned.

"You can't play sick forever. You're going to have to tell him. And your mother, too," I added.

"That's going to be the hardest part." Her eyes narrowed and she tilted her head coyly. "Do you remember last week, Bonnie, when you promised you'd think about talking to her?"

Her voice had grown softer, more girlish. This was a crafty young woman. Smiling, I shook my head. "That's something you're going to have to do. I remember a lot of promises last week. Most of them weren't kept."

"You're still mad at me?" She threw herself back into the cushions. "That makes everybody. Carmen isn't friends with me anymore. Galena yelled at me Sunday night when I left the stage, and Michael—boy, was that awful. He said I had something special and I was wasting it. He talked about giving me a solo in the second movement of the Balanchine ballet." She rubbed her forehead as if trying to erase a painful memory. "Chris isn't speaking to me, either," she added carelessly.

"Chris?"

"Yeah. That's okay, though. I want to find a boyfriend who reads something besides his own reviews. We were never that serious. I think he was going out with somebody else."

"Why isn't he speaking to you?"

"He blames me for talking him into snorting cocaine before the performance. Actually, he would have been okay if he hadn't gotten nervous and taken something to bring him down. Chris never uses drugs when he's going to dance. He's afraid he'll mess up."

"That's a pretty realistic fear, considering what happened. But I thought Chris was a heavy user."

Jonquil shook her head. "He likes to talk big, but he's not. When I met him last summer all he ever did was smoke a joint every now and then. He got turned on to coke in the fall. For a while he was bragging about it, but underneath he's like the rest of the company. He cares about dancing more than anything else." She picked up one of the catalogs. "I'm going to find something I care that much about. I have an appointment with a counselor at NYU this afternoon. I don't want to be something boring, like an accountant. What do you think of being a writer?"

"Now that's practical. A wide-open field."

Grinning, she said, "I could do articles on dance: 'The Rise and Fall of Nikolai Koslov.'"

"You may have something there," I said with a smile. "But speaking of accounting . . ."

"Right!" She slapped her hand to her forehead. "Your money is hidden in the bedroom closet. I didn't want to have to explain it to my mom."

While Jonquil was in the bedroom I went back to the wall of shoes. I can't explain why, but they were so much more fascinating than a collection of autographed photos would have been. These shoes, some of them not much more than shreds of silk, had encased the feet of the most famous dancers of the last thirty years. Margot Fonteyn's shoe was pinned to a yellowing program from *The Sleeping Beauty*, and—I lifted a pair of shoes from their hook. How glittery they were, covered with a sparkling paste.

"Those are my mom's glass slippers," Jonquil said as she walked into the room. "She danced *Cinderella* with the Atlanta Ballet when they went on tour."

How surprising! I knew that Abigail had studied but I had no idea she'd reached the performance level. "She never talks about that time in her life," I said.

"It makes her sad. She met my dad right after that tour. They got married and I was born and she decided to take a year off, and then my grandmother got sick and Mom had to take care of her. . . ."

"Her mother?"

"Yes. My Granny Foote. Anyway"—she shrugged—"that was the end of it. The problem with ballet is you can't take a couple of years off and do normal family things."

Jonquil counted out ten twenty-dollar bills for me. "I was a pretty crummy roommate, wasn't I?"

Tucking the money into my purse, I started for the door. "The worst."

She looked sheepish. "I'm not usually like that. Things will be different once I'm doing what I want to do."

The phone rang while we were in the foyer. Jonquil grimaced. "What if it's Michael?"

"You can't stay hidden."

She picked up the phone as if it was a hot potato. As she listened her expression darkened.

"I've been out a lot," she said quietly. "Yes, sir. Let me get some paper." She pulled a pad of paper from under the phone—a Gala Affair notepad. Glancing my way, she whispered, "Mom brought home tons of these," then turned back to the phone. "Where is your office?"

The foyer was so small that I couldn't miss the address she wrote on the tablet. It was one I knew well: the address of Tony's precinct.

Carmen had planned to see Tony earlier that week. Now he wanted to talk to Jonquil. It had to be something Carmen had said, but what? Had she somehow implicated Jonquil in Niki's murder? Or in pushing her into traffic? Jonquil was capable of sneaking into her roommate's wallet for money. Would she have been capable of sneaking into a prop room and cutting Niki's hitch? Did Tony know that her blood type matched that found on the cut hitch?

As I hurried down Columbus Avenue toward Lincoln Center I grew more and more concerned. Jonquil and I had our problems, and she wasn't about to win any Miss Reliability awards from me, but I hated to think of her as a murderer.

It was almost two o'clock when I walked into my office. I had a desk full of work but I could hardly keep my mind on it.

Abigail was doing what she generally did with the papers on her desk: stacking them, moving them, staring down at them glassy-eyed. Still, I found myself looking at her differently. It was not a grudging respect I felt or even understanding. Maybe it was that trace of affinity. Like me, this woman had once managed to put heart, soul, and body into her own future as a dancer. Like me, she hadn't made it. As she bent over the bottom drawer of a file cabinet, I studied her.

Physically, there was almost nothing to suggest Cinderella, even before the glass slippers. Though she was not fat, her waist had thickened with time. Only the muscles in her calves hinted at the ex-ballerina. And her feet. That easy turnout.

Why had I always kept Abigail on a "back burner" of suspects? One reason was that she'd refused the pass I'd offered her. Not that returning to the office unseen and taking a pass from my desk would have presented much of a problem for her, but . . . Abigail? The woman who could barely maneuver a piece of paper out of an envelope and into a file cabinet? Hatching a plot and carrying it through takes energy.

In a way, though, Abigail's entire existence was a scheme. Wasn't she always calculating, trying to manipulate anyone who might help Jonquil's career?

"Abigail?"

She turned slightly to the right. Her left foot stayed planted on the floor.

"Forget it."

I moved my officemate to a front burner.

All afternoon I kept telling myself that Tony was on the job, that he didn't need my assistance. I gave myself stern lectures about interfering. They didn't help. By four o'clock my amateur detective demon was in control.

Michael was rehearsing the new ballet in the same studio where I'd first seen Niki. The class was just breaking up when I got there. Boys and girls, towels around their necks, were slipping on the leg warmers and sneakers that littered the edges of the floor. All of them looked tired and a couple, miserable. Galena, that pillar of strength, was holding her sides and panting. As I walked to where Carmen was sitting against the far wall, I passed a girl wrapping bandages around bleeding toes and a boy rubbing his calf and cursing quietly.

Carmen was lacing her tennis shoes. She was soaked with perspiration, but compared to the others she looked good. I sank down next to her. "Can we talk for a second?"

She nodded. Though she didn't look up, her elated smile was obvious. "Sure. I've got to tell you something." She glanced around furtively. "I've got to tell it to somebody."

"What is it?"

"I'm the best one," she said softly. "A little while ago Michael made everyone watch me because I was the only one doing Balanchine's steps fast enough and getting them right. You know what, Bonnie?"

"What?"

"There's a pas de trois in the second movement, two boys and a girl. The girl does a long solo and Michael keeps rehearsing me in her steps." She tightened the bow on her sneakers. "This is mean, but I'm glad Jonquil's sick. Just because she has longer legs Michael would probably give her the part even if she couldn't do it."

"I doubt that. Did you see Detective LaMarca?"

"Sure. On Tuesday. Why?"

"I thought you were going as soon as you got back. You're awfully casual about your life."

She answered with a shrug. "I gave him your note. He said to give you this," she added, reaching into her bag. "I stopped by your office with it yesterday but you were out."

I ripped the envelope open. Thank God I didn't read it aloud. "Thanks," he'd written. "But Chris Lansing's alibi checks out and your information from Brighton Beach is all hearsay. Now drop it, PLEASE!" "PLEASE" was underscored three times. The bastard! After the way I'd helped him in the past. Not to mention the fact that he'd indirectly met his future wife through me. I just hoped Amanda went through every dime he brought home.

"I told him everything," Carmen was saying. "The stuff I told you, and the other stuff."

"Other stuff?" I gave the girl a long look. "You didn't tell me about 'other stuff.'" Silly, but I was hurt. I took pride in my detecting ability.

She looked away. "I was scared you might tell somebody

and pretty soon the whole company would know. I mean, I trust you, but . . . you know."

"So tell me now," I said, hoping I sounded detached. "What's the 'other stuff'?"

She shook her head. "I promised Lieutenant LaMarca I wouldn't talk about it."

"I'm sure he didn't mean you couldn't talk to me."

"He said especially you." A big grin spread over the girl's face. "Lieutenant LaMarca said that sometimes you get in over your head and you should let the police do their job."

"He said that about *me?* So let him do his damn job! Who wants to talk about that boring nonsense anyway."

"Yeah," she said, getting to her feet. "Let's talk about clothes. What are you wearing to the Spencers' on Saturday night?"

"I don't know. Tricia said to dress up but the invitation said 'casual.'"

"I'm not going casual, not to their apartment. They're so rich they even have their own pool. Wait until you see my dress. It's unbelievable!"

"They don't have their own pool. They rent their condo pool for the afternoon."

"It's almost the same thing."

We had reached the hall. Carmen's "other stuff" was still knocking around in my head. I couldn't let her go without a last try. "Did you tell Lieutenant LaMarca something to make him want to question Jonquil?"

"I told him the truth," she said defensively. "I'm not trying to get her arrested or anything. I wouldn't lie just to get a role." She started walking away.

"What's the truth about Jonquil?"

"I told you I'm not supposed to talk about it."

"I think everybody's going to know pretty soon. He's called her down to the precinct."

Carmen turned back to me. "It's her own fault," she

grumbled. "Do you swear you won't tell anybody else, not until the police know for sure?"

"I swear."

"When I went to see Lieutenant LaMarca he asked me who else knew that the woman I saw near Props might not be the Polish lady. Well, there was you, but you didn't find out until after I got kicked into the street. The only other one was Jonquil. I told her on Wednesday afternoon, the day after I saw the television special about Niki. Somebody tried to kill me the next night."

16

"Another gin and tonic, miss?"

I opened my eyes. One of the young bartenders stood over me, smiling. The late afternoon sun beamed through the glass enclosure that covered the Spencers' pool, shading his face, shining on mine.

My swim had relaxed me until I felt as if I would melt into the padded chaise longue. Another gin and tonic and I just might. I smiled at the bartender. "Yes, please."

That morning the prospect of appearing in a bathing suit with this crowd had given me a good-size anxiety attack. It is disturbing, to say the least, when you're one of the few people around who can "pinch an inch." I must have looked okay in my bright blue maillot, though. Derek's eye hadn't roved too far afield.

"What time is it?" asked Galena. She was stretched, a long sinew in a black one-piece, on the chair next to mine.

"Almost five-thirty, madame."

Galena was a "madame." Her muscle-fat ratio was in better shape than mine but I was still a "miss." The waiter placed the fresh drink on the little white platform attached to the arm of my chair. "Thank you."

Five-thirty. Almost time to start dressing for cocktails. It seemed only minutes earlier that I'd settled into the chair. The invitation had read, "Surf's up at the Spencers', from three till the wee small hours." Derek and I, arriving a stylish hour late, had found the party in full swing. Swimming is one of the few sports ballet dancers can indulge in, and Gotham's dancers— particularly the younger ones—were taking full advantage of the Spencers' generosity. The activity in the kidney-shaped pool showed no sign of letting up.

Derek, in the deck chair on my other side, leaned toward me: "This has to be costing a fortune. How many restaurants does this guy own?"

"Two that I know of. He can take this party as a tax write-off," I added knowingly.

It really was some party—the kind that makes society page gossip columns. The idea of living in a building with a rooftop pool was incomprehensible to me. To rent that pool, complete with dressing rooms for an afternoon and evening, to hire waiters to indulge your guests' every need—write-off or not, this was an expensive proposition. Downstairs in the Spencers' reportedly lavish condo a staff of kitchen help was slaving over a buffet dinner for us.

Billy Spencer looked my way from across the pool. He was mixing drinks at a bar that had been set up on the wood deck. Our introduction had been mechanical, but when I smiled he waved back so affably you'd have thought we were old friends.

I'd expected an older Billy Spencer, fawning, maybe a little dotty. That would have fit my idea of a rich husband with a wandering wife. I certainly hadn't been prepared for Billy. He was a big, rock-jawed type with a thatch of prematurely white hair and a terrific tan. His build was that of an ex-athlete, gone paunchy. There was a certain polish to him, but it hadn't turned him into a jewel. He struck me as a stone rubbed smooth on its surface but still rough at the core.

Our hostess was at the shallow end of the pool talking to Carmen and some of the other young dancers. Isabella Spencer was quite taken with the dancers—more so than her husband. She may have been as silly as Tricia claimed but I found her pleasant enough. Her tinkling laugh continually floated over the pool. She was always in motion, a flutter of nervous mannerisms. In a malnourished way she was attractive. Her light brown hair framed a face that, when younger, must have been like that of a cute ten-year-old, with tiny features and almost translucent skin. But at somewhere around forty that gamine look showed strain. When I'd seen her at the gala she'd looked better—not necessarily younger but fresher. Now there were dark hollows around her eyes and her face seemed drawn. Maybe it was too many parking lots and too much Chris.

Speaking of Chris, he was unusually subdued, hardly stirring from a deck chair. Jonquil wasn't the only one the company black sheep was ignoring. Isabella got the same treatment. I watched her climb from the pool and walk past Chris. He purposefully closed his eyes.

When the group at the shallow end broke up, Carmen dog-paddled breathlessly to the side where we were sitting.

"This is the kind of apartment I'm going to live in when I get married," she announced, hanging on to the edge with both hands.

"Me too," Derek and Galena chorused.

Picking up my gin and tonic, I said, "Marry well."

"Of course," Carmen responded, as if anything else was inconceivable.

"We all do," said Galena. "Once or twice."

Turning her back, Carmen dog-paddled away. Like many city kids she wasn't much of a swimmer. At the deep end of the pool she stayed within a cautious foot from the edge.

Jonquil was poised on the edge of the diving board,

fingertips touching over her head. Her white bikini had cost its manufacturer, at most, a square foot of cloth. Though Jonquil wouldn't have admitted it, I suspected the suit was a slap at her mother. Abigail hadn't arrived. When she did she would be the only parent at the party, something that could not have made her rebellious daughter happy.

"Such a performance last week," Galena said, nodding at the girl on the board. "Michael threatened to suspend her."

"Why didn't he?"

"He likes that 'coltish' look of hers. All legs. A shame the way he's neglected some of the others trying to bring Jonquil along. She doesn't work hard enough."

"I'm not sure she cares. And Chris? Did Michael do anything about him?"

Galena shrugged. "Male dancers are not so plentiful as female. Male dancers who are good partners are rare creatures. I doubt if Michael did more than talk to Chris. Perhaps Chris has learned his lesson. He was dreadfully embarrassed about his performance. He called me and apologized the next evening. Took me to dinner." She grinned mischievously. "A shame he's not older."

I laughed. "That might not matter to him."

"Ah," she said, looking across the pool at our hostess. "You've heard those rumors too."

"Galena. Here you are. My favorite ballerina."

Galena gave our host a twenty-watt smile. "But you say that to all of us, darling."

He did. That was only one of Billy Spencer's conversational oddities. There was also his strange habit of reverse bragging, and of throwing in the listener's name at every opportunity.

"You people doing okay? Enjoying this little mud puddle of ours, Bonnie Jean?"

He glanced away before he finished the sentence, and I was only half sure I'd heard right. Bonnie Jean? Where in the world had he come up with that? The only time I use my middle name is when I'm trying to be forceful. Had I actually introduced myself as Bonnie Jean Indermill?

"Nice bunch of kids, aren't they, Galena?" he said, watching Jonquil make a smooth dive. The girl swam as if she had learned young and well. As she crossed the pool she passed the panting, paddling Carmen without slowing.

"Did you get to any of our performances last week?" Galena asked. "You have a house in the Berkshires, don't you?"

"Shack's more like it. I made opening and closing night. Most of the time I was driving back and forth to the city watching out for things here. Isabella's the real fan. She went to almost every performance."

As he was speaking, a sickish feeling began knotting my stomach. "This is Bonnie Jean Indermill," I heard myself shouting into the phone at Primrose Cottage. "I know what you are and . . ."

"You must have had two cars up there," I said.

Galena frowned, bewildered by my comment. Billy didn't seem the least bewildered. He answered readily.

"We drove up in my wife's BMW, Bonnie Jean. I keep an old wreck up there for running around in."

He was looking me right in the eye, and there seemed to be a challenge in his cold stare. It almost dared me to ask what kind of "old wreck" he kept. I was so shaken by this that I was mute. Looking past me, Billy said, "Derek, I hear you're an artist. You exhibiting anywhere? We've picked up a few little pieces here and there, but there's always room . . ."

"Well, in fact—" Derek began.

"Billy!"

The voice that carried from the other side of the pool, interrupting Derek, belonged to my boss. Tricia, of the great self-control, rushed our benefactor with arms outstretched, a thousand-watt smile lighting up her face. She was in a disastrous mauve print dress that made her skin look yellow and her figure squat. I don't know why, but Tricia's clothing mistake made me feel kind of sad for her.

In her field she made no mistakes. She was an artist. She gave a Billy for every Tricia she got. "I hope you're making your famous barbecue sauce for us this year, Billy," she said, shamelessly courting the man she'd described as a Neanderthal. "I've looked forward to it for weeks." When the two wandered off arm in arm, I glanced at Derek. He must have recognized the confusion in my expression but he gave it his own interpretation.

"I may kill that woman," he said under his breath. "Who is she?"

"My boss. Please don't kill her."

Galena laughed. "You'll get another chance at Billy later. Or his wife. She's the art lover. He's the money." Sighing, Galena waved toward the waiter. "For me, this could be a long evening. Not one available man over thirty. I may become quite drunk."

I stood up. Maybe Billy had gotten that Bonnie Jean business from the address list. I'd seen the list before Elliott sent it over, and I was almost positive my middle name hadn't been on it. To be sure, though, I had to look at my invitation.

"Where are you going?" Derek asked.

"To the dressing room. I want to change."

The women's dressing room was at the far end of the pool, away from the elevator and reception area. The attendant wasn't at her desk when I walked inside, but she'd propped a gray metal chair against the door to the locker area to hold it open. I retrieved my things and went straight into my purse.

Bonnie Indermill. That's how my invitation was addressed. Not Bonnie Jean. Tucking the envelope away, I took a fluffy white towel from a rack. As I let the warm shower rain over me, my mind was in a frenzy of speculation.

Could it be that Chris was getting more than anyone realized from Isabella Spencer? When Chris had climbed into the BMW in the church parking lot, maybe my initial notion had been right. Maybe he *had* been meeting a drug contact. Isabella had been backstage the night of the gala. Twice, in fact. Had Isabella put the drugs in Niki's dressing table? Was she the reason for Chris's questions about the investigation? And while she was on the lower level, had she made her way into the prop room?

"And this is Billy's study," Isabella Spencer said.

Our hostess was leading some of her first-time guests from room to room, letting us admire the results of her efforts at conspicuous consumption.

I've never had the money to give serious thought to decor. As a child my taste was molded at Sears. It was later honed to its fine edge at secondhand stores and flea markets. I was probably not Isabella Spencer's ideal audience.

There was a glossy magazine–spread look to the Spencers' apartment—a rather "California" look of pastel fabrics and modern paintings in light, airy colors.

"Isn't that abstract over the desk amusing?"

We all nodded dutifully, amused as anything. *Amusing* was one of Isabella's words: "I thought this fabric was so amusing"; "Ordinarily I don't care for ultramodern, but this chair is amusing."

"I picked it up in Soho." As she walked behind her husband's desk to straighten the picture, she nodded at the wall behind us. "Those photos are Billy's restaurants."

We turned obediently to a series of framed black-and-white photos. How amusing. Billy behind the bar, cocktail shaker aloft, Billy drawing beer, Billy smiling over a chef's shoulder, Billy greeting celebrities, Billy greeting—I did a double take—Nikolai Koslov and his starlet date at Dos Sombreros.

"El Sombrero in the Village was the first," she said. "Early this year we opened Dos Sombreros. I chose the decor. Mexican's so amusing, isn't it?"

Hilarious. I'd had no idea Billy owned Dos Sombreros. I leaned close to the photo. "I think I was there the night this picture was taken." The night, though I didn't say it, that Chris disappeared into the restaurant looking for the Old Man.

Isabella's smile sagged. She clasped her fingers almost as if she was praying. "Poor Niki. I still cry when I think about him. I was backstage before the gala." She loosened her fingers and gazed sadly at them. "He kissed my hand. Such a beautiful man."

I nodded agreement, looking at yet another hand blessed by those hot Russian lips. Such beautiful hands Isabella had. Probably never touched a dirty dish or— "Oh!" I said suddenly. "Your gloves. I just remembered them. Did you get them back? I found them after the gala."

Isabella's damp gloves had come back to me in a leap of memory. I wasn't trying to startle her. But there was an all-but-invisible flinch, a sudden recoiling of her head. Or did I imagine it? She was a nervous woman.

"Gloves?" she responded after a hesitation. "I don't know what you mean. You must have me confused with someone else." Nodding at the photos, she said, "Billy spends a lot of time in his restaurants. Tending bar amuses him!"

A bell rang somewhere in the apartment. "Din din," our hostess said brightly.

I may have imagined the flinch but I hadn't imagined the gloves. They matched her gown. Why would Isabella lie about them? As she crossed the room I scooted from behind a chair so I could watch her walk. It was impossible. Her feet poked from beneath long, wide-legged turquoise pants. My effort must have been pretty obvious, though. Halfway across the rug she paused. Glancing up at her face, I realized she was staring down at her feet. She looked back at me, mystified.

"I was admiring your shoes," I said quickly. "They're lovely."

Her shoes were the least conspicuous item on her person: black patent sandals.

"Thank you. They're Italian. From Milan, you know."

Of course. Where else?

Sunset from the Spencers' terrace was a red-and-gold spectacular. After that came a twilight of soft, cool breezes and a million flickering lights as New York City put on its nightly show.

The show inside the Spencers' apartment almost rivaled it. Casual? No way. I'd made do with new rose linen slacks and a pink silk shirt. I was adequate but no showstopper. Carmen was.

A photographer's flash caught the girl as she sauntered into the living room in four-inch heels and that glittery red number I'd had my eye on in the Berkshires. Her dark hair had been teased into a mass of wanton curls. She looked five years older than she had in the pool.

Derek and I were at a table on the terrace. He stared through the open doors in disbelief. "That's the same kid? She's seventeen?"

As she walked across the living room she took a glass of champagne from a tray. By the time she reached the terrace she'd finished it and taken a second one from a passing waiter.

"That's quite a dress, Carmen," I said.

"You don't think I went too far, do you?"

She was looking my way but her eyes kept sneaking over to Derek. "He's cute," she had whispered to me at the pool. His approval mattered more than mine.

"You look spectacular." He pushed an empty chair toward her. "Join us?"

"I can't sit. I don't want to wrinkle my dress." She downed the second glass of champagne, then said with a giggle, "Oooo, I'm getting bubbles in my brain. I had one of these while I was dressing. This makes three."

Once a chaperone, always a chaperone. "You're supposed to sip it," I said.

"Not tonight. It's now or never. If I don't get a date I'm

through trying. I'll devote my life to my art." She waved her empty glass at the waiter. He quickly replaced it with a full one.

"You may get more than a date."

"I better. When my daddy sees the bill for this dress he's going to have a fit. I didn't dare show him the dress. Do you think Joey noticed me?"

"I'm sure he did. Look." I nodded across the room. Joey and a few other dancers had gathered around Michael and Galena on a big, curved sofa. "He keeps glancing this way. Why don't you go join them?"

She considered this, then shook her head. "I can't talk to Michael."

"You talk to Michael all the time," I said.

"That's about dancing. I couldn't have a real conversation." She slumped against my chair. "Would you go over there and mingle, Bonnie? You could whisper a message to Joey."

"No way. You whisper your own message. I'm going to mingle around the food."

At that moment Isabella Spencer joined Michael and the others on the sofa. Derek abruptly put down his glass of champagne and pushed back his chair. "It's now or never for me, too," he said. "I'm going to engage Mrs. Spencer in a talk about *my* art. What's your message, Carmen? I'll deliver it."

He took her arm and they left the terrace together. At the other side of the glass doors she whispered in his ear. A second later Derek joined the group around the marble table. Pulling Joey aside, he said something. Joey nodded, glanced at his watch, and turned back to Michael.

When I recall the next part of the evening there's little order to my thoughts. For a while the sick fear I'd felt earlier disappeared into the swirl of lights, laughter, and music. My memories leap about as the Spencers' party did, in ever-changing bursts. At its height there must have been fifty or sixty people in the living room alone. I remember the continual swirl of movement, the ebbing and flowing of voices. A crowd on the terrace one moment, an empty terrace the next. Guests clustering briefly and then breaking apart, wandering, food and drinks in hand.

Some vivid random memories: Tricia gleefully holding up a sesame-dipped chicken leg and calling to Elliott, "Wouldn't Niki have enjoyed this!" And Isabella Spencer's hand resting against Derek's arm as he jotted his name in her address book.

I briefly found myself in the peculiar position of watching Chris and Isabella Spencer pretend they hardly knew each other. "Of course I remember you from last year. I've become familiar with your work," she cooed. "I absolutely adore your Siegfried."

Ah, yes. His Siegfried. And his pectorals and his surfer smile. So amusing. I'd thought Chris impervious to embarrassment. He wasn't. He blushed.

I remember Elliott, looking like Howdy Doody in a bow tie and plaid jacket, scowling as he watched Carmen down another glass of champagne. "I suppose I'm the only one here who thinks we should put her in a cab and send her home," he grumbled. How carelessly I answered him: "I'll keep an eye on Carmen."

And I recall the reporter who sported an ID badge from a well-known magazine, how he interrupted Elliott to ask if we were "anybody." We weren't, but many guests were. The reporter had a photographer companion whose bursting flash gave the party a Fourth of July feeling.

"Looks like she's trying to change her image," I heard a soloist say when Jonquil walked into the room.

She looked almost touchingly young and innocent. The high lace collar on her blue dress played up her youth. Her red hair, pulled back by a blue satin headband, hung past her shoulders. Alice in Wonderland had replaced the punk girl in the tight black pants.

From that point, my memories are more crystallized, some of them into sharp, brutal points.

Abigail arrived just a few minutes after her daughter. I remember I was with Tricia near the table where a chef was serving Billy's barbecued ribs. Isabella was a few feet away, again talking to Derek. How far would he go to get one of his paintings on her wall, I wondered?

"The life of the party has arrived," Tricia muttered sarcastically.

Abigail had made an effort. Her green dress looked new and she'd had her hair done. Her gray, like mine, was momentarily vanquished. She crossed the living room, latched onto her daughter's arm, took a plate of food from Jonquil's hand, and lost no time steering the girl toward the photographer. Her movements were so deliberate she might have rehearsed them.

Unlike me, Abigail knew exactly what she wanted from life. She was a mess, certainly, but she was a focused mess. Had she been a wonderful Cinderella, I wondered? Had the audience been in her palm as the clock struck twelve and she fled her prince, slippers glimmering across the stage?

Glass shattered behind me, startling me back to the present.

"Oh!" our hostess cried softly.

I glanced over my shoulder. Tricia was helping Isabella wipe a spot of barbecue sauce from her blouse.

"No, no. Ignore it," Isabella said absently as Derek bent to pick up the plate she'd dropped onto a marble table. "The maid will get it."

Isabella's translucent skin looked almost ashen. Her gaze was directed across the room, where, in front of the fireplace, the photographer was snapping Jonquil's picture. Abigail stood by, talking to the reporter.

"You must have met Jonquil Jeffreys in the pool," said Tricia, amused. "You didn't recognize her in that dress."

"And the other woman?" Isabella asked.

I didn't hear Tricia's answer. Billy Spencer was at my side, all suntan, smirk, and red Hawaiian print shirt.

"What do you think of those ribs, Bonnie Jean? That sauce is my own recipe."

"Delicious. Please call me Bonnie. I don't often use my middle name."

He smiled. There were small pads of fat at the corners of his mouth. I found his smile scary—a smile the class bully gives a cowed sixth grader. "But you do sometimes, don't you. Enjoy your ribs, Bonnie Jean. Tricia," he said pushing past me, "I hear it costs a bundle to underwrite a new ballet. I know some people who wouldn't mind putting in a few bucks. Let's go hide out in my den. . . ."

The queasy feeling was back, a dozen times worse. Was I going nuts or what? Either my perceptions were totally messed up, or this man knew I knew it was his answering machine I'd left a threatening message on. And he didn't care!

The room suddenly seemed too crowded, too noisy. I ditched the ribs into a waste can and began wandering slowly toward the back of the apartment.

At a quiet corner in the hall I stood for a moment, trying to assemble my thoughts. It wasn't hard to imagine Billy Spencer dealing drugs, but it was almost impossible to visualize his wife cutting Niki's hitch. With Chris's instructions she might have been able to get into Props and find Niki's hitch, but my mental picture went fuzzy when it got to Isabella tugging the harness from the shelf, taking a razor from her bag, and slicing through those nylon threads. Isabella was not the tugging and slicing type, and the job wasn't one she could have given to the maid.

I needed proof; I had none. I'd lied to Elliott about the dents in the van. How could I change my story and tell him that a patron—a patron who might underwrite a new ballet yet!—had tried pushing the van off a cliff? And it would amount to career suicide to even hint that the Spencers and

Chris might be tied to Niki's murder and to an attempt on Carmen's life.

I thought again of Isabella's lily-white hands, and those fine, damp gloves. Why had she lied?

For a moment the fuzzing cleared. A scenario appeared as if on a theater screen.

Isabella has worn the gloves to the gala. When she goes into Props, she leaves them on as a precaution to avoid getting prints on Niki's hitch. As she cuts through the nylon stitches, she gashes through a glove, deep into her flesh. Crimson blood seeps into the heavy silk. Isabella blanches. (Isabella would blanch.) She finishes and hurries to a rest room to rinse the glove. Speed is vital. She was seen earlier at the reception. She has to get back before she's missed. In her rush the glove becomes soaked. The blood stain clings. Later, during the chaos of the gala, Isabella misplaces the telltale glove.

Here's where the picture on my screen blurred again. Which was more dangerous for Isabella? Would she retrieve the gloves, thus identifying them as hers? Or would she leave them in the lost and found and live with the fear they and the damning bloodstain might be discovered?

What would I have done? In her place I probably would have retrieved them. Of course, in Isabella's place I would have destroyed them instantly, too. In Isabella's place, when I really considered what her place was, I wouldn't have cut the hitch at all! Isabella Spencer wrestling a harness from a shelf? For what? For love? To get rid of her boyfriend's competition? To get rid of a possible threat to her husband?

As I leaned against the wall, lost in thought, a couple of ballerinas passed. They were coming from the rear of the apartment.

"Wouldn't you kill for a bedroom like hers?" one of them was asking.

Someone had put rock music on the stereo. The party was growing more boisterous. I was sure nobody noticed when I bypassed the guest bathroom and slipped into the back hall.

The Spencers had their own rooms. On our tour Isabella had called them "chambers." "Anyone here?" I said softly at the door to Isabella's chamber. The room was quiet. Floor-length white chiffon curtains billowed in from the terrace. The walls and the thick carpets were white, the bedspread pale lavender. I went in and closed the door, blocking the bright light from the hall.

The room was dim now, lit only by a thin pink bulb shining from a bedside lamp. I turned the lock, crept across the floor, and peeked into Isabella's gigantic bathroom. It was empty. Black porcelain fixtures shone eerily in the pink light.

My chances of finding Isabella's gloves, much less of finding them with bloodstains, were slim. I had to try, though. I went through her two closets quickly. The Empire gown was in a plastic cleaner's bag. Lifting the plastic, I ran my hands over the cloth. It poured through my fingers like fresh cream. I felt across the hanger for a pair of gloves. They weren't there.

Isabella's modern chest of drawers opened easily, almost soundlessly. The music concealed the slight noise I made as I went through it. I searched through scarfs in the top drawer, lingerie farther down. I bent to reach a bottom drawer.

A noise startled me. My heartbeat quickened. Spinning, I looked around the room. It was empty and ghostly, with faint light and billowing curtains. I turned back to the drawer.

Sweaters, in the softest cashmeres imaginable, in so many colors I was mesmerized.

I didn't see anyone behind me, but I felt someone and then there was a thing, a looming shape. A powerful hand clamped over my wrist. My face grew hot and my legs quaked.

"What the hell are you doing?" Chris whispered.

I collapsed onto the carpet. "If you don't let go I'll scream," I said weakly.

Chris knelt beside me, his face inches from mine. "You'll scream? You're the one who's going through our hostess's clothes. I doubt if anybody would hear you from back here anyway, with that music."

I tried to pull my arm free. He held tight. "I was looking for something," I said weakly.

"What? Maybe I can help." He stared into my eyes and for a moment I was frozen by fear. Chris was so strong. If he put those hands around my neck . . .

"How did you get in?" I asked, a meaningless question, but I needed time to collect my wits.

He glanced at the billowing curtains. "The terrace comes around this side of the building. When you were talking to Billy you looked upset. You disappeared back here and I got nervous."

His grip had loosened. Pushing my heels into the carpet, I scooted back until my spine dug into the dresser. Chris looked down at his hand. "You're afraid of me? I'd never hurt a woman." He let his fingers go almost slack.

I didn't say anything.

"If I let go," he said softly, "can we talk calmly? I'd like to settle this mess before it gets worse."

I couldn't imagine things getting much worse, but I nodded. He dropped my wrist.

"All right," he said. "Tell me what you think you're doing in here."

I took a deep gulp of air before I spoke. "Your friend Billy Spencer is the Old Man, isn't he?"

Chris shrugged. "So the guy has a little side business. What's the big deal?"

"The big deal?" I repeated, incredulous. "He tried to run my van off the road. That's the big deal. And you're the one who told him how to find me, aren't you?"

A flicker of pain creased his forehead. "Bonnie, I swear I didn't know what he planned to do. He asked me if I knew Bonnie Jean Indermill. I've talked to him since then. He doesn't want trouble. He's happy to drop it if you are."

Chris smiled, that same surfer smile. "Think about it," he said. "There's no real harm done."

I was jolted by a memory. Given a different night,

different surroundings, I might have ended up in the Thritty Inn with this shallow kid. My fear subsided, anger taking its place.

"No real harm? How can you say that? You and Isabella are involved in such a terrible mess—"

"What are you?" he demanded. "The Moral Majority? Billy doesn't care who she fools around with. Why should you? Tell you the truth I wish I'd never seen either of them. She won't leave me alone and he scares the hell out of me." As he said this his gaze wandered. He looked past my shoulder and raised his hand to his head.

I turned to see what had distracted him. Good God! There was a full-length mirror on the door next to the chest. Chris was admiring his own reflection.

"Sorry," he said when he caught me watching him. "A professional hazard. What have I been doing with Isabella that's got you so upset, anyway? I thought you weren't interested in me."

I had never figured Chris for overly sensitive or, for that matter, overly intelligent, but could he possibly be this indifferent to murder? I went on, but the theory I'd put together minutes before was being eroded by doubts.

"Let's start with the books Niki had in his dressing table," I said. "He had just checked them out of the library. You weren't backstage all day but you knew the titles of those books. Gift-wrapped drugs were found in the drawer with the library books. Your girlfriend and her husband deal drugs."

He started to say something. I held up my hand. "Let me finish. Isabella Spencer was on her way to your room with a bon voyage present. She wandered into the wrong dressing room."

"Okay, okay," he groaned. "The drugs were for me. The note was for me. Isabella saw the books and asked me why I was reading them. What's so . . ." Suddenly Chris straightened. His eyes widened. "Oh, no. You're not thinking Isabella went into Props?"

I nodded. His handsome features drooped. He opened his mouth in protest but there were no words.

"She was wearing gloves," I said. "She got blood on one of them while she was cutting Niki's harness. She tried rinsing the glove. I found it later. It was still wet." And then I lied. "I saw the stain but I didn't realize it was blood."

Chris's head was moving slowly back and forth. "You're wrong," he said, but there was a note of desperation in his voice. "You're right about the drugs but you're wrong about the rest of it. She wouldn't any more kill Niki than you would. She thought he was terrific."

"Then why did you keep asking me about the investigation? It wasn't just curiosity."

Chris hesitated. I spotted the beginnings of that surfer smile. I glared and it vanished. He averted his eyes and stared into space as if a struggle was going on in him.

"Isabella might have seen something while she was on the lower level," he finally admitted. "All along I told her she'd be better off going to the police. She didn't want to because so many people knew about us. She was scared somebody would connect her with the drugs. Some of Billy's friends aren't exactly strangers to the police," he added.

No doubt the same friends he was telling Tricia about right then, the ones willing to finance a new ballet. "What was it Isabella saw?" I asked.

"Are you going to your policeman friend with this?"

"Probably."

Chris leaned back on his elbows and began flexing his feet. "What the hell! I'm tired of worrying about this. It's messing up my concentration. When Isabella left Niki's room she got her directions screwed up. It's easy if you've never been down there," he added, as if defending her. "She was looking for the stairs so she could get back to the reception when she saw a woman going through an exit door. The woman didn't notice her. Isabella decided maybe she was better off going outside and walking around to the theater entrance. When she grabbed the doorknob, her hand slipped. Isabella thought she'd gotten stage makeup or paint on her glove until it came out in the news that there had been blood on Niki's hitch. Then she realized she might have seen the murderer. The woman Isabella saw—she wasn't that KGB officer."

I felt as if an icy hand had gripped my spine. "Paige Davenport," I whispered. I went numb thinking about what I'd overlooked. It was a moment before I could push myself to my feet.

"Who? Where are you going?" Chris said as I unlocked the bedroom door. "You're not planning to cause trouble here, are you?"

Dread energized me. I was already out the master suite door, racing down the carpeted hall.

The music was loud, the lights turned down. Some couples were dancing. The living room was more crowded than ever.

Tricia was talking to Isabella. I hurried over to her. "Have you seen Carmen?"

She looked around, then shook her head.

Where had Derek gone to? Our host was with Michael. So was Carmen's friend Joey. I didn't see Jonquil. Or her mother. I finally spotted Derek by the kitchen door. Pushing through the crowd, I grabbed his arm.

"I can't find Carmen. What was the message you gave Joey."

"'I know where Mrs. Spencer keeps the key to the roof. Meet me at the pool at ten.'" He glanced at his watch, then looked across the room. "It's ten after. Joey's going to be late."

"Please come with me. I've got to be sure she's okay."

The rooftop door was open. Derek and I had just stepped through it when we heard the splash. We ran past the deserted clubhouse reception desk, past the men's locker room, straight for the pool.

The lights were out. Across the roof a shadow darted near

the women's locker, then everything was still. The pool shimmered under the moonlight, and at the end where the water was deepest a solitary figure floated facedown on the surface. A shaft of light played across shining red cloth and lit a floating black halo of hair.

I was around the deck and in the water in an instant. Derek was only seconds behind. I reached Carmen first and yanked her face above the surface. Between us we pulled her to the side. I was climbing onto the edge when there were footsteps on the deck.

"Carmen? What's . . . Oh, man!"

"Joey," I gasped. "There's a phone at the desk. Call the police quick."

We got the girl out of the water and stretched her over a deck chair. Water poured from her mouth and nose. A stream of blood trickled across her forehead. There was a cough, and another. She gagged, struggling for breath.

"The cops are on their way," Joey said as he hurried back. Squatting next to Carmen, he put his hand on her shoulder. The girl caught her breath. A moment later she was sobbing.

Rising, Derek started for the men's locker. "I'm going to get some towels."

I sat with Carmen until her sobs quieted. When her breaths were deep and regular I left her with Joey and walked toward the women's dressing room.

Stepping past the deserted attendant's station, I paused at the door to the lockers. It was still propped open by the metal chair.

"Abigail?" I called.

Only the *plonk plonk* of a dripping shower broke the quiet. At the entrance to the locker area I slid my fingers along the wall, hunting for a light switch. There was none. The switches must have been at the attendant's desk. I stepped through the door into semidarkness. The only light came through narrow windows near the ceiling. They were crisscrossed by black bars. She was still here.

"Abigail?" I called again. I moved quietly around a bank of steel lockers. The row beyond them was empty, but something had changed. I strained to hear. The rhythmic dripping had stopped. A moment later the familiar *plonk plonk* returned. Taking a deep breath, I tiptoed to the shower room door.

There were three shower stalls. I crouched and saw her feet in the stall farthest from the door. As I straightened, voices broke the quiet. The police were at the pool.

"Abigail?" I said. "Nobody's going to hurt you."

There was no answer.

"Paige Davenport," I called softly. "Are you there?"

She moved slowly out of the shower. In one hand she held something that picked up points of light. She raised her other hand slowly to her head. A strand of hair had fallen across her face. She grasped it and pulled it back.

"My hair was lighter then. I wore it in a topknot with the most beautiful gold crown. The *Fort Worth Globe* said, 'Paige Davenport is a magical Cinderella.' In Little Rock I got three curtain calls. And you should see what the reporter for the Memphis paper said. I still have the clippings if you'd like to read them."

The dim light caught the luster in her eyes. As she moved slowly toward me I made out the thing in her hand. It was a champagne bottle, swinging lazily. A thought—she'd never hurt me. Then I saw Carmen's face, and Niki's. I backed through the locker area into the attendant's room. Closing the door, I jammed the metal chair under the knob to block it.

Tony read part of my statement back in a monotone. "Abigail took the pass from my desk. Maybe she went home. I don't know. Maybe she went to the park and spent the afternoon on a bench. But she practiced signing my name on a Gala Affair notepad until she had it right. Then she forged my signature on the pass and went through the lower-level entrance using her old stage name, Paige Davenport. Abigail knew everyone would be one flight up at the reception. While she was cutting Niki's hitch, she got a deep gash in her hand. She stayed out of work the beginning of the next week so nobody would notice it."

Tony looked up. "That's it?"

I shrugged. It was late and I was exhausted. Derek and I had gone to my apartment for dry clothes before going to the precinct. "You know the rest," I said. "Carmen told Jonquil that the woman leaving Props had a turnout, Jonquil told her mother, and Abigail decided she better get rid of Carmen."

"And you guessed Abigail was Paige Davenport?"

"Not at first," I admitted. "I should have. Abigail didn't meet her future husband—Ned Jeffreys—until after she toured as Cinderella. Foote was her maiden name, but she would never have appeared professionally as Abigail Foote. Think of the openings that would give a critic: foot sore, footloose, flat foot, foot on a banana peel, two left feet. When Chris told me that Isabella had seen the murderer, and I remembered how Isabella reacted when she saw Abigail, it all came together for me."

"Crazy," Tony shook his head. "She doesn't look dangerous."

"What does dangerous look like?"

He forced a smile. "Touché!"

"That's okay." My glance fell to the top of his desk. A manila folder was lying directly under my statement. I nodded at it. "I guess you're not going to let me take a look at Carmen's statement."

I'd already asked once. Tony had already told me no once. "You never stop, do you?" he said, and he looked so exasperated I actually felt guilty. He picked up his paper coffee cup and pushed back his chair. "I've got to get another of these. You want one?"

I shook my head.

"We're about through, but why don't you wait for me to get back." He looked down at the folder. "I'll be a few minutes.

I may have to make a new pot." As Tony left his office he pulled the door shut.

I reached across his desk and slid Carmen's statement from the folder.

"I noticed Jonquil's mother looking at me at the party," it began. "She must have seen me take the roof key out of the dish on the Spencers' mantel. I had to stretch to reach it and when I turned around, she was staring. I thought it was because of my dress or because I was drinking too much champagne. A second after I got to the pool I heard the elevator door. I thought it was Joey but it was Mrs. Jeffreys. She had a champagne bottle with her. She pretended to just be talking and looking at the water but she was acting weird. She kept staring at me real hard. I got scared and said I was going back downstairs. Then she said, 'You know who I am, don't you?' I said no but I did by then. She hit me on the head with the bottle and shoved me in the deep end. The only thing I remember after that is thinking, 'I won't get to do the Balanchine pas de trois.'"

— Six Weeks Later —

Carmen danced her solo the night before last. Derek and I had orchestra seats. The audience loved her. In this morning's *Times* the reviewer said, "The young Carmen Garcia made a splendid debut in the pas de trois. Her execution is fearless, her speed exciting." She got her date, too. I saw her leaving the theater hand in hand with Joey.

I haven't seen Abigail since the Spencers' party. I understand she's still undergoing psychiatric evaluation. Jonquil fled to Atlanta for a few weeks. Who would blame her? She's back now, living in the apartment she shared with Abigail. A few days ago she stopped by the office and showed me an acceptance letter from New York University. I asked if she had seen her mother and she said no, she couldn't handle it yet. "I will soon," she promised. I think she meant it.

Chris was promoted to principal dancer with no fanfare. One day his name was in small letters, the next day in big ones. And that was that. Galena still talks about retiring, and still dances. She has a new White Knight, an attorney whose resemblance to Robert Redford would be amazing if he were only six inches taller. She smiles fondly down at him. He gazes up, captivated. White Knights come in all sizes.

I'm not sure what happened to the Spencers. I learned from Tony that the Drug Enforcement Agency had been watching them for some time. Several weeks ago a metamorphosis occurred on Broadway. Dos Sombreros, amusing decor and all, vanished after closing one Thursday. Two nights later another restaurant materialized in its place. It's called Swamp Things. God knows what they serve. I'll wait for some good word of mouth before I try it.

As for me, I'm still with Gotham. Tricia took the loss of the Spencers' patronage in stride. Michael did not. He doesn't speak to me. I suspect he'd rather have a new ballet underwritten by cocaine money than no new ballet at all. He has no reason to fire me, but I'll bet he'd love to see me go.

I may oblige him. The part-time help Tricia mentioned hasn't materialized. (As Tricia points out, neither has my uncle—but that's another matter entirely.) The pace of the fund-raising office is so frenzied that by evening I'm asleep on my feet. While there have been times when I would have sacrificed my evenings for a job, this isn't one of them.

Home is now Derek's loft. Moses made the transition with less fuss than I did. He's found two mice and lives in an ecstasy of tail-switching anticipation. Washington Heights has faded from his memory. It still lives in mine. Seized by caution, I refused to give up my apartment. One of the dancers has sublet it.

Today that caution seems foolish. The Indian summer sun warms Tony's backyard in Queens. Autumn has turned his one stunted tree gold and orange. I'm color-coordinated. My bridesmaid's dress is russet. The wedding is bigger than he and Amanda originally planned, and guests have trampled a flower bed. Maybe Amanda will develop a green thumb.

Amanda looks wonderful in an ankle-length white gown. The women all talk about what a beautiful bride she is. The men talk sports. There's Derek, a guy who spent at least a couple of minutes of his flaming youth pitching Molotov cocktails at the police, talking baseball with a bunch of New York City cops.

Every day we grow more comfortable with each other. I'm not quite ready to tell that dancer she can have my lease, but . . .

Oh! Something is happening in the house. There's a commotion. I have to hurry inside. Amanda is getting ready to throw her bouquet.